# A Ship is Dying

*by the same author*

A FLOCK OF SHIPS

A PLAGUE OF SAILORS

THE DAWN ATTACK

A WEB OF SALVAGE

TRAPP'S WAR

# A Ship is Dying

Brian Callison

**COLLINS**
St James's Place, London, 1976

William Collins Sons & Co Ltd
London · Glasgow · Sydney · Auckland
Toronto · Johannesburg

First published 1976
© Brian Callison 1976

ISBN 0 00 222461 5

Set in Monotype Imprint
Made and Printed in Great Britain by
William Collins Sons & Co Ltd Glasgow

You gentlemen of England
Who live at home at ease,
How little do you think
On the dangers of the seas.
Martin Parker
?—*1656*


. . . and how little we've changed,
In three hundred and odd years.

# Prologue

She was just an average ship.

With an average crew, an average cargo, and embarked on an average voyage across a pretty average winter sea.

She could have been a Greek. Or a Scandinavian. Perhaps a German or an American, even a Russian.

She could have been built in Helsinki or Hamburg. Maybe Kobe, or Melbourne.

But it so happened that *Lycomedes* was British. Her port of registry was Liverpool. She'd been built on the Tyne with swearing and love and the constant threat of strikes. And with a very great pride by very great craftsmen.

She had a crew of fifty-two British seamen and one Chinaman.

Plus a pretty average dog. And a parrot.

She was twelve years old. Which is a fairly average age for a merchant ship. She was four hundred and seventy-eight feet in length with a gross registered tonnage of seven thousand three hundred, and maintained an economical service speed of fifteen and a half knots.

She was an archetypal splinter from the three hundred million tons of shipping sailing across today's oceans. Yet how many land-bound people ever give a thought to them – to any of those merchant vessels just like *Lycomedes*. Or to the hazards they face?

Probably very few. Because they're . . . well . . . they're so *ordinary*.

Come to that, even when disaster does overtake one of their number it still doesn't warrant much more than a casual mention in a newspaper here and there. Not unless it happens

7

to be a passenger ship, of course, with real people like you and me aboard. Or a leaking super-tanker threatening to pollute our favourite holiday beach for weeks ahead.

But not when it's only an ordinary ship. With only ordinary sailormen living and breathing and laughing, or being sad, in her.

And anyway, that kind are foundering or stranding, or colliding or burning or just plain disappearing-without-trace every day of the week. So what's particularly special, so extra-ordinary about yet another vessel's dying, then?

Probably nothing at all, really.

Unless, of course, you yourself just happen to *be* one of those sailormen.

During one of those average days aboard one of those pretty average ships. Such as the Motor Vessel *Lycomedes*.

When it *is* all so routine and dull. And so ordinary.

Until . . . the Cataclysm!

# Chapter One

Suppose that we, tomorrow or the next day,
Came to an end – in storm the shafting broken.
*C. Day Lewis*

## CATACLYSM MINUS THREE MINUTES

The second mate saw it first.

Fine on the starboard bow, almost bisected by the P.P.I. heading marker and roughly three-quarters of a mile away.

One fuzzy, luminous blip. Only barely detectable on a radar display harassed by legions of other mini-blips. All frenetically claiming the electronic attention of *Lycomedes'* smoothly whirling scanner as, for one brief splinter of time, the foam-streaked and curling peak of each individual storm wave reflected its own personal image, its own physical identity, before collapsing again into that welter of constantly shifting nuclei called the North Sea.

Fuller blinked hard. Deliberately compressing his eyebrows into a corrugated vee to squeeze away the neon-induced fatigue of the constant radar viewer. Then he opened his eyes again and, bedding his forehead more firmly into the soft rubber cup of the console hood, stared ferociously. Searchingly.

At that fuzzy, luminous blip. Only slightly more apparent than its fellows. Hanging momentarily on the screen like a small orange flare yet fading from the very milli-second of its conception while the constant, clockwise rotation of the trace continued one more revolution of the force ten turbulence surrounding *Lycomedes*.

Until the trace had spun full circle, returning once again to

9

twelve o'clock vertical. But there wasn't anything there any more.

Apart from that myriad of identical, featureless, non-threatening mini-blips.

But Second Officer Fuller still maintained his concentrating frown and, without lifting his head, fumbled for the knurled control marked *Anti-sea clutter*. Caressing it gently he reduced the wave effect until the whole screen now presented an almost opaque orange saucer of light.

Still no contact, though. Nothing even suggesting menace in *Lycomedes'* path. Merely the constantly re-forming speckle echoing back from a multitude of rearing watery facets.

Which was precisely what one would have expected because, after five days of steadily deteriorating wind and sea conditions, not many vessels of much under *Lycomedes'* bulk were likely to be bucketing around the North Sea. Not even an East Coast seine-netter. While at a half-mile range anything larger would be filling the wheelhouse windows like an ocean-going cathedral . . .

However, Second Officer Michael Fuller was a careful, as well as a conscientious young man, so he clung resignedly to the grab handles flanking the Decca console while *Lycomedes* buried her flared bows into yet another thirty foot trough then, allowing the motion of the ship to propel him at a staggering half-gallop towards the starboard clear-view screen, deftly snatched his binoculars from the varnished box under the ledge and focused ahead, through the constantly sheeting curtains of spray, out past the plunging fo'c'slehead to where the monochrome rollers leaped and reared in enormous anticipation of *Lycomedes'* passing.

Just a routine visual check on an electronic eye.

To make absolutely certain there *wasn't* a bloody cathedral in the way.

Of course there wasn't one.

A cathedral. Lying in wait, half a mile ahead of *Lycomedes*.

Because if there had been, then either Chippie or the bosun or deck hands Bronson and Falls would have seen it too, situated as they were at the forward end of the centrecastle alleyway and just waiting for the ship to regain some semblance of an even keel before dodging for the lee of number three contactor house.

Then from there even farther forward. Down the ladder to the well deck followed by a nerve-racking dash along the starboard lifelines to the break of the fo'c'sle while all the time those monstrous white-capped breakers would be rearing and roaring high above their heads with the tumbling peaks atomized into horizontal clouds by the fifty knot shriek of the wind . . .

At least, that was how deckhands Bronson and Falls saw it anyway. To the carpenter and Bosun Skinner it was a routine and necessary part of a sailorman's life – merely the daily responsibility of the ship's carpenter to sound all compartments, tanks and bilges, and to enter the depths of water in each on the appropriate chalk board situated in the engineroom. Thus avoiding the statutory wrath of the Department of Trade and Industry, Sea Transport Branch; the bleakly aloof gleam of censure in the eyes of Chief Officer McRae; and a general disagreeableness from the rest of *Lycomedes*' crew when they found their boat sinking because it had filled up with water and nobody had bloody well noticed.

However, on account of the weather, Bronson and Falls had also been detailed to accompany the carpenter while he precariously manipulated his shiny brass sounding rod.

And Bosun Skinner just happened to be going forward, too. Though if the truth were known it was really because he didn't reckon he could trust either Bronson or Falls on anything more unstable than a concrete block of flats, and because he'd been shipmates with Chippie for seventeen years and loved him like a brother.

So he just stared calculating ahead while *Lycomedes* hesitated on the crest of a roller, shielded the spray from his eyes with the back of a calloused mahogany hand, and growled sombrely, 'Two at a time when I says "Go". You first, wi' Chippie . . . an' mind an' keep close-hauled to them lifelines. Savvy?'

Falls muttered, 'Yes, Bosun.' Nervously.

Deckhand Bronson didn't say anything. He was too scared.

Chippie just grinned an amiable grin and winked at his friend behind the seamen's backs. Then the grin faded a bit because Skinner had suddenly frowned, lifting his chin and narrowing his eyes in the way he always did when things weren't quite right.

Swivelling, the carpenter followed the bosun's steady gaze forward, out over the grey serried ranks of the wave crests ahead.

'See something, Willie?'

But Skinner didn't answer for a moment, still searching curiously as *Lycomedes* reared skywards out of the trough with the white water streaming and babbling aft, forming a fuzz of impacted spray against the windlass before the storm took it again, whipping it further astern to spatter the men's yellow oilskins with a frustrated sigh.

Then the bosun shrugged dismissively and said, 'Jus' remember them lifelines, you two!'

So Chippie gripped his sounding rod and line a bit more firmly.

And Bronson and Falls hunched even more miserably under the icy flail of the wind.

While the bosun disregarded what he'd just seen, or thought he'd seen maybe seven, eight cables ahead. For a start, waves didn't *have* sharp, solid corners. Apart from which they were forty or fifty miles clear of the nearest coastline with its attendant rocks and shoals and buoys and other identifiable hazards.

And anyway – *Lycomedes* did have radar.

'Get ready, lads!' the bosun sniffed.

The door slammed open as the ship juggernauted out of the trough and Kemp stumbled over the coaming, skidding awkwardly across the non-skid deck before grabbing desperately at the bookshelves for support. A large yellow-covered edition of *Regulations for the Use of the International Code At Sea* tumbled deckwards, carrying with it the W/T-room copy file of *Navigational Warnings*.

Bentine swivelled in his chair, headphones hooked casually round the back of his neck, and said cheerfully, 'Good afternoon, Chief Radio Officer.'

Kemp muttered 'Shit!' and bent down to pick up the litter.

'Whatever turns you on, Chief.' The second sparks sucked a hollow tooth that had been niggling for three months then added inconsequentially, *'Vejarbejde.'*

'Eh?'

*'VeJARbejde!* It's Danish for "Road works ahead". I've been learning the local lingo f'r when we dock.'

Kemp grinned sardonically and rubbed his knee cautiously. 'With your mind, laddie, you should be figurin' out how to say, "How much" and, "Now let's turn over an' do it the other way, Ingrid." '

Bentine looked interested. 'Who's Ingrid then?'

The chief sparks ignored him irritably. 'Get the forecast, did you?'

'On the file. Copy to the bridge. Same as before – Severe gale, nor'east to east continuing in Forties, Fisher and Germ . . . '

'Shit!' Kemp muttered again.

'Oh, I do like a bit of intellectual conversation. Helps to pass the watch . . . Raised a W/T urgency call twenty minutes ago, by the way. Some Dutchman with steering failure getting nervous. Asking anyone handy to stand-by him.'

The chief radio officer picked up the signal pad. 'And?'

Bentine shrugged. 'Fifty miles west according to the bridge. Two or three ships answered, closer to him.'

'No distress follow-up?'

*Lycomedes* rolled heavily and a pencil rattled across the desk.

'Not yet,' Bentine said meaningfully.

'Yeah, well we've all got problems.'

Kemp bent down, balancing on one knee as the ship returned to the horizontal. He picked up the *Navwarn* file and hung it back on its hook below the bookshelf.

He didn't bother to glance at the top copy. He didn't have any reason to, for that matter.

While, even if he had, he couldn't possibly have realised that the neatly pencilled text explained a lot of things.

Such as Second Officer Fuller's frustratingly vanishing radar blip. And Bosun Skinner's wave with the curiously sharp corner.

'Anyway, what *about* this Ingrid bird then?' Second Radio Officer Bentine probed hopefully.


'Dried blood, David!'

The captain unhooked his cap from the back of the master's day-room door and waved it commandingly at the mate.

'There isn't a tomato worth picking that hasn't been reared on dried blood. Write and ask Maureen to get some. Fork it in on your next leave, then stand well back, by God.'

McRae grinned. 'In between decorating the kids' bedrooms and re-wiring the garage, eh?'

*Lycomedes* shuddered, digging her bows in. A scurry of spray rattled the forward windows. The Old Man glanced out momentarily and looked petulant. 'Jennie'll probably have me rebuilding the damn fence when I get home . . . Everything all right on deck?'

'Checked the hatch-locking bars myself this morning. Chippie should be sounding the wells sometime about now – if Skinner stops fussing long enough to let him do it, that is.'

'Skinner's an old woman. Always worrying.'

'He's a good bosun. Worries about all the right things.'

*Lycomedes'* master opened the door and stood there for a moment, swaying easily with the movement of the ship while squaring his cap away. Without it he could have been anyone – a surgeon, a miner, an architect, even a farm labourer if you noticed the weathered lines forming around the grey eyes. But once framed under the oak-leaved peak Captain Graham Shaw was undeniably a seaman. He also happened to be a good one. The total professional.

'I'll take a turn up to the bridge and see how Fuller's coping,' he said crisply as McRae followed him out into the internal alleyway.

His chief officer smiled triumphantly, but there was no disrespect. 'What was it you said about Skinner?'

The Old Man looked solemn. '*And* I worry about all the right things as well, Mister McRae.' He lifted his arm. The gold braid gleamed softly under the glare of the overhead lights. 'These four rings give me a pension in two years' time, a steward of my own . . . and a lot of responsibility.'

McRae pulled the master's cabin door shut with a firm click and turned aft. 'I've only got three. They mean I'm the one who has to sweat over the Copenhagen loading plan . . . '

*Lycomedes* barrel-rolled to fifteen degrees. From somewhere below the smash of breaking crockery carried up the internal stairway.

The mate hesitated. 'We're still on full revolutions, sir?'

Shaw noted the slight doubt in his chief officer's tone and nodded. 'We don't alter course off Hanstholm Light until midnight. Then we'll have a beam sea all the way into the Skagerrak. The quicker we get there the less time it'll have to increase – which it will do according to the forecast.'

He placed one foot on the stairway to the bridge, then swivelled back.

'You remember, now. Dried blood's the only thing that makes tomato-growing worth while, David.'

The sigh of the waves against *Lycomedes* racing steel flanks almost drowned the steady hum of the accommodation blowers.

It was all part of a pretty average day. Aboard a pretty average ship.

The fuzzy, immediately-diminishing blip on the radar screen flared up once again. But no-one on the bridge saw it this time.

Second Officer Fuller was still trying to hold his binoculars steady for long enough to make even a little sense out of the tossing hysteria ahead of the bows.

First-trip apprentice Rupert Cassiday, huddled out on the starboard wing, was still so overwhelmed by the drama of it all – the exhilaration of being a real sailorman standing a real watch aboard a real ship in a real storm – that he wouldn't have noticed anything amiss if *Lycomedes* had suddenly sprouted sails. But three weeks ago Rupert had still been a schoolboy.

Quartermaster Ernest Clements, riding easily and comfortably on splayed legs behind the wheel, was plain browned off with a matelot's life on the ocean wave. However, Ernest had been browned off for eight lousy years, come to that, so he was single-mindedly switched-on to maintaining *Lycomedes*' gyrating heading of zero three two degrees true.

And anyway, it wasn't his job to keep look-out for anything in *Lycomedes*' path. Not even a bloody cathedral . . .

This time the blip hung tenuously to its electronically-induced life for three complete revolutions of the trace.

*Lycomedes* had now covered a distance of six hundred yards since that first infinitesimal warning.

She only had one thousand yards – precisely one half nautical mile – left to travel.

## CATACLYSM minus TWO MINUTES

Captain's Steward Huang Pi-wu didn't care at all about elusive radar contacts, waves with unaccountably solid peaks or chief officers with cargo-planning problems.

For Huang Pi-wu was asleep. Blissfully, romantically, and dedicatedly asleep.

Tripping with ethereal grace through an eternal panorama of sweet-scented jasmine and gently swaying cherry blossom, hand in hand with the beautiful Yeh Chun whom he had loved with undiminished passion since their days of childhood in the autonomous region of Kwangsi Chuang, in the People's Republic of China.

Not that Huang Pi-wu was a Communist. Not in any sense of the word. In fact, even during those first triumphal days which heralded the coming of the great proletarian cultural revolution, young Huang had seen the writing on the wall for potential capitalists such as he, and had bugged-out accordingly, plitty damn quick, to the bureaucratic oasis of British Hong Kong, whereupon he had signed on as steward aboard a Blue Funnel liner homeward bound for that supreme capital of capitalism – Liverpool.

And ever since then Huang Pi-wu had been scrimping and saving to realize his second happy dream – when he could open the very first establishment in a theoretically endless chain of Cathay Chinese restaurants; proprietor and licensee – Huang Pi-wu, Esq.

But, even more important, Huang was not only a dreamer. The sum of one thousand, three hundred and sixteen pounds sterling lay locked in a hand-painted tin box secreted under the little steward' bunk. Not even Officers' Steward Eddie Ferguson knew about that, and Eddie was Huang Pi-wu's greatest friend aboard *Lycomedes* as well as being his cabin mate.

Perhaps Huang was foolish. Perhaps he should have invested his hard-earned savings in a more secure and interest-earning potential than a hand-painted tin box could offer.

But perhaps, also, Huang Pi-wu still retained just a little of the true proletarian deep inside him. Which meant an instinctive mistrust of those totally capitalistic institutions such as banks, insurance companies and the stock market.

And anyway – what could possibly happen to his dream aboard a ship?

Aboard an ordinary ship. On a very ordinary voyage.

'Simple Simon met a pieman . . . ' the chief engineer recited in clear, utterly distinct syllables.

'Bloody hell!' the parrot said, succinctly.

'Perhaps he's not in the mood, sir,' the second engineer murmured consolingly. 'And all said an' done, Hermann's a German, remember.'

'Then why . . . ' the chief demanded cleverly . . . 'why does it . . . he . . . swear in English, then?'

'Maybe it . . . he belonged to someone from the British Consulate in Hamburg. Or from the Yank Embassy or somewhere.'

The second engineer shuffled impatiently. All he wanted to do was sort out what the chief required in the way of routine maintenance while they were alongside in Copenhagen, then get below and check on the third's progress with the injector change on the port generator.

'He couldn't have,' the chief announced with devastating logic. 'Diplomats don't swear for a start, and that's all that bloody bird ever does.'

'Fuck you!' the parrot confirmed with enormous relish.

'And you . . . In fact, *especially* you!' the second engineer thought with heartfelt sincerity. But he didn't actually say it out loud. Not while the chief was there, because the steely-eyed bird with the lethal beak and all the bald patches where it had tried to pick itself into total nudity – it was the one thing calculated to convert Chief Engineer William Barraclough from being a reasonable man into a raving, wild-eyed lunatic.

Because he'd bought the creature in Hamburg two years before. A present for Mrs Barraclough, to keep her company while her husband was away at sea. It had been a nice gesture, a generous thought from a devoted husband. Until Hermann went and opened his beak.

And revealed that he was the most foul-spoken, obscene, vulgar and utterly depraved bird that had ever donned feathers.

Which had meant that Chief Barraclough hadn't dared take Hermann within earshot of Mrs Barraclough, so was forced instead to ship the wretched creature everywhere *Lycomedes* went. Northwards, southwards, criss-crossing the oceans of the world in a screaming, blaspheming continuity of squawks. A sea-going ball of feathered vituperation. The Flying Dutchman of birdland . . .

'I'd like to strip down the lube oil purifier soon as possible, sir,' the second suggested hopefully.

'Simple . . . Simon . . . met . . . a . . . pieman . . . ' the chief pronounced doggedly.

The parrot glared at his master with baleful hatred. 'Bloody hell,' it counter-attacked shrilly. 'Bloody hell bloody hell bloody *hell* . . . !'

'Bloody PARROTS!' snarled the chief engineer of the Motor Vessel *Lycomedes*.

'Yes, sir!' the second engineer agreed. With feeling.


'Go *on*, then!'

Deckhand Falls took off like an apprehensive rocket, seaboots splaying little spurts of seawater across the deck as he headed for the shelter of the contactor house at the forward end of number three hatch. Chippie watched him silently for a moment then said, 'Trouble with youngsters today, Willie, is that they haven't never seen real bad weather.'

The bosun waited until the other two had made it then followed at an easy jog-trot, making small alterations of course every few steps to compensate for the roll of the ship. Arriving in the lee of the steel housing he turned and glanced up at the bridge high above his head, a streamlined white horizon swaying in slow arcs across a scudding grey sky with the halyards and ariels bent in wide curving strands under the pressure of the wind.

A small head cut above the starboard dodger – that new apprentice, Skinner thought absently. No doubt relishing every sensation, every uncomfortable detail of what would soon become the routine boredom of life at sea . . . and another figure in the wheelhouse, the second mate. Peering ahead through binoculars, as usual.

*Lycomedes'* bosun sniffed disapprovingly. In his opinion binoculars were an outdated affectation still clung to by all deck officers. Like sextants, when they had miracle inventions like Loran and RDF and Decca Navigation systems . . . and Consol or whatever it was, to tell them precisely where the ship was at the flick of a switch.

His eye caught the movement above the bridge – the radar scanner, steadily rotating in a mesmerising sweep. 'Now that's God's *real* gift to the mariner,' the bosun reflected appreciatively. 'No need for glasses when you got an electric eye to do your seeing for you. And just as efficient even if there's fog or spray or pitch darkness.'

'Second mate's bein' a sailorman again,' he grinned to Chippie.

The carpenter shrugged, mopping at a trickle of seawater which had found its way inside the collar of his oilskin. 'They got to show the personal touch sometimes, Willie. Keeps up the mystique, sort of. To prove that not everybody can be an officer.'

'That's it,' Skinner nodded agreeably. 'Mystick, jus' like you say . . . Ready for the well deck, then?'

'Quicker we go, the quicker we're back, Willie.'

'Yeah . . . well.'

Skinner stepped out of the lee of the housing and stood at the top of the ladder. The wind buffeted him warningly but he ignored it with lofty familiarity, watching for the right moment ahead. The period when the seas come in predictable, regular swells with a lot less risk of a rogue wave ambushing them on that exposed stretch of lower deck, rearing unexpectedly and tumbling inboard over the bulwarks in a thundering smash of almost solid water.

He'd just started to emphasize, 'Remember them lifelines, you two . . . ' when he broke off abruptly. Disbelievingly.

In fact, Bosun William Skinner was the first man aboard *Lycomedes* to feel the chill of incomprehending fear.

Because, this time, he wasn't mistaken.

And there *was* something out there.

Right ahead of *Lycomedes*' plunging bow.

## CATACLYSM MINUS ONE MINUTE

She carried an average sort of cargo.

Steel plates in numbers one, two and five lower holds, consigned for Stockholm. Cash registers, machine tools, television sets, Irish linen tea-towels, rubber tyres and twenty-four brand new tractors for off-loading in Copenhagen. Seed potatoes, jute products, cigarettes, custard powder and two hundred tons of dynamite for Malmö, Sweden. Sixty tons of Scotch whisky for a thirsty Finnish importer . . .

She'd sailed from the Port of Swansea precisely fifty-three

hours and fourteen minutes before Second Mate Fuller first saw that perplexing little flair on the radar display.

Until then it had been an uneventful, slightly uncomfortable North Sea passage. Just the same as all the other voyages *Lycomedes* had made during her twelve years of service.

Not one man aboard gave even a passing thought to the possibility of anything going wrong. No more than a passenger travelling on the same bus route that he's travelled for the whole of his working life would anticipate a fatal collision. Or a young housewife would give to the chances of being killed while crossing the road to the local shop.

Certainly nobody sailing in *Lycomedes* on that routine winter's day ever imagined for one minute that he might even die in the very near future. And in an extremely violent, and most extraordinary manner.

For an ordinary seaman, that is.

Aboard an ordinary, run-of-the-mill merchant ship.

Shaw walked through the screened chartroom at the after end of the bridge and into the wheelhouse itself. It was an act the captain had performed hundreds of times in the past, yet it always gave him a warm glow of satisfaction, a feeling of accomplishment. That he was master on his own bridge, aboard his very own ship.

And *Lycomedes* was a good ship. A well-found ship.

Shaw was very, very proud of her.

Quartermaster Clements, lounging comfortably behind the wheel, saw the captain first and straightened up smartly. But he also sucked a hollow tooth noisily and made a point of eyeing the course board above the steering compass just so's the Old Man would see that Ernie Clements wasn't too chuffed at *Lycomedes* running on manual steering when she was fitted with a perfectly good automatic pilot.

It was a gesture which the captain did notice, but completely ignored. Automatic systems were superb, but they couldn't think. They couldn't anticipate in the way that a seaman could, for the moment when the rogue sea – the legendary seventh wave of a seventh wave – started to build ahead, gathering its strength, calculating that precise second in time when it could rear high above the fo'c'sle, forcing the ship's bows away and exposing her insignificant well deck freeboard to the clambering tons of water which might easily smash downwards and into her forward hatches.

But seamen could. Even truculent, bolshie seamen like the man Clements. And begin to apply that extra half turn of the wheel in advance, bringing *Lycomedes*' head round to forestall and nullify the always present treachery of the sea.

So Shaw merely walked over to the binnacle and equally pointedly looked at the swinging compass card, letting Clements see that he, the captain, was aware that *Lycomedes* had been allowed to yaw three degrees off course in the few moments the quartermaster's attention had been diverted towards his silent protest . . .

. . . until he caught sight of Second Officer Fuller, strangely tense at the wheelhouse window. And immediately forgot all about recalcitrant helmsmen.

But he was only half way across the space between them when Fuller whispered disbelievingly, almost hypnotically.

'Oh, my *God* . . . !'

The dog sat in the wire-netting pen they'd built for it under the shelter of the poop housing and stared gloomily at the boy through unblinking brown eyes.

'D'you want a biscuit, then?' the boy said coaxingly.

The dog just sat there.

'Christ,' the boy thought ruefully. 'Two an' a half years' apprenticeship gone towards my second mate's ticket and they give me command of a dog!'

23

He smiled softly, a little wryly, and poked the biscuit temptingly through the diamond mesh. 'C'mon, dog. It's a cream biscuit. I saved it 'specially for you.'

The dog blinked. Just once. It wasn't a very active dog.

*Lycomedes* plunged her bows into a trough. The stern rose skywards like an express lift and the boy felt the shuddering rumble transmitted through the deck as the screw rose towards the surface. The Red Ensign gave a flapping crackle under the added flail of the wind and the dog pricked up one ear warily.

Then the ear subsided again like an empty velvet purse while the dog continued its unblinking scrutiny of the boy.

'You're the funniest cargo I've ever seen,' the apprentice murmured conversationally. 'Most pets go by air, I suppose. But maybe you're being shipped by sea because they reckon you can't stand flying.'

He waggled the biscuit appetizingly. 'Which makes you a very nautical dog. A proper sea-dog, eh?'

The dog gave a deep sigh. Its nose glinted blackly against the brown shiny muzzle. It didn't seem very interested in the biscuit, though. Not even when the boy stuck it through the wire mesh of the cage and left it there hopefully.

'And I'm standing watch with you.' The boy grinned as a thought struck him. 'I'm standing the dog watch, in fact. With a real dog.'

His name was Michael Standish. He was an only child. He had broken his mother's heart when he'd gone to sea two and a half years before, but she'd never let Michael know that. And he'd never really thought much about it because he'd always wanted to be a sailor, and he was still too young to understand proper sadness.

The after end of *Lycomedes* plummeted again, sinking deep into the heaving white wake astern.

'Or maybe you're seasick, Seadog?' the boy said, suddenly concerned.

But the dog didn't answer.

It just sat there. And looked disconsolate.


Chippie stared anxiously as Bosun Skinner stood, apparently transfixed at the head of the well deck ladder and totally oblivious to the sheeting spray.

'What d'you see Willie?' the carpenter snapped, suddenly aware of a growing nervousness. 'What the hell *is* it f'r Chrissa . . . !'

But suddenly Skinner whirled round to face aft, waving frantically up at the bridge before cupping his hands together in a desperate, frighteningly urgent roar.

'Object dead *ahead* . . . ! Right under the bow an' DEAD AHEAD!'

The wind seemed to increase in ferocity, screaming with excitement, snatching at Skinner's voice and flinging it outboard, tearing and shredding it into an unintelligible whisper of fractured syllables.

Looking down from the high bridge wing, first-trip apprentice Rupert Cassiday saw the stocky, romantic old seaman waving at him from the deck and smiled with pleasure.

It was as he'd always imagined it would be. Men against the sea. Comradeship. A rugged, select brotherhood in combat against the elements . . . !

He waved back. Positively swelling with pride.


Fourth engineer Chisholme ever so carefully withdrew the number two cylinder injector from its seating and handed it over to middle-watch greaser Carbon Black to put in the tin box with the others.

Then he laid his head even more carefully against the cold metal of the generator block and closed his eyes. Just for one brief moment.

Because Bert Chisholme felt sick. Utterly, unmercifully and gut-wrenchingly seasick.

But he always did. Every time there was a bit'f heavy weather. Every time he caught one whiff of that insidious, stomach-turning mixture of hot air, hot oil and hot paint which constitutes the atmosphere of a ship's engineroom.

Mind you, after six years at sea the smell itself had almost become bearable – excluding the odd taint of exhaust gas which unerringly followed Fourth Engineer Chisholme like a heat-seeking missile – but take all those pollutants, add the constantly pounding cacophony of a medium-speed *SEMT-Pielstick* marine diesel engine thundering within a few feet of you, enclose the ingredients within a brilliantly-lit steel box.

Then tilt the whole fiendish arrangement through a shuddering, roller-coasting forty degree arc every few seconds . . .

. . . and – if you've got a delicate stomach like Bert Chisholme's – *you'll* feel sick.

Bloody sick!

The third engineer came strolling along the chequer-plated walkway looking disgustingly fresh in spotless white overalls. He squatted and looked under the guard rail to where Bert knelt in the oily sludge swilling around the generator sump.

The third winked knowingly at Carbon Black, who smiled back conspiratorially. It was a wide, enormously evil smile.

'Feeling a bit dodgy are you, Bert?' the third asked sympathetically.

Bert opened one eye and said succinctly, 'Piss off, Bowman!'

Carbon Black shook his head sadly. 'Mister Chisholme's gotter grave disability f'r a sea-goin' engineer, sir. With that stummick've his.'

Then he took his teeth out and, with sly ostentation, started to clean assorted lunch time debris off the back of the plate with a long condemned scrap of oily cotton waste.

'Rotten bastards!' Chisholme screamed hatefully, then put his head down and heaved uncontrollably.

The third engineer and the greaser turned away respectfully. I mean, you've got to let a chap have a bit of privacy when he isn't feeling very well.

The blip on the bridge radar display flared again. And, again, no one was there to observe it.

Only this time it was with an unconcealed and mocking incandescence. Orange-bright and totally apparent as a pulsing blur disfiguring the die-straight line of the heading marker – thus finally winning its battle for individuality against all the other tiny, insignificant wave echoes clamouring for electronic recognition.

The trace whirled full circle. The contact glowed with recharged radiance. And again . . . and again . . .

Until it had almost touched the centre of the P.P.I.

Was almost merging with the pin-point source of the trace indicating *Lycomedes*' own steadily advancing position.

' . . . dead AHEAD!' the bosun screamed, hating that starry-eyed, totally unresponsive little bastard of an apprentice up there on the bridge with every fibre in his body.

The carpenter kept on snarling, almost pleading, 'What *is* it, Willie f'r . . . what the hell *is* it, man?'

For he couldn't see whatever it was for himself. Not now. Because the cause of Skinner's panic was already hidden by the rising sheer of *Lycomedes*' forecastlehead.

Deckhands Bronson and Falls didn't even try to look.

They just started to run blindly aft. Away from the origin of that unspecified threat . . .

Chief Cook Dempster lifted the lid from the three gallon skillet and sniffed with professional appreciation.

27

'Nice drop o' soup there, Second Chef!'

'Old Man's favourite – mulligatawny.' The second cook jerked his chin. 'Just check the oven, Norrie. See the flamin' main course hasn't rolled right out the tin, eh?'

Dempster dropped the pot lid, noticing how the whole massive utensil slid sharply from side to side every few moments before bringing up against the stainless steel bars of the hot plate fiddles with a metallic click. Even down here in the galley, immediately abaft the officers' saloon, the ship was working heavily.

'Bloody weather,' he remarked, wrapping his apron round the knob of the oven door.

The second cook chopped an onion almost absently, the blade of the knife echoing a blurring rat-tat-tat within a hairsbreadth of his fingers. 'Maybe we should sign on P an' O or a Cunarder next time, eh? Winter cruisin' in the Caribbean on a floatin' gin palace.'

'Sin palace, more like.'

Dempster opened the door to a blast of aroma-laden heat. Bending at the knees he peered in. The meat was just beginning to brown to a soft golden shade, the electric heating elements below glowing dull red as the thermostat cut in.

Roast leg of lamb for the officers and ratings of *Lycomedes* tonight. Lamb, roast potatoes, mint sauce and two veg.

The ship wallowed heavily and a trickle of mulligatawny soup slopped over the rim of the skillet to hiss warningly on the hot plate. The crouching man at the open oven door swayed awkwardly and growled an irritable 'Damn!'

It meant that, for the next few unstable seconds, Chief Cook Dempster would be caught off-balance . . .

. . . and then the captain saw it for himself.

Now less than two hundred feet ahead and directly under *Lycomedes*' streaming, plunging bow.

A great steel pyramid, almost awash. Rust red and hideous, with one line of rivets slashing diagonally towards its peak and the white water clutching and boiling with enormous glee around the base of the barely visible apparition.

Until the sea suddenly fell away into a trough of black, sucking grue and the pyramid became a sheer, all but vertical wall of metal squatting like some grotesque and monstrous sea-cliff across the racing ship's track.

Shaw's eyes dilated. Showed bewilderment. Just for that first sickening moment of frozen incredulity.

And then he whirled with the fear a tight fist of pain and in the certain hopeless knowledge that he was too late – already far too bloody late – to save *Lycomedes*.

'Hard to starboard, man . . . !'

The quartermaster, Clements, jerked with the shock of it. Blinked back owlishly. Still occupied with resentment over the Old Man's bloody-minded indifference to a bloke's discreet protest . . .

' . . . God dammit I said hard to STARBOARD!'

Shaw started to move towards him savagely, hands outstretched as if to seize the wheel, and Clements squealed an unnerved 'Hard a st'bd aye, *AYE* SIR!' before flinging his weight on the spokes, spinning the wheel in frantic, unreasoning response to a madman's whim.

The captain halted with a conscious effort of will. Then slowly he turned back to stare, almost sorrowfully, at the hypnotized figure of the young second officer, still transfixed behind raised glasses.

'My God, Mister Fuller . . . ' he whispered in a dull, utterly drained voice. 'My God, but what have you *done* to us . . . !'

# Chapter Two

A huge peak, black and huge,
As if with voluntary power instinct
upreared its head.
                    *William Wordsworth*


## CATACLYSM MINUS THIRTY SECONDS

The ship started to turn. Swinging to starboard almost imperceptibly at first, the black flare of her bow smashing into the building seas while great gouts of water flung skywards to be snatched by the storm and dragged, slashing and hissing, across her fo'c'slehead.

And then faster. Until the dazed watchers on her bridge could begin to detect the pendulum arc of her foremast cutting a path across the misty, jagged line of the horizon. Feel her heeling with ever increasing momentum.

Three degrees . . . four . . . five . . .

Starting to sheer bodily sideways now, responding to the combined forces of angled rudder and the transverse thrust of her right-hand-turning propeller, yet still moving at full speed through the water.

Shaw didn't try to stop her. Not right away. Deeply loaded as she was *Lycomedes* would require a minimum of six times her own length in which to come to rest, even with her engine going full astern.

While that monstrous steel belly-hook now protruded from the sea less than a quarter of her length away.

*Lycomedes* was already condemned. Shaw only had one defensive tactic left to stay her execution. To use what cumbersome manœuvrability her forward momentum could afford him . . .

'Wheel's hard a st'bd, sir!'

Clements bending at the waist, forcing the spokes of the wheel down against the stops as if his conscious effort of will could make *Lycomedes* answer faster while watching the captain apprehensively from the corner of his eyes, still unaware of the reason for the apparent brainstorm.

Until the second mate lowered the binoculars and, without turning his eyes from the hypnotic fascination of the sea immediately ahead, started to shake uncontrollably.

'Almost awash . . . ' Fuller intoned in a low, curiously resentful voice. 'Virtually submerged . . . so's I wouldn't see it on radar . . . '

'Ring the engine to "Stand-by", Mister Fuller!' the captain snapped. 'Quickly, now!'

'Oh Christ!' Clements muttered involuntarily, slowly beginning to understand that this was for real.

' . . . the lousy weather! Lousy, rotten seas . . . ' The second mate's voice rose strangely. ' . . . masking the contact . . . screwin' up the bloody *radar* . . . !'

'God *DAMMIT*, MAN!' Shaw roared, lunging for the handle of the telegraph.

*Lycomedes* only had fifty feet of searoom left to cover.

The clang of the telegraph in the restricted volume of the wheelhouse was shocking – heart-stopping almost – in its impact.

A long way from the bridge, separated by half a ship, the dog suddenly gave a low whimper.

It still sat there, though. Gazing mournfully at the boy through limpid brown eyes.

Perhaps it was the first living creature aboard *Lycomedes* – apart from those few who had already observed the immediate sea ahead – to sense the coming of the Cataclysm.

Though other men quickly became aware that something was amiss, too. Even before the warning jangle of the telegraphs echoed below decks. And despite the fact that the ship was already wallowing in an unpredictable and random manner because of the weather.

For there is still a feel, a crazy regularity about the movement of a ship steaming a straight course. In a head sea she pivots longitudinally, roller-coastering from trough to trough with the slow rise and fall period dictated by the distance between each oncoming crest. In a beam sea she rolls, sometimes quite sickeningly, yet with a ponderous, rhythmic inevitability. In a quartering sea, where the crests angle in under her stern, lifting and surfing her ahead, she progresses in an unsettling series of sheering rushes.

Only in a confused, undecided storm sea – such as that surrounding *Lycomedes* on that winter afternoon – does she barrel and corkscrew without any real pattern at all.

But even then a seaman will still detect the moment when she starts to alter course. To turn to a new heading. He will immediately sense the changing angle of the wave forms as they meet her swinging bow, and the very slight addition to her normal inclination as she heels outwards under the centrifugal pressure of the turn.

And there were a lot of seamen aboard *Lycomedes*.

During those last moments of that last minute. Of what had been, up to then, a pretty ordinary, pretty average voyage.

'Nyhavn's the place for you,' the chief radio officer offered knowledgeably. 'Copenhagen's swinging sin centre. Booze, birds an' brothels.'

'All right, is it?'

Kemp shrugged, flicking idly through the W/T log. 'Depends on what you're after. And what you've got to spend. Or there's the Minefelt district . . . full've queers and fairies.'

'Aw, thank you *very* much . . . ' Bentine scratched his head and yawned, leaning well back in the operator's swivel chair. 'There's racing at Kempton Park today. Or d'you fancy a feast of pop music on Radio One . . . '

He hesitated, then said, 'We're altering course. Must be going into the Kattegat.'

The chief sparks frowned. 'Skagerrak. It's the Skagerrak that cuts across the top of Denmark. Then we turn south again into the Kattegat . . . ' He looked up at the bulkhead clock. 'Anyway, it's only fourteen twenty – we won't be altering east for another ten hours or so.'

The ship rolled jerkily as a sea took her on the beam. Bentine clung to the arms of the chair and said, 'Oooooops!'

'Still turning,' Kemp muttered curiously. 'Quite a bit of wheel on by the feel of it.'

The jangle of the bridge telegraph sounded distant, but very clear.

'Bloody hell!' the parrot squawked stridently. 'Bloody hell bloody hell bloodeeeeeee *hell*!'

It broke off triumphantly and pulled another two feathers out, all the time eyeing the chief engineer with a calculating glare of provocation. The feathers floated to the bottom of the cage and Hermann looked just a little bit more like an oven-ready chicken.

'What was it you wanted to look at, Charlie?' the chief asked distantly, glowering back at the fowl.

'The lube oil purifier.'

'Put the fourth on to it then. Soon as they ring down finished with engines . . . Wonder what the Danish for "millet seed" is?'

The second engineer sighed. 'You could ask the second sparks, sir. He's got a Danish dictionary.'

'Bentine? Aye, and he'll probably have a lot more Danish books by the time we sail again. Mrs Barraclough would be horrified if she knew a young lad like that could be so obsessed by . . . '

The chief broke off, listening.

'Who's a silly bugger?' the parrot enquired temptingly.

The second stared pointedly at the top of the chief engineer's slightly balding head. It was the nearest he dared to giving Hermann a straight answer.

'Just altering course,' Barraclough remarked, satisfied that *Lycomedes*' changing attitude wasn't anything to do with his engines.

'Must be someone coming the other way,' the second commented, following up quickly with, 'Do you want anything done about that suspect packing on the main . . . '

The telegraph clanged from the bridge almost directly above the chief engineer's cabin. Barraclough jerked his head up, frowning interrogatively at his assistant.

'The Old Man never warned me he might be reducing the revs. You know anything about it, Charlie?'

The second shook his head. 'Maybe going on stand-by. For fog.'

'In *this* wind . . . ?'

*Lycomedes* juddered to the slam of the beam sea but she didn't quite come back on an even keel. Still didn't feel quite loose. Still angling over fractionally to port.

'By God but we're still turning!' Barraclough snapped, suddenly displaying a tenseness that the second had never detected before.

But Chief Engineer Barraclough had been at sea a very long time. And he could feel things – almost anticipate events – by adding up all the little occurrences, insignificant in them-

34

selves but together forming an out of the ordinary sequence.

Which, in turn, presupposed an extraordinary, and therefore potentially dangerous situation.

He started to reach for the bulkhead telephone above his desk. His finger hovered undecidedly between the engineroom and bridge call buttons . . .

Huang Pi-wu turned on his back and smiled. It was a beautiful, seraphic smile of pure joy.

Because this was the bit he enjoyed best in the whole of his dream. The bit where they had reached the perfume garden, had floated on legs of thistledown all the way from the Gate Of A Thousand Happy Lovers to the lush green bank of the river where the carp and the goldfish traced thread-like furrows across the placidly drifting surface.

And here he lay down, sun-bronzed and eternally youthful. While the ethereal form of the lovely Yeh Chun towered above him like a vibrant young forest animal. Adoring him. Worshipping him. Caring for and protecting him . . .

The deposit for the Huang Pi-wu Restaurant chain was pretty well protected, too. All one thousand, three hundred and sixteen pounds worth in its tin box under the bunk.

It wasn't terribly erotic in itself. But it made sleeping with the wondrous Yeh Chun every afternoon a lot more reassuring.

Huang never felt the ship entering her turn. Or the distant shock of the telegraph.

Because Yeh Chun was bending over him now. Smiling down at him. Reaching out with yearning hands . . .

And that bit was the *very* best bit of all.

It was the worst bit as far as Fourth Engineer Chisholme, still retching spasmodically into the sump tray under the generator, was concerned.

Not connected with the unbelievably desirable Yeh Chun, of

35

course. Bert didn't know anything about her and he didn't personally go much on Chinese birds, for a start.

Or not now, anyway. Not after that long-haired raver he'd met during the time *Lycomedes* was on the Singapore run. The fantastic creature with the swimming, anything-but-inscrutable black eyes and the blue shiny silk *cheongsam* stretched like a drumskin between uptilted and incredibly-sculpted young breasts . . .

. . . which episode really tore Bert up and almost destroyed his psychological stability even to this day. When he discovered that the libidinous and animal-passionate Lola Chang had one major, and basically insurmountable flaw.

In that Lola finally turned out to be a . . . well . . . a *bloke*, actually.

And even more shattering than the actual discovery of his bed-mate's true hormone structure was the lengths to which Bert had already carried the affair before he *did* find out that she . . . he . . . Lola was a feller.

But it was his first trip out east. And nobody had thought to tell him about the rather unusual young creatures of Singapore's Boogie Street . . .

Anyway, the worst bit about being seasick for Fourth Engineer Chisholme was the distance – mostly vertical – that he had to cover to reach fresh, reviving sea air, Bert usually choosing to be overcome by nausea while in the lowest part of the engineroom.

So he just knelt there in the oily sludge and felt the ship sway and plummet, and reflected miserably on the endless soaring flights of steel-runged ladders between him and a breathable, life-supporting atmosphere.

And wished the bloody ship would sink. Quickly!

*Please?*

Until the third said curiously, 'We're altering to st'bd, d'you reckon?'

And Carbon Black advised knowledgeably, 'Prob'bly givin' way to some southard-bounder I'd say, sir . . . Now come on, Mister Chisum. Get a grip've my arm here . . .

Then the telegraph clanged shockingly, blood-freezing in its unexpected clamour which slashed right across the thunder of the fourteen cylinder *Pielstick*.

The third muttered 'Jesus!' and started to run back along the catwalk towards the control room.

Chisholme watched him go, whiter than white against the glare of the lights, and swallowed convulsively, willing the nausea to leave him in peace. Praying for it to.

Because – quite unaccountably – he suddenly felt very, very scared.

That unexpected beam sea that buffeted *Lycomedes* in the first few moments of her emergency turn also caught Chief Cook Dempster – already off balance at the open oven door – and swayed him even farther into an unstable, half-crouching posture.

It was a small incident. The sort of thing that happens to everyone aboard a ship during rough weather, and the reaction to this temporary loss of equilibrium is invariably automatic – you wait until you know precisely which way the bloody deck's going to go, then you take corrective action.

Which Dempster did.

Watched by a grinning Second Cook Stan Young he just snorted a good natured 'Aaaaah *shove* it!' and stayed exactly where he was.

It was only because Officers' Steward Eddie Ferguson – staggering into the galley with an armload of company-crested plates and cannoning off the door frame as he did so – added a not-so-good-natured 'Effin' boats!' that the chief cook even realized they were turning.

He didn't give it a second thought. Not even when the telegraph rang.

He merely concentrated on shielding his eyes from the heat of the oven while maintaining the knees-bent posture of a Cossack dancer frozen half-way through his act.

Bosun Skinner, also dancing in agonized frustration at the top of the forward well deck ladder, suddenly saw the Old Man's face appearing at the wheelhouse window high above him. Then the face disappeared abruptly and, a moment later, *Lycomedes* began to swing urgently to starboard.

Skinner stopped waving, muttered a shaky 'Thank *Christ*!' and whirled to face the apprehensive eyes of the carpenter.

Chippie pleaded for the tenth time, 'What *is* it, Willie boy?' but Skinner grabbed him by the arm, shoving him aft with a muttered, 'I dunno . . . Somethin' . . . a wreck in the water. Right under our *bows*, matey . . . '

Then, without realizing it, he, too, had started to run for the purely psychological and illusory safety of the centrecastle accommodation. Thereby falling prey to the same blindly unreasoning fear of deckhands Bronson and Falls.

He didn't – couldn't immediately – appreciate that whatever happened to *Lycomedes* would inevitably affect every man aboard, no matter where he chanced to be at the time. And that a roof over your head wasn't going to matter a damn – would even be a disadvantage in fact – if your ship rips her guts out and just keeps on steaming straight down to the bottom of the sea . . .

'C'mon,' Skinner snarled tightly. 'Come *on* f'r Chrissakes . . . !'

So Chippie began to run, too. From what he didn't really know. He hadn't even seen it, for cryin' out loud. But he'd seen the look in Willie's eyes an' that was more than enough . . .

Until his seaboot-clad foot skidded in a shiny patch of oil and

38

seawater spreading around the base of a winch. He felt it go from under him and started to fall headlong. But just as he hit the deck in a flailing, involuntary dive *Lycomedes* rolled unexpectedly, shying sullenly away from a vagrant beam sea . . . adding further momentum to the carpenter's uncontrollable descent . . . propelling him across the ice-rink deck in a starfish bundle of gleaming yellow oilskin.

He felt his nose shatter as his head slammed precisely into the gap between the winch barrel and the steel casing, the skull imprisoned as firmly as a wedge in a vice. He started to convulse, giving out little animal cries with the shock, the agony, the ultimate horror of it all . . .

Skinner bellowed, 'CHIPPIEEEEEEEE!'

The ship wallowed sullenly, rolled again, skittering the spreadeagled man sideways. The carpenter's neck snapped with a crack that echoed above the buffeting of the wind and the hissing rumble of the sea. The frantically scrabbling legs ever so slowly straightened out while his hands fluttered briefly, then relaxed . . .

The carpenter was the first man to die aboard *Lycomedes* on that ordinary, average day.

Even before the Cataclysm finally overtook her.

The dog suddenly whined again. A soft, mournful cry almost overwhelmed by the crackle of the ensign over the taffrail and the buffeting moan of the wind.

Certainly the boy never heard the warning clamour of the telegraphs. Not that far away from the bridge. But perhaps the dog had still been able to. Perhaps it had also detected the horror in Bosun Skinner's appealing bellow from the forward deck.

Or even the keening, short-lived agony of the carpenter.

For certain animals reveal an uncanny, finely-tuned awareness. Like the sea dog, in a wire cage on that stormswept deck, which seemed to sense so much more than the boy who knelt beside it.

Because this time the dog kept up its uneasy, repetitive lament.

Right up to the moment when *Lycomedes* herself began to scream.

Apprentice Cassiday, looking down from the height of the starboard bridge wing, saw one of the seamen on the deck below take a pretty nasty tumble under the winch and worried a bit because it seemed as though the chap might have hurt himself quite badly.

He also noticed at the same time that the ship was turning, and pretty fast at that, which did strike him as a little odd because Rupert could hardly make out the horizon at all, never mind another ship or land or anything.

But he thought he'd better tell someone about the accident, so's they could enter it in the log or whatever they did, and turned towards the open wheelhouse door.

Then stopped. Abruptly!

Feeling suddenly very uncertain of himself. Even a little apprehensive . . .

When the captain, apparently staring with ferocious concentration through the wheelhouse window, took an abrupt – almost an involuntary step backwards – and said strangely, 'She can't *do* it, Fuller . . . '

And then added, with a terrible sadness, 'I'm sorry, but . . . we're finished!'

# Chapter Three

When stately ships are twirled and spun
Like whipping tops and help there's none
And mighty ships ten thousand ton
Go down like lumps of lead.

*Ralph Hodgson*

## THE CATACLYSM

The apex of the wallowing sea-pyramid entered *Lycomedes'*
number one hold some thirty feet abaft the bow.

Had she not been swinging hard under full helm – had she,
instead, taken the initial impact of the blow full on her reinforced
stem – then she would have crumpled, flooded her forepeak
tank, breached the collision bulkhead, even breached her
forward hold space . . . yet *Lycomedes* might still have survived.

Many ships collide. A considerable proportion of those
sustain grievous, but not invariably fatal wounds. But *Lycomedes*
was also turning, exposing her flank. Sacrificing the protective
ram of her reinforced forefoot and bow section . . .

So the object she'd struck entered the comparatively light
shell plating of her port side instead, clawing a railway-
carriage length laceration which exposed both her numbers one
and two lower holds to the instant rush of the sea.

And she screamed then, agonizing in a shuddering, screeching
cacophony of severing metal which searched out and encroached
on all the secret, silent places in the ship. And men turned
suddenly shocked faces towards the outboard side of their
separate compartments, each undergoing his own private version

of hell as he anticipated that frail protection, too, imploding under a roaring cataract . . .

. . . until the ship began to veer crazily, but this time to port, pivoting uncontrollably on the lynch-pin of the submerged thing which penetrated her. And the masts which had previously leant out to port now swung in a great gyrating arc until they lay to starboard – just as the avalanching ingress of the sea blew the hatch cover clean off number one forward hold with a shattering roar of compressed air and spiralling cash registers and spewing bags of seed potatoes and atomized spray . . .

And a man screamed 'Oh dear *Jeeeeeeesus* . . . !' yet no man aboard would ever remember having cried out at all during that first brain-freezing instant of the Cataclysm.

Until – suddenly – the bedlam of rending metal stopped. Dead! Leaving only a deathly hush broken by the rumble of flooding water and the soft moan of the wind.

But *Lycomedes* didn't. Because she was still driving ahead, still under full engine power and compelled by her several thousand tons of forward momentum while finally wrenching that underwater spike from the wound in her stricken hull . . .

Only then, instead, was the period of The Hammer.

The unearthly, blood-chilling clangour of a great object striking the bottom of the ship. A recurring submarine rumble as *Lycomedes* passed over the monster, rolling and compressing it in her wallowing, slewing passage. Crushing back at the thing below her belly like some unreasoning juggernaut.

And so the ship continued, driving and plunging into the piling seas on the crest of that sepulchral thunder as, all the time, the muffled booming passed farther and farther aft. Under number two . . . clean under number three . . .

. . . a screeching stridency as steel plates lacerated yet again somewhere under the bridge itself, then The Hammer once more. Piledriving in under the cofferdam . . . oil fuel bunker, switchboard flat . . . along the underside of number six double bottoms . . .

A greaser in the ratings' mess closed his eyes and fumbled for the words of a prayer. *Any* bloody prayer f'r . . .

Someone else wondered what drowning would be like, and maybe he should go for his lifejacket now an' not wait for someone else to pinch it. But he didn't move. Not one muscle.

. . . booming sonorously . . . grating . . . passing farther aft under the pipe tunnel. Half way along number six double botto . . . !

'Oh NOOOOOOOO!'

The still anonymous submerged finger erupted into *Lycomedes*' engineroom precisely under the after gearbox mounting, displacing it and instantly shearing both the propellor shaft and crankshaft couplings. The main engine, abruptly relieved of any load at all, immediately over-ran the governor in a rapidly escalating thunder of power which almost drowned the triumphant rumble of imploding seawater.

Only nine interminable seconds had passed since the moment of the Cataclysm.

And only then did *Lycomedes* finally begin to slow, abruptly slewing to rest under the drag of the monstrous sea-anchor transfixing her belly. Already the first seas were beginning to break green over her rapidly settling fo'c'slehead.

The ship – in the space of a few revolutions of her still-scanning radar eye – had now become a powerless, eviscerated hulk.

Yet to the men on board they all seemed to take a very long time. As if experiencing a slow-motion replay of a high speed event.

Those few violent moments when *Lycomedes* actually began to die . . .

The first thought that flashed into Chief Officer McRae's mind

43

– already preoccupied with cargo plans and stability factors – was that the dynamite in number four had exploded.

He had still been in the officers' accommodation, one deck below the bridge, and heading for the mate's office when the door of the shower room opened and Mickey Wise came out wearing a bath towel and fluffy red carpet slippers with yellow pom-poms on them.

The third officer grinned 'Afternoon, sir,' from the middle of a cloud of steam, then hesitated, looking a bit embarrassed as he caught McRae's somewhat pointed downward gaze.

'Slippers, sir,' he'd added informatively, lifting one foot. 'Bought them for my mother in Hamburg an' then found I'd none myself . . . Quite comfy actually, except they're a bit small.'

The mate had nodded gravely. 'And they make you look very pretty, Three Oh. Rather sexy, in fac . . . !'

Then *Lycomedes* reared in agony . . . tearing herself apart . . . and the dull thud of an explosion from forward almost immediately . . .

'Dynamite!' McRae said dazedly, 'The bloody *dynamite's* gone up . . . !'

But he couldn't really believe that because dynamite wasn't an unstable cargo, and it was secured in a specially constructed magazine with no electrical wiring, only copper nails and . . .

And then the nerve-racking booming. From under the ship. Until she reared again . . . started to sheer violently and at the same time decelerate with a savagery that propelled the shocked third mate – still balanced on one foot – in a white-faced hop, skip and jump to bring up with a crash against the ladder leading to the bridge.

Temporarily stunned with disbelief McRae blinked as the young officer slid down in an untidy heap then, almost immediately, got up on his hands and knees again, dazedly scrabbling around with bright red blood cascading from his nose to form little whorls on the compo deck. 'Towel . . . I got to get my *towel*, sir . . . !'

While McRae, equally confused by the suddenness of it all, muttered in relief, 'It's O.K., Three Oh! It's not the dynamite . . . We've only hit something . . .

Until realization swamped over him.

*Collision!*

He cleared the third mate's grovelling nudity in one leap. Running for the stairway to the bridge . . .

On the forward centrecastle deck Bosun Skinner started to run back towards the winch, and towards Chippie. But he'd heard the vertebrae snap clear as a bell and seen the way the carpenter's legs had suddenly relaxed, and there was only a dull certainty in the bosun's mind . . . and a slowly growing misery.

So he just knelt by Chippie's side and held a wet hand, and dimly felt the ship spitting herself on the thing he'd seen ahead of them, but he didn't give a damn right then. He never even raised his head when the forward hold blew out and a great slab of hatch board smashed into the deck less than ten feet away.

And maybe Skinner even cried a little while *Lycomedes* was suffering her mortal wounds, though you'd never have been able to tell because the leather-tanned face of the old man was already shiny wet from the rain and the spray and the oil . . .

But it was only when the ship had finally stopped screaming and lay exhausted in the water that Bosun Skinner gently placed Chippie's hand by his side and, slipping out of his yellow oilskin jacket, spread it neatly to cover the obscenely-angled shoulders of his friend before rising unhurriedly to his feet and looking down for a moment longer . . . Just remembering . . . Until *Lycomedes* slid sideways into the trough of a wave and he felt her stagger with the shock of it.

He glanced bleakly at the piling seas already sweeping the foredeck. His voice was quiet. Almost matter of fact. 'Likely

45

there's a lot of us due to pay-off in a little while, Chippie . . . an' then you'll be in company . . . '

Then Skinner turned, standing very erect. And walked aft. Towards the ladders leading to the bridge.

Both the dog and the boy Michael Standish took the whole thing very calmly, considering.

Though there wasn't a lot of noise down aft, and what little sound there was had been muffled and distorted by the sea and the wind, and probably the most frightening symptom of the impact was the way *Lycomedes* abruptly slowed and started to swing beam on all at the same time. But even when a thing like that happens, you don't really believe it's more than a major engine breakdown. Or perhaps a minor collision, at the worst. Especially when you're not even nineteen years old yet, and being lost at sea only happens to sailing ships rounding the Horn or some other chaps in an undermanned Liberian or Greek with unserviceable radar and an elderly drunk on the bridge.

Certainly it didn't feel all *that* disastrous. And certainly not like the prelude to a Cataclysm . . .

So the boy just muttered anxiously, 'Oh lord!' and began to head for the ladders to the after well deck and his emergency station. Then he sensed, rather than actually felt the ship getting heavier and heavier by the head and, almost without thinking, turned and went back to the wire pen.

Opening the door he unhooked the slip chain and said tentatively, 'C'mon, dog. Maybe you'd better stay with me, eh?'

He was a bit surprised and pleased when the dog came out right away and sat in front of him, staring trustingly up into his eyes. It still looked gloomy, though. But a little more lively.

As soon as he slipped the lead over the animal's head the dog got up, sort of leaning against the boy's leg and ready to go.

Then it pointed its nose forward and gave a tiny, anxious whimper. Almost a plea to hurry.

'Don't be silly, Seadog,' the boy said doubtfully. 'There can't be all *that* much to worry about . . . C'mon, then. Heel!'

They started off towards the well deck together.

The dog kept very close to the boy.

Chief Cook Dempster was whimpering, too. But that was largely because he was being roasted and scalded, all at the same time.

Actually he'd been screaming quite loudly at the start. When the ship had struck, slowed with such abruptness and cata-pulted him – already off balance – head first into the open oven.

But steward Eddie Ferguson, originally struggling through the galley door with his load of plates, stole the show in the first instance by disappearing back into the alleyway again with a startled yell fusing into the crash of breaking crockery . . . and it was only after *Lycomedes* had ripped herself apart and finally slewed with every moveable item in the galley tumbling and bouncing and smashing to the deck that the dazed second cook Young – totally bewildered and still gripping his chopping knife in frozen fingers – suddenly noticed a pair of kicking legs, clad in chef's black and white check trousers, projecting from the oven.

Just as the soup from the simmering skillet above, especially made for the captain's dinner, slopped out of the pot, piled up against the back of the stove in a brown steaming flood, and then ran aft with a great hissing to pour over the edge of the hotplate and down in a boiling cataract on to the scrabbling legs below.

Which was when the man in the oven stopped shrieking and just lay quietly burning, with only the tiniest of occasional whimpers to show that he was still alive.

While the second cook, finally galvanized into frantic haste by the super-horror before him, screamed, 'Here, Eddie . . .

f'r God's *sake*, EDDIE!' and ran forward to grip Dempster's legs.

The steward appeared at the door for a second time, with a bleeding gash in one hand and a look of fury on his face, and snarling, 'What the fucking he . . . !'

Then he saw what Young was doing and muttered, 'Oh, Christ . . . !' in an appalled voice, and stumbled towards the oven just as Stan pulled at the cooking man. And the whole bloody lot came out together – oven shelves, roasting tray, super-heated fat, gently-browned leg of lamb . . . chief cook Dempster . . .

Stan Young sobbed, 'What do we do, Eddie . . . What do we *do*?'

But Ferguson just took one look, choked, 'Oh *Christ*!' again . . . and started to be sick.


Huang Pi-wu was still smiling seraphically.

He never heard *Lycomedes* rolling over the monster. He didn't feel the shock as she finally dragged to a halt. He wasn't even aware of the rising crescendo of the run-away main engine not far below him and the cabin he shared with Bert Ferguson.

Because Yeh Chun was actually caressing him now. Running her thistle-down fingertips with indescribable gentleness across his forehead; over his closed eyelids; toying for one exquisite moment of tenderness with the manly gloss of his hair and then on to his lips – aggressive perhaps, but not cruel – his chin, his throat . . . still downwards to his sun-bronzed and immensely powerful shoulders . . .

He could sense her mounting excitement. The passion, barely under control. Her burning desire for him, revealed by the intensity of her breathing – the quickening rise and fall of her statuesque and enchanting young breasts . . .

And who could blame her . . . ? For not only was the dreaming

Huang Pi-wu utterly irresistible and attractive – but he also possessed the vast sum of one thousand, three hundred and sixteen pounds.

Sterling.

In the radio room some fifty feet away from the bridge both Kemp and Bentine seemed to guess instinctively that *Lycomedes* had struck a submerged object.

Chief operator Kemp even went a bit further than that. He was also the first man aboard *Lycomedes* to guess at the precise nature of the submerged object which they *had* struck – by suffering an immediate flash of intuition which linked the tearing and booming underneath the ship directly with a message he himself had received earlier and passed to the bridge . . . just before filing his own routine copy in the clip on that hook labelled *Navigational Warnings*.

But Kemp was a practical, as well as a perceptive man, so he instantly forced the speculative past from his mind and concentrated on the more urgent future.

'Get out've the chair,' he snapped, even while the ship was swinging, wallowing monstrously. Still screeching under their feet. 'I'll take the key. You try an' raise the bridge on the phone!'

But Bentine just stared at him and looked bewildered.

'We've hit something . . . ' the youngster blurted, almost accusingly. *Lycomedes* heeled a few more degrees to port then started to come upright – and then lie over the other way. Bentine grabbed for the edge of the table and again demanded unsteadily, 'We've bloody *hit* something, haven't we?'

Kemp saw the fear in the kid's eyes, noticing the way they kept darting towards the door, and thought grimly, 'Christ, but I hope he's not goin' to panic . . . ' so he swallowed his own terror and forced a tight grin.

'Sounds like it. And the Old Man won't want to keep it

49

secret either, so just get out of the chair, Johnny, an' let me earn my extra money, eh?'

'It was right underneath us, though. It was bad, too. I could tell by the way she swung . . . '

Kemp detected the rising note of hysteria and deliberately kept his own tone very, very calm. 'Just get out of the chair. Please, Johnny?'

Bentine closed his eyes for a moment and Kemp allowed himself a quick glance round the cabin to see if there was anything handy to hit the kid with if he had to, but then Bentine opened his eyes again and seemed to take a deep breath. He slipped the headphones off and handed them over without another word.

Kemp said, 'Thanks, Johnny,' very casually and eased into the swivel chair while Bentine reached for the phone. His hands were shaking.

The chief radio operator checked that the transmitter switch was on full power and the frequency selector set to 500 kilocycles, then he leaned back in the chair and started to whistle softly. Waiting.

'Aren't you going to do anything?' Bentine asked anxiously. jabbing at the call button on the phone. 'Aren't you even going to key the auto-alarm or something?'

Kemp stopped whistling and glanced at the clock on the bulkhead. It stood at 1421 precisely.

'They'll have a lot on their minds on the bridge right now,' he said. 'We'll give 'em a few minutes to decide whether they want an urgency or distress transmission.'

He began to whistle again, still thinking bitterly about that *Navwarn* message.

But it was hard to seem so bloody casual. With the fear such a tight, burning knot right down in his belly.

And even more so when he had such a clear impression of the size of the thing they had smashed into at full speed.

And what it must have done to them below the waterline.

The chief engineer and the second engineer collided in the cabin doorway, both aiming with single-minded determination towards the engineroom in the very first instant of *Lycomedes'* agony.

Until Barraclough literally hauled the second out of the way by the scruff of his neck and was heading the scramble for the head of the ladder even before the awful measured booming of the submarine hammer had passed.

They were the only two men on board who were deliberately driving themselves below decks at a time when most others only wanted to see a clear sky above their heads, but they were ship's engineers, and ship's engineers always have had a very distorted opinion of where they should be during times of crisis.

The door to the chief's cabin stood open.

A voice – a vituperative, not-quite-human voice from inside remarked petulantly, 'Bloodeeeeee *hell*!'

But then again, who could have blamed Hermann for swearing at that moment.

Trapped in a wire cage, in an already sinking ship, as he happened to be.

Though others were also confined, if not actually trapped inside the hull of *Lycomedes* during those first agonizing seconds of the Cataclysm.

It was even a bit like being in a wire cage as well if you saw it through the eyes of fourth engineer Chisholme, frozen in a crouching position beside the generator at the moment of impact and still staring upwards as the whiter than white figure of the third made it half way up the first flight of shiny steel-web ladders in response to the 'Standby' command of the telegraph.

And then the ship started to reverberate, and explode and

spiral and rip apart all at the same *time* f'r Chrissakes . . . while
the whole bloody engineroom floor level seemed to erupt in a
raging smash of fountaining water and spray with great gouts
of foam hurling high above him towards the glaring deck-head
fluorescents . . .

The third seemed to half-turn with the fright of it, staring
back down towards Chisholme with his mouth sagging disbelievingly and one hand still stretched upwards to grip the
shiny, oil-bright handrail of the ladder until *Lycomedes* rolled
heavily, unexpectedly, and Bowman's foot skidded off the rung
to bring him tumbling all the way to the bottom again in a
flailing rag-doll dazzle of bleached laundry.

Carbon Black, standing over Bert, blurted a shattered
'*JE*sus!' then dropped his teeth and started to run for the
ladder. Chisholme screamed a frantic 'Gimme a hand out've
here you bast . . . !' until the thunder of the run-away *Pielstick*
and the grating of tortured steel and the tumult of the imploding
North Sea all got too much for his ravaged nervous system so
he clung to the generator casing and sobbed and tried to haul
himself up and vomit all at the same time . . .

. . . just before a hissing tidal wave of fuel oil and water
rampaged along the catwalk, slammed him violently against the
cold steel block, ripped his shoe cleanly from his left foot and
finally submerged him in a gurgling shroud of claustrophobic
horror.

One starkly etched image of a frantic Carbon Black struggling
with single-minded self-preservation to climb the ladder . . .
but with a sobbing third engineer Bowman clinging equally
dementedly to the greaser's leg while shrieking, 'My back's
*broken* f'r Christ's sake! My back's been BROKEN an' I can't
move my . . . !'

Then Bert Chisholme started to drown.

The captain didn't move at all during the Cataclysm.

He'd just taken that one involuntary step backwards as he realized without any doubt at all that *Lycomedes* was going to hit, and then the sadness and the futility swamped over him – and the utter certainty that quite a lot of his crew must die in a very short time from now because men – ordinary, average men – couldn't reasonably expect to survive in thirty foot, just-above-freezing seas without the kind of luck that ordinary, average men don't normally warrant.

And in brutal fact, that the only doubtful outcome of the next few hours would be not so much a question of 'How many might live,' as 'Could *any* men live . . . ?'

Because the captain already knew that *Lycomedes* was going to sink very quickly. He knew because he was himself a part of her, and because every time her hull was breached by the monster a little bit of Captain Graham Shaw died too . . .

. . . so he just said, 'I'm sorry!' again. And waited until the ship had stopped shrieking. And then the young apprentice who'd been standing out on the starboard wing turned a white frightened face towards him and cried, 'We've hit something, sir! Hit something hard . . . !'

The captain hesitated at that moment. He wanted desperately to reassure the boy, to promise him he'd be all right, and that somebody would always be there to look after him. Only he was coldly aware that it could prove to be a meaningless charade, and that the time would come soon when men might barely hope to save themselves.

Because the Cataclysm sneers at selflessness. It demands the acceptance of reality, while icy-cold reality in its turn perpetuates the traditional absolution of '*Every man for himself!*' from the bridges of foundering ships.

So the captain simply nodded and said, 'Thank you, son.'

Then, even though *Lycomedes* was already powerless, her

53

control out of his hands, he turned abruptly and grasped the shiny brass handles of the telegraph.

And swung it firmly to STOP ENGINE!

For the very last time.

# Chapter Four

Me howling blasts drive devious, tempest-tossed,
Sails ripped, seams opening wide, and compass lost.
*William Cowper*

## CATACLYSM plus ONE MINUTE

The anonymous sea-pyramid penetrating *Lycomedes'* engine-room – the precise identity of which only chief radio operator Kemp had been able to guess at until now – was itself mangled and ruptured out of all recognition.

Within sixty seconds the remaining air within it – the trapped air which had given the monster sufficient buoyancy to hover in wait for *Lycomedes* just below the surface of the North Sea – that air had vented free, adding its exhausting roar to the bedlam in her flooding engine space.

The peak of the sea-cliff then withdrew, sinking vertically towards the ocean bed twenty-six fathoms below.

And as it plummeted downwards trailing a gigantic spiral of twinkling bubbles it also created the effect of a cork being drawn from a wine bottle.

What had originally been a flood of seawater trying to drown the shocked Bert Chisholme, the berserk greaser Black and the appallingly-injured third engineer Bowman now became a thunderous torrent.

The air in *Lycomedes'* engineroom also became compressed by the rising level of the water. It started to whistle at first, then to squeal and finally to shriek out of the open ventilators leading towards the deck.

Only those outlets weren't enough to cope with the volume of air being displaced. So the air pressure inside the central compartment of the ship gradually increased until it became a tangible danger – totally unnoticed by the men already fighting for life within her but a lurking, unsuspected hazard to those on deck . . .

But the first shock was wearing off. All through *Lycomedes* men began to shrug out of that bewildered paralysis which had marked the coming of the Cataclysm. Reflex action began to take charge. Bedlam mutated to a more ordered chaos in all parts of the ship not instantly threatened by the sea as crewmen hurried to their usually only vaguely recollected emergency stations.

Or simply hurried towards the open air, obsessed by the subconscious horror of being trapped in a foundering steel crypt. Perhaps not even giving thought to what they would do once clear of that most immediate prospect of death.

Though there were the exceptions to the rule . . .

For instance the galley abaft the officers' saloon wasn't evacuated right away.

As Eddie Ferguson gagged convulsively beside the cooked cook Dempster until Stan, looking white as a slab of dough, pleaded, 'Help me, for God's sake, Eddie. Help me get 'im up on deck, *please*!'

The steward sniffed shakily and wiped the back of his slashed hand across his forehead. It left a wide bloodied smear which immediately began to fuzz at the edges as it fused with the sweat on his brow. He forced himself to turn again and look down at the softly whimpering Dempster, but when he whispered, 'Oh, Christ!' for a third time it was with compassion and not revulsion.

Almost absently, without really taking his eyes off the injured man, he felt for a carving fork lying in the skating-rink mess on the deck and stabbed it into the leg of lamb.

'Now what're you doin'?' the second cook asked, watching him uncomprehendingly.

'Eh . . . ? Well, I din't want it to get spoiled in all that . . . !' Then Eddie realized what he was doing and dropped the fork with a hopeless gesture before asking apprehensively, 'Shouldn't we get 'im on deck, then?'

'That's what *I* said. Just in case she's goin' to go down . . . You take his arm, O.K.?'

Ferguson swallowed nervously and reached out, tentatively closing his fingers around the lobster-red limb. A sliver of blistered flesh slid away under his thumb and Dempster screamed. Just once. The steward dropped the arm abruptly and jerked back in fright.

'Oh JEEze!'

The ship rolled heavily and the lamb went skittering and sliding to starboard with the fork still stuck upright in it like a silver mainmast. A slow trickle of brown soup formed an erratic tributary towards the dishwasher with a thousand tiny, gradually-congealing fat boats passaging down it.

Stan Young began to cry. It was difficult to tell whether it was with fear or frustrated sympathy.

'What do we *do*?' he started to ask. All over again.

Huang Pi-wu knew precisely what *he* was doing. Or at least, what the lithe, sun-kissed fantasy image of himself was doing anyway.

And that was to open one eye – one arrogant, all-seeing and hypnotic dream eye that was – and allow it to roam with blatant appraisal over the bending, worshipping form of Yeh Chun.

He also allowed his lip to curl contemptuously . . . but not *too* contemptuously. Just enough to draw, with superbly calculated finesse, the tiniest of concerned breaths from her exquisite throat. Just enough to make her unsure of his need for her. Just enough to prevent any hint of complacency from blunting her superlative skills in the techniques of serving her lover . . .

*Lycomedes* gave a sudden violent swing, falling away into the troughs of the seas. And then another. The drawer under the sleeping escapist's bunk slid open to reveal a neatly folded tier of freshly laundered underwear, a leather mah-jong case decorated with inlaid gold dragons . . . and a hand-painted tin box.

But still Huang didn't wake up. He didn't even stir. He just lay moving gently from side to side against the raised bunk boards.

With, perhaps, the very tiniest suspicion of a smile on his lips. A curling, slightly contemptuous smile.


And of course chief engineer Barraclough and the second were still going down while nearly everybody else was coming up.

Which was why, when half way along the corridor between the ratings' mess room and the steel door to the machinery space itself, they virtually collided with a tidal wave of humanity, all apparently dedicated to heading in the other direction.

But Barraclough didn't really see them as people, more as obstacles, so he just roared, 'GerroutthebloodyWAY . . . !' and kept on going until someone grabbed his arm and swung him round in an apoplectic arc which brought him face to face with the shocked features of the man Halliday – a greaser whom the chief didn't like anyway and didn't have any damn time for even when the bastard wasn't using an irrelevant excuse like a collision to assault his senior officer.

Until Halliday stuttered, 'She's holed, sir! They've all 'ad their lot down below . . . ' and the chief could see he wasn't being aggressive – just terrified out of his mind.

Someone else from behind him said agitatedly, 'We've got to

get on deck. We got to get to the boats . . . !' before the second engineer's snarl cut the voice short with a vicious 'You'll do what you're told, Donaldson. An' *when* you're bloody told!'

Barraclough eyed the door at the end of the alleyway hungrily. Every nerve in his body was screaming for him to open it, to assess for himself the precise nature of the wound to *Lycomedes* – especially to *his* part of *Lycomedes* – but he was also a strong man, an understanding man, and he could sense the panic building around him.

And, also being a practical man, he knew that incipient panic at this stage would lose the ship even more surely than any natural hazard, so he just said quietly, 'I've got lads down below. I'm going down for them . . . anyone else coming?'

The greaser, Halliday, gazed at him with wild eyes. Only there was a hint of truculence there now, behind the fear.

'You givin' us an order then, Mister Barraclough?' he demanded on a note of rising hysteria.

Barraclough closed his eyes for a moment, feeling the hopelessness swamp over him. He already knew – he could hear and feel, almost taste the indications that *Lycomedes* was finished. The subterranean rumbling of the sea; the higher, throbbing roar of the SEMT-*Pielstick* which told him the main engine had separated from the shaft and was only held back from running amok by the hydraulic governor . . . the way the ship was already falling into the troughs of the seas and fractionally down by the head yet not much more than a minute could have passed since they'd struck . . .

'No . . . ' he snapped bleakly, tiredly. 'No, I'm not giving you an order!'

Then his concern for those watchkeepers possibly trapped below became too much for him to bear. He pivoted abruptly without another glance at the men in the alleyway and began to hurry towards the machinery space door. He didn't realize – couldn't possibly have been aware of – the accumulating air pressure lurking behind it . . .

The second hesitated, eyeing the group coldly. There were three seamen and the two greasers, Halliday and Donaldson. He jerked his head at the deck ratings, who just blinked back uneasily, out of their element. 'Topside! You lot get topside where you'll be some use!'

He didn't even glance at the two remaining greasers. Just shouldered his way roughly past and started to run again, trailing the chief. Donaldson looked at Halliday and Halliday glowered back at Donaldson until the little greaser dropped his eyes diffidently, almost in embarrassment.

'Yeah . . . well . . . ' he muttered, shuffling a bit. 'Maybe they'll need a hand like they say, eh?'

Then he turned, too. Following reluctantly.

Halliday stared after them through glinting tears – too scared to go back, too ashamed of his terror to turn and simply run away.

'Fucking *heroes*!' he roared unforgivingly.

But by then Chief Barraclough had reached the engineroom door. Only the handle seemed strangely stiff.

Rather as if someone, or something, was exerting pressure against it from the other side.

Chief Officer McRae – having left a temporarily dazed third mate Wise in reflex search for his towel – arrived at the top of the bridge internal stairway just as the captain swung *Lycomedes*' engine telegraph to 'Stop!'.

'Sir?' he blurted apprehensively. There didn't seem any need for a more specific question, not in view of the situation.

But Shaw simply raised his head and blinked at the mate. There seemed to be a vagueness about his expression, the way his brows were drawn together, almost as if he still wasn't quite sure whether he was awake or locked in a nightmarish fantasy world.

'*Sir!*' McRae said again, more sharply this time and with a note of appeal to it which emphasized his own uncertainty – his slowly growing fear that he would himself prove inadequate to cope with the responsibilities which must come shortly. And that, without Shaw's strength and experience to bolster him, he might even fail totally to withstand the pressures of the Cataclysm.

For it *was* the time of the Cataclysm. McRae sensed that much, even before he could make any assessment of *Lycomedes*' condition for himself. The shocked attitudes told him; the still disbelieving faces; the almost tangible air of guilt that emanated from the men around him – the men who had been on *Lycomedes*' bridge during those past moments of disaster and who, accordingly, had carried the responsibility for her safety, and the well-being of her crew.

Like *Graham Shaw; Master*: Guilty by tradition. Whether by default or not really didn't matter. As *Lycomedes*' captain he bore the burden of detached accountability.

And *Michael Fuller; Second Officer*: Guilty by neglect. The senior bridge watchkeeper at the time when *Lycomedes* suffered her death blow. The fact that he was also conscientious and careful and subject to ordinary human limitations didn't really matter either. Fuller would never shake off that guilt for as long as he lived . . . or in the short time before he was scheduled to die.

Then there was *Rupert Cassiday; Apprentice*: Guilty by virtue of being a boy. And, because he was young, of being blinded by romance. Rupert had good eyes and nothing to do but use them as he'd been told to . . . yet all he'd noticed was a friendly wave from a rather odd old seaman.

And, finally, *Ernest Clements; Helmsman*: Guilty by resentment. Because he *could* have been looking ahead, out past the compass card, while Fuller was engrossed in his radar screen. But Clements hadn't bothered – it wasn't his responsibility to keep a watch over the bow. Not even if there was a bloody cathedral in the way . . .

'Oh, for God's *sake*, sir!' McRae blurted urgently, virtually snarling.

Because he didn't give a damn right then about whose fault it had been. Not when he and the rest of *Lycomedes'* crewmen were liable to be struggling for survival in a Force Ten maelstrom very shortly, with lungs dissolving under retching gulps of fuel oil and the ship capsizing in a great, obliterating holocaust of rending steel and whipping wire, widows' grief and children's tears.

All of which did make the finer apportionment of guilt seem a little academic . . .

'Casualties, Mister? Any injured must be brought to the boat deck immediately . . . '

McRae snapped from his chilling reverie into sudden awareness as he noticed the Old Man eyeing him with a more normal, almost brisk expression. 'But what *was* it, sir?' he asked involuntarily feeling, at the same time, absurdly grateful for the change in the captain.

Then just for a fleeting instant he feared Shaw was going to slip back into his brooding, introspective trance until *Lycomedes'* master shrugged imperceptibly, shaking his head.

'I don't know. But it was big, David, damned big. It's hurt us terribly . . . '

Shaw swung abruptly and snapped, 'Mister Fuller. I want our present position and likely rate of drift . . . Quickly, please!'

But the second mate, who'd been standing transfixed before the wheelhouse windows all this time, suddenly swivelled and blundered past them, heading blindly for the chart space and muttering, 'I couldn't have seen it . . . Clutter! The radar masked by sea clutter so's *nobody* could've seen it . . . '

McRae called 'Mike!', shaken by the wild expression on the second's features but Shaw gripped his arm and said quietly, 'Leave him. Just for a minute.'

Then Quartermaster Clements shouted, 'Wheel's still hard to st'bd, but she's not answerin' the helm no more.'

The Old Man turned and nodded calmly. 'Midships . . . Secure the wheel but stand-by for the present.'

'*Christ* but you've got us in a right bloody mess,' Clements blurted. The glow from the binnacle reflected against the sweat on his brow while his knuckles, white with tension, still clamped around the spokes of the wheel.

The mate started to snap, 'Belay that, Clements!' but Shaw just repeated firmly, 'Midships the wheel, lad. Then lash it securely, if you please.'

The quartermaster seemed to hesitate, glaring at the two of them nervously, almost accusingly. Then he let go of the wheel abruptly and began to secure it in the loop of the telemotor lanyard.

Shaw didn't add anything further but there was a growing sense of urgency about him now, of returning competency. He, in common with every other man aboard *Lycomedes*, had suffered from that initial paralysis of stunned disbelief but it was easing gradually, losing its grip. The pain would come later. If the captain survived.

'Where is Mister Wise?' he asked irritably. 'Surely to God the man knows to report to the bridge right away.'

'Still below – looking for a towel!' McRae answered, feeling ridiculous as soon as he'd said it. The captain stared at him for a moment, frowning absently. Then he actually began to smile, even though it was only a fleeting, humourless sort of smile.

'Which does seem a very practical thing to do, at that. Though perhaps a little optimistic . . . under the circumstances.'

The telephone from the Radio Room began to ring anxiously.

The bulkhead clock was approaching two twenty-two in the afternoon.

It hadn't been an ordinary, average day aboard *Lycomedes* for two whole minutes.

And so the sequence of events following the Cataclysm progressed. Some men reacting almost instantly, others taking a little more time to adjust . . .

For Kemp and Bentine in the Radio Room there had been only a momentary inaction. But they were high above the water and isolated from the worst of the shock. They couldn't make any assessment of the full gravity of the blow, not right then, yet Kemp, ironically, was still the only man aboard who appreciated the identity of their submarine assailant.

For Chief Engineer Barraclough and the second there had been virtually no immobility at all. They were moving towards the engineroom even while *Lycomedes* was still blundering over the sea-cliff. But they, more than any others in the ship, were aware of the horror that such a disaster could bring on men who spend their lives working deep in the bowels of ships at sea, and of the urgency with which help might be required.

On the bridge itself the period of frozen inaction had, perhaps, existed for longer than anywhere else. But they, in turn, were more aware of what had happened than those others below decks. They were the ones shocked by the additional realization that – had they been even a little more competent – then they might have avoided the disaster in the first instance. They were also the ones best situated to appreciate just how grievously *Lycomedes had* been wounded . . . and evaluate, with seamen's eyes, the future prospects for survival in the storm force maelstrom surrounding them.

And there were still some men who just didn't *know* what to do, not even when the first horror had passed. Like Second Cook Young and Steward Ferguson, kneeling helplessly beside the critically burned man in a puddle of soup. Or like Greaser Halliday, who didn't have the courage to follow his mates into the flooding rat trap of the engine space yet, at the same time, couldn't face being labelled a coward either. Or young Michael Standish on the after well deck, who found himself taking a dog for a walk on a sinking ship.

One man didn't even try to do anything. But Huang Pi-wu was still being willingly seduced by his fantasy lover, with a sardonic smile on his lips and a tin full of money under his bunk. It made him a pretty special person in a way. Because *he* was the only man aboard *Lycomedes* who'd thoroughly enjoyed the past two minutes of her voyage.

And finally there were men who'd been busy right from the very instant of the Cataclysm.

Simply fighting to stay alive.

Like Fourth Engineer Bert Chisholme . . .


## CATACLYSM plus TWO MINUTES

It wasn't peaceful at all under the water. Not like Bert had always imagined it would be, somehow.

Though it wasn't really a thing he'd ever given much thought to before the Cataclysm – drowning. And certainly not drowning while he was still *aboard* the bloody ship f'r Chrissakes! Yet oddly enough he didn't feel so panicky any more, not now it was actually happening, because somehow he couldn't believe this was the finish of everything . . .

Not . . . well . . . not of *everything*, surely?

So he just tried to hold his breath and not waste it by screaming like Third Engineer Bowman and the ship were doing, while at the same time he didn't fight against the swirling tidal wave which held him hard against the generator block – he just reached up and felt for a handhold with the vaguely-

c

formed idea that if he could only manage to pull his head above water he could maybe float until the level of the flood reached the deckhead . . . and then sort of swim straight out on deck . . . maybe step into the boat they'd be bound to keep waiting because they'd know Bert had been delayed a bit . . .

It never actually occurred to him that by the time the water level did reach the top of the engineroom *Lycomedes* would already be half way down towards the bottom of the North Sea. Or that, under the storm conditions prevailing outside Bert's king-sized ocean-going crypt, they'd be lucky if they even managed to launch a lifeboat, never mind hang around and wait patiently for the odd flotsam engineer to float by . . . or up . . .

And then his hand did close around the lifting lug on the after end of the genny – and suddenly the panic came back even more overwhelmingly than before while Bert gave up being a drowning philosopher and clutched frantically at life as represented by a welded, half-inch steel plate instead.

Until his head broke surface, and the roar of the *Pielstick* and the thunder of the sea again battered his senses while he stared upwards into the glaring lights feeling a hysterical rage because he heard himself shrieking, 'Somebody *HELP* meeeeeel', which was the one thing he'd promised himself not to do . . .

. . . then Third Engineer Bowman floated past all mixed up with a great swirl of foam and whirlpooling rubbish, and he must have been screaming, too, because his mouth was open like a wide, crimson wound against the pallid skin – much whiter now than the overalls, Bert noticed vaguely, which were wet-dulled and smeared with oil and grease from the treads of the ladder – but he couldn't hear what Bowman wanted for the madhouse uproar of the Cataclysm.

Though he knew already, come to that. So he forgot about yelling and gave a last convulsive heave which left him lying precariously over the polished heads of the generator, then

66

stretched out his arm in a half-hearted attempt to arrest the third's macabre passage, with one part of his mind crying out in horrified sympathy while the rest of it bellowed, 'Let him go, let him *go* you misguided bastard an' don't lumber yourself with a part-corpse around your bloody neck . . . !'

Until Bowman's head came up, and he looked at Bert as if he knew what the fourth engineer was thinking. Only there was another expression on the lost man's face, too. A macabre, spine-chilling mask suffusing the slowly spiralling death's-head.

As if the third was pleased about something. Sort of . . . satisfied.

Almost as if he was actually smiling. Triumphantly . . .

But then *Lycomedes* seemed to give a tremendous roll and the free-surface effect of the water flooding the engine space caused it to rumble over to port, piling up against the side of the main engine in a clambering breaker and carrying all the rubbish and the spreading oil and the third engineer with it.

For a moment – just for a moment – Bert felt sad, and almost ashamed. And terribly, terribly relieved . . .

Then Bowman lifted one arm high above the surface, except there wasn't a real hand on the end of it any more – only a suppliant claw with the stubs of the fingers red raw and groping blindly because the third's head was under water now as he spun in the maelstrom.

Just before the ship hesitated at the end of her roll, Bert vaguely realized that what had avalanched to port was shortly due to return starboard side with the progressive certainty of death following life, and that the temporary reduction of the sea level around him offered the only chance he would ever get . . .

. . . so he wriggled frantically along the generator head and literally fell off the inboard end in a crazy lunge for the handrail of the catwalk – a solitary lifeline charting his passage towards the bottom of the ladder some fifteen feet astern – then shrieked with the terror of it all when he missed it and slipped into the well surrounding the genny . . . before his head broke surface again while he felt his fingers finally close over the precious tubing . . .

Somehow he scrambled over, or grovelled his way under the barrier sobbing hysterically, 'Not like Bowman got taken . . . Please *God* but not like Bowman . . . '

His knee slammed hard down against the floor of the submerged catwalk, bruising agonizingly along the chequered steel plating. It was the most exquisitely welcome pain Bert had ever felt in his life.

Blindly he began to stagger aft, dragging his numbed body arm over arm, floundering and slipping in the torrent which threatened to sweep his legs from under, not even daring to lose the slender security of one single hand-hold to wipe the cloying hair from his eyes because *Lycomedes* had already begun to roll to the vertical . . . the flood would return at any instant and he knew he couldn't fight any longer.

One single myopic vision of an ascending steel ladder . . . alternating with the haunting memory of a nightmarish arm rising above the deluge . . . The Quick and the Dead.

But only if you were *very* Quick.

Mind you – at least Fourth Engineer Chisholme didn't feel seasick.

Not any more.


The parrot crooned, 'Hello sailor . . . Jig a jig?'

Then he cocked his head to one side, his black little starboard eye coldly fixed on the open door as if waiting for the reappearance of the chief, and a joyous return to mutual hostilities.

But nothing happened, so he plucked another green feather from under his wing, cracking and shredding it in the pugnaciously hooked beak before discarding it with masochistic contempt. The overall effect was hardly noticeable – it just made the bottom of the cage look that bit fluffier and Hermann that shade more revolting.

*Lycomedes* rolled slowly, reluctantly. Hanging over to port with the door curtains and the telephone cord and Chief Barraclough's floral dressing gown on the back of the bedroom door all suspended at a disturbing twenty-four degree angle from the vertical.

It didn't disturb Hermann, though. Not with all the sea-time he'd logged. As the cage began to tilt he just performed a series of reflex back-steps, allowing the perch to revolve under his claws like a lumberjack rolling a floating tree trunk.

Only this time the return roll wasn't quite even. *Lycomedes* didn't pendulum quite so far back to starboard. Almost as if she was already aware of the added weight of water in her belly. Losing her designed ability to remain stable . . .

'Bloodeeee hell!' Hermann shrieked.

But it wasn't genuine apprehension. The words didn't mean anything.

Not to a parrot.

Bosun Skinner finally caught up with deckhands Bronson and Falls, waiting white-faced and hesitant in the starboard centre-castle alleyway.

They watched his approach with apprehension, too, but theirs was a real emotion, not like Hermann's. The only obscure thing about the nervousness in their eyes was whether it was for what had happened to *Lycomedes* or what Skinner was about to do to them for running out on him.

The bosun's expression was bleak. Uncompromisingly bleak. Bronson took an abrupt step backwards, unconsciously allowing Falls to come between him and the closing seaman with the big fists and unsettling demeanour. Just for a moment he even thought wildly about opting out once again at high speed, but where the hell d'you run *to* aboard a ship . . . ? Especially a crippled ship like he'd suddenly found himself in, which suggested that hiding below deck would be like jumping from the frying pan into the grave . . .

'We got scared, Bose,' he called appealingly. 'The way you was yellin' . . . then the explosion an' that . . . '

But Skinner didn't hesitate. He just came on with that cold, unnerving expression – fists clenched, knuckle-white and threatening. Falls suddenly realised he'd been manœuvred into the front line and stepped aside, too, jostling for back-up position with Bronson.

'Yeah, well, we'll get forr'ad again, on the double . . . ' he said tentatively, eyes glued on Skinner's fists. 'Give Chippie a hand like you said . . . '

The bosun reached them. Bearing down like a battleship steaming into action. Not even deviating from his course to humour the roll of the ship. Bronson whispered tightly, 'Watch 'im, Archie, f'r Chrissake . . . !'

Only Skinner was suddenly past – and still going. No word, no glance at the two nervous seamen who stepped adroitly out of his way, not even a sideways blink to acknowledge their existence. Just continuing towards the upper deck ladder with an awful, harrowed look suffusing the lined face.

'Where's Chippie, d'you reckon?' Falls muttered uncomfortably.

But Bronson didn't answer right away. He merely stood watching silently as Skinner turned at the bottom of the ladder before climbing upwards with slow measured steps. While the bosun didn't look threatening any more. Only listless now, and somehow grieving.

Bronson shivered.

'We couldn't have hit that bad, could we?' he said uneasily. 'Not bad enough to *sink*, I mean?'

Which was roughly what Steward Ferguson was wondering

when he felt the ship roll in that not-quite-regular way to port and then hesitate just a little too long before she began to come back.

While the engine didn't sound right, either. There was too much vibration in the deck and even the muted throb of it seemed louder, running at a higher pitch than before. And they were stopped, too. You could tell that much by the way *Lycomedes* was working before the seas.

So why hadn't anybody come down to see they were all right – which they bloody well weren't! Or was the rest of the crowd all busy out on deck . . . Out on the *boat* deck, even . . . ?

The chief cook began to moan softly, flapping his burned hands in vague fluttering movements. Stan Young said nervously, 'Oh Jeeze but he's going to come round . . . How d'you treat burns, anyway. Bad ones?'

The steward bit his lip. 'You . . . we don't. He needs a hospital. Doctors. Maybe an operation even . . . Look, we got to get on deck, Stan. The ship's not right an' I've got a nasty feeling about it.'

'But we can't leave 'im . . . ' The second cook stared up, suddenly getting panicky as Eddie rose to his feet. 'Where are you going, f'r God's sake?'

'To get help. And a stretcher. It's the only way we'll manage without killing him, Stan boy.'

Dempster groaned and lifted one arm as if trying to ward something off, then his eyelids twitched and the arm dropped back across his chest, one thumb catching in a ragged, black-charred hole. He jerked and whimpered like a hurt animal before the hand freed itself and flopped back into the mess on the deck.

'Well go *on*, then!' Stan snarled urgently.

Ferguson turned away feeling sick again and headed for the door. Just before he got there the second cook called, 'Eddie!'

Reluctantly he swung back, suddenly conscious of an overwhelming desire to reach the alleyway leading to the deck outside. Stan was looking at him anxiously. Appealingly.

'You will *come* back, Eddie. Promise me you will, eh?'

*Lycomedes* shuddered. It felt like a whole sea sweeping the fo'c'slehead. It also had the feel – the pathos of a whimper. Like Chief Cook Dempster was doing. And Dempster was very badly hurt indeed.

'Say you'll come back for us, Eddie. Please?'

Officers' Steward Ferguson dropped his eyes and stepped across the coaming, out into the corridor so's he wouldn't have to look at Stan.

'I'll . . . try an' get some morphine or something. While I'm up there, Stanley boy.'

Under normal circumstances when you open a door inwards, towards you, you merely depress the handle, pull automatically like you've done a million times before in your life – and it swings on a gentle radius with the hinged edge as the fulcrum.

You don't expect it to do anything else. Opening a door conforms as naturally to the routine pattern of living as the acceptance that when you have a shower the water doesn't suddenly turn to super-heated steam and scald you to death, or that when you drop a piece of toast it may always fall buttered-side down – but it doesn't also explode and blow your legs off.

So you don't approach each door warily. Hold it under tight control in case it runs amok. Stand well clear as the juggernaut is released.

You just . . . well . . . you just *open* it.

Which was really what triggered Greaser Halliday into making his final decision on what action to take – stay, or go. Head engineroomwards to selfless heroism while offering succour to his shipmates in hazard – or shuffle smartly deckwards to number three lifeboat station while ensuring his higher survival potential under an unencumbered sky.

Because he'd stood there in the alleyway, shaking with resentful frustration at being the only bloke with any properly balanced appreciation of reality out of the whole bloody crowd, while Barraclough an' that supercilious pig of a second mechanic acted like he, Halliday, was some kind of disease just 'cause he didn't go much on suicide as a quick way of paying-off the bloody boat.

An' then even Donaldson himself – Oggie Donaldson, who'd got more yellow streaks than a Bengal Tiger up his spineless little back – even *he'd* opted for the flamboyant way of a hero. But then again, Oggie never did have proper guts. Not the kind needed to live up to Halliday's conviction that a man's first responsibility is to his wife and children.

And there was a pretty fair chance Greaser Halliday might very well get married. Some day!

Just as soon as he found a bird worth savin' himself for . . .

. . . so he was almost decided on which route to take towards the boat deck when he saw Barraclough take hold've the door handle, try it, then let go again like it was eggshell china, f'r cryin' out loud. Then the chief hesitated and put his ear to the door instead, frowning. And then the *second* had a listen, too, before he gingerly tried to turn it, standing well back as if he expected it to spit at him.

While Oggie orbited uselessly around the debating brains of the engineering department like a satellite with flat batteries asking nervously, 'D'you hear it, Mister Barraclough, sir. Is it floodin' down there then . . . ?'

Which was when Halliday really began to get mad.

I mean, after the way they'd treated *him* like a leper because he hadn't gone bull-headed for the glory. Because he'd acted sensible an' thought about his duty to the ship an' not gone galloping down below to leer helplessly at a few bastards who'd probably got the deep six already anyway.

Only now the chief's own Charge of the Light Brigade had run out've steam when it came to the bit . . . Whereupon all Greaser Halliday's barely-controlled resentment and hatred of authority and a whole lifetime of being a born loser came welling to the surface.

So finally he was going to make *his* mark. This was going to be Halliday's Cataclysm, when the men sorted themselves from the boys, an' the boys stood behind shut doors while shipmates screamed for Halliday from the other side . . .

He began to run, feeling nothing but contempt for the gutless and pride in himself . . .

'D'you guys want to live for *ever*?' he snarled, suddenly unable even to credit the thought. It wasn't really his phrase, of course. He'd read it in a book once, but it had a nice ring to it. A dramatic flavour. The sort of thing they'd remember later, and talk about. Especially in the newspapers.

'LEAVE IT!' the chief roared.

But Halliday just grinned, shoving his way past the trio. It was a tough, capable grin. With precisely the right suggestion of a sneer to it.

He didn't hear the warning that had alerted Barraclough and caused him to delay acting for the few seconds required to create a stand-in hero. That steady, sibilant hiss which shouldn't have been transmitted through the door – and which spelled caution.

And Halliday hit the handle. Still grinning.

The catch slid back.

The accumulated pressure inside the engine space – only slightly higher than in the rest of the ship perhaps, but still enough to assert a considerable force over an area as large as a door – took charge immediately.

The heavy door slammed open with a sharp *phut* of escaping air. Greaser Halliday, caught totally unprepared in his moment of supreme glory, acted instead as a shocked and incredulous

74

buffer between the inflexible alleyway bulkhead and the rampaging steel plate.

It snapped the wrist holding the handle and smashed both kneecaps. It impacted his head against the waiting bulkhead and fractured his skull. It instantly transformed Greaser Halliday into *Lycomedes'* third serious casualty outwith her engineroom.

It wasn't possible, looking down at his mutilated features, to tell whether or not he was still grinning any rugged, deprecating grins.

Oggie Donaldson whispered, 'Oh, *Christ*!' and turned away.

The second simply turned away – before gazing utterly appalled down into the engineroom and *then* blurting, 'Oh . . . CHR*IST*!'

Chief Barraclough didn't say anything at all, for a moment of shocked time. But he'd seen accidents aboard ships many times before, and there wasn't a lot he could do for Halliday – not right then – while there were other men still facing the Cataclysm down below. Men who perhaps couldn't survive alone.

So he simply passed a shaking hand across his forehead, and said in a tightly-controlled voice, 'You'll have to do what you can, Donaldson. The Robertson stretcher in the control flat . . . try and carry him out on deck . . .

Which *was* pretty ironic, really.

Considering that was precisely where Greaser Halliday had wanted to go. Right from the very start.


The clock above the radio operators' table was just closing twenty-two minutes past two when Bentine hung the bridge telephone back on its hook.

Kemp stopped whistling and said, 'Well?'

It wasn't possible to keep all the tension out of his voice, not even to encourage Bentine to stay calm.

The second sparks turned to face him. He was frowning

slightly, but it wasn't so much an expression of thoughtfulness as the look of a man still trying desperately to catch up with reality.

'It was the Old Man himself,' Bentine muttered. 'He says we're to try an' raise any ships in the area . . . '

Then the kid swallowed nervously. His eyes flickered, fixed on the transmitter key almost hypnotically. Chief Radio Operator Kemp knew what he was going to say before he'd even started.

'Request them to suspend all radio traffic, maintain a listening watch . . . and prepare to receive our SOS.'

# Chapter Five

Throw out the lifeline, throw out the lifeline,
Someone is sinking today.
                                        *Edward Smith Ufford*


## CATACLYSM plus THREE MINUTES

The ship lay dead in the water now, all forward way lost and
lying at an angle of some forty degrees to the troughs of the seas.

And each succeeding roller pushed her a little farther to port,
sweeping in under the sheer of her fo'c'sle to explode in a
raging gout of white spray which immediately disintegrated
under the shriek of the storm into a horizontally drifting cloud
hanging downwind, the curling crests of individual waves lost
for moments in the opaque fuzz before re-appearing as sliding
black walls moving monstrously through their self-generated
gloom.

While the farther *Lycomedes* fell away from the seas the more
erratic became her motion. She was corkscrewing now, but it
wasn't the lively, barrelling progression of a vessel under power,
simply a staggering, restless oscillation which seemed to lose
any suggestion of rhythm as her ruptured forefoot slid into
trough after trough, bringing up with a staggering impact
transmitting itself through every frame and every plate of the
passive hulk.

And she was noticeably lower in the water. Lower, and
settling by the head. Already she was unable to rise to the seas
as she'd done incalculable times before, responding automatically to those laws of buoyancy and equilibrium and displacement

which had governed her progress across the world's oceans since the moment of her inception.

Because her designers could only hope to contrive that she would withstand all reasonable, and perhaps even a measure of unreasonable natural forces acting outwith her welded frame. Yet no conceivable planner's strategy or slide-rule equation could afford *Lycomedes* immunity from the ultimate disaster. From the Cataclysm itself.

In which her underwater shell was breached. And the enemy advanced within . . .

McRae watched the captain replace the radio room telephone on its hook with an absurd feeling of detachment. Almost as though he were a witness to someone else's happening – some other rapidly escalating event which didn't really concern him directly.

'That bad?' he said calmly as Shaw turned to face him again.

The Old Man looked at him. There wasn't a flicker of doubt or uncertainty in the steady grey eyes.

'She's sinking, David. Finished. And we might not have a lot of time left . . . '

Then Second Mate Fuller blundered out of the chartroom waving a sheaf of paper and snarling, 'Two days. Two bloody days that thing was waiting for us out there so how the hell was I to know it could still be a hazard, eh . . . How the hell could *any* of us?'

Shaw snapped sharply, 'I asked you for our position, Mister. Where is it?'

But Fuller didn't seem to hear him, he just thrust the paper under the captain's chin and shook it wildly. 'Look . . . read it for yourself, dammit! Two days southerly drift when it should've sunk – an' we go an' hit it while *I'm* on the bloody bridge . . . '

'No doubt about it, but the world's going completely berserk,'

McRae reflected, still with that outlandish slow-motion sense of being merely an observer and not really involved in the scene that was playing around him. 'The Old Man quite calmly announcing that *Lycomedes* is going to sink – which means she'll probably drown most of us when she does – while nobody has even bothered to phone from the engineroom yet, to ask what the hell's happened . . . and the chief officer – me! – simply refusing to believe the evidence of his own eyes . . . Then a second officer who seems more bloody interested in *what* we hit, an' who's lousy *fault* it was . . . '

But only three minutes had actually passed since the end of his average day at sea, and it does take a little time to accept the fact that you could very possibly be dead long before the next one dawns.

'Priorities, Mister . . . ' Shaw was saying doggedly. 'Our distress position, damage state, casualties, crew muster, boats prepared for launching – and *then* the post mortems, Fuller . . . '

'READ IT!' The second mate shrieked in a high-tensile, almost pleading falsetto.

McRae wallowed back into reality, suddenly aware of the atmosphere building to a guilt-ridden peak in the wheelhouse around him – supercharged to a point verging on hysteria, with the Old Man glaring furiously at the still utterly stunned second mate, who in his turn had retreated into an anguished obsession concerning the cause, rather than the effect, of *Lycomedes*' situation. While the boy, Cassiday, and Quartermaster Clements hovered threateningly on the periphery of the conflict – threatening because if the apprentice's inadequacy and Clements's barely-suppressed bitterness was transmitted to the rest of the crew, then they were lost before they'd even begun to fight . . .

. . . so McRae desperately gripped the second mate's arm, spun him round in a wild-eyed arc until he slammed against the

79

bulkhead, and snarled grimly, 'Shut up, Fuller . . . an' gimme that!'

He snatched the papers from Fuller's unresisting hand, but before he even glanced at them jerked his head towards the watching men. 'Clements. Break out the signal flares in the chartroom and bring them through here . . . Cassiday, you go below and find the third mate. Tell him to get dressed first, then report to the bridge – but he's to get dressed first, remember! OK, lad?'

The apprentice blinked at him vaguely for a moment, then he seemed to gather his wits with an effort and nodded, almost brightly. 'Aye, aye, sir' he said and went scuttling towards the chartroom and the internal stairway.

Ernie Clements just nodded sullenly, eyeing the dazed second mate with barely-concealed contempt before following the boy. But there was a relieved look there, too, as if his own resentment at what had happened was mitigated by the analgesic of positive action.

Then McRae turned to face the captain and Fuller. He looked down at the sheaf of papers in his hand – the bridge copies of the *Navwarn* messages forwarded from the radio room. The top one hit him almost immediately. He'd seen it before – they all had – as part of the routine watch-relieving procedure, but it hadn't struck him earlier as being anything other than an expensive but commonplace incident occurring in an adjacent area – expensive to the underwriters insuring the casualty, but all too commonplace to seamen.

Too average, and too ordinary for special note. Like *Lyco-medes* herself. Before the Cataclysm.

It was a *Securite* signal – a navigational warning. The date-time group of receipt, neatly entered in Chief Operator Kemp's precise handwriting, indicated it had been received nearly two days before, just after they'd sailed from Swansea. It commenced with the safety prefix of TTT, repeated three times.

'Relayed through Stonehaven Radio. To all ships. Following received from United States tug *Cherokee Indian* at zero two two five GMT today . . . '

McRae continued to read aloud in a flat, dogged monotone. The captain was right – of course he was right – that their real priorities were to prepare for the ordeal ahead rather than speculate over the immediate past. But they would also need the second officer's help. And Fuller wouldn't be able to exorcise his obsessional guilt until he could at least share it with the rest of *Lycomedes*' navigating complement. Because if there *had* been a rogue threat lying in wait for them – one which they had already been advised of in a warning message – then they were all equally responsible for a failure to anticipate, and to take corrective avoiding action.

' . . . THREE HUNDRED FOOT LONG OIL RIG SERVICE BARGE NEMCO IV PARTED TOW IN HEAVY SEAS 1745 GMT YESTERDAY. RADAR CONTACT LOST 0150 GMT TODAY WHEN BARGE BELIEVED TO HAVE SUNK BUT VESSELS IN IMMEDIATE AREA ADVISED TO KEEP CLOSE WATCH. LAST OBSERVED POSITION . . . '

'I'd already plotted it. When it came in during the middle watch, night before last . . . ' Fuller broke in bitterly. 'It happened thirty-seven miles clear of our course line. Thirty-seven bloody miles clear – an' yet we hit it smack on the nose.'

'Three hundred feet long,' McRae muttered. 'Jesus but that makes it damn near as big as we are . . . ' He looked up at Fuller and snapped nervously, 'Anyway, how d'you know *what* we hit, Second. As presumably you didn't see it anyway?'

Fuller glared back at him incredulously. 'Oh come *on*, Mister. How many floating wrecks big as that do you think there *are* in the North Sea, f'r cryin' out loud?'

'But thirty-seven *miles* . . . and without even being seen by anyone else?'

'I told you – it couldn't *be* seen. Not by visual, not on radar, Dave. Not until we were close enough to damn well collide . . . '

Fuller broke off abruptly and stared out through the wheelhouse windows to where the water raged in foaming slabs across *Lycomedes*' settling fo'c'slehead. Shaw took the file from McRae and glanced at it briefly.

'Thirty-six hours,' he said quietly. 'Drifting under the surface at slightly over one knot . . . it is just possible, David. If you add wind, submarine currents and damnable luck.'

He shrugged like a tired old man and lobbed the file carelessly on to the ledge below the window. It fell off but nobody moved to pick it up. 'We'll probably never be certain,' the captain added. 'Not that it really matters. Not at the end of the day.'

Fuller said, 'It matters to me, sir. It matters a lot.'

Shaw picked up the engineroom telephone, then turned back to face the second mate. Fuller was watching intensely – almost appealingly McRae thought . . . 'Let him off the rack, Captain,' he urged silently, 'Let the poor bloody kid at least have a chance of fighting for survival without having the prospect of half a hundred dead men on his conscience . . . !'

'You have always been an efficient and highly capable officer, Mister Fuller,' the captain said before he pressed the call button on the phone. 'Nothing you have done up to this moment in time has given me any reason to modify my opinion of you . . . '

The second mate relaxed visibly, under the circumstances an oddly out-of-place relief apparent in his eyes. 'Thank you, sir,' he said; then began, at last, to move urgently towards the chartroom. 'I'll plot our Mayday position. Should get a range and bearing from the Vyl Light Vessel from my last DR.

Shaw kept his finger on the engineroom button. Only the tip of it showing white under the pressure betrayed the tension within him. Nothing happened, though. Nobody answered. His eyes met those of his chief officer's and he jerked his head, still calling.

'Sound the emergency signal, Mister McRae. I'd like everybody assembled on the boat deck as quickly as possible, please!'

McRae nodded silently, reaching for the whistle lanyard above his head. It was the one act he'd never ever thought he'd have to perform for real. Not outside an especially hellish nightmare.

'Three hundred feet *long* . . . ' he reflected, starting to feel cold and shivery again.

'Ohhhh Lord, but you've really got it in for us, haven't you . . . '

The dog managed to claw its way up the first few steps leading from the after welldeck to the centrecastle, then its paws started to skid frantically and it ground to a halt, staring round and down at the following apprentice, pink tongue lolling out and panting with excitement.

The boy grinned. He couldn't help it, even despite the worry in his mind. 'Stuck, eh?' he said remonstratively. 'Only there's not much point in being a sea dog if you can't climb ladders, is there?'

He placed his shoulder against the dog's bottom and heaved. Scrabbling with enormous enthusiasm the dog shot up the ladder then turned at the top and began to lick Michael's face with great wet slurps of the pink tongue. The boy giggled, trying to push it away and feeling pleased again all at the same time with the dog's obvious affection for him.

'Don't get too full of yourself, Seadog,' he spluttered. 'There's a lot more climbing to do before we get to the top deck an' without me it looks like you're good an' stuck, eh?'

The dog suddenly stopped licking and sat looking up at him with bright, suddenly alert eyes, almost as though it could understand what he was saying. It was quite active now, not at all listless and disinterested like it had been in the cage on the poop. Standish abruptly remembered the cream biscuit he'd left stuck in the wire mesh and wished he'd brought it with him. Seadog would probably have enjoyed it, and realized canine co-operation had its advantages.

'C'mon, then.' He jerked the lead experimentally. The dog immediately got up and walked obediently beside him towards the bottom of the next ladder. 'D'you reckon lions and things would be as easy to train as you . . . ?' the boy asked conversationally.

But he was really only talking for his own benefit. To try to keep his mind off what had happened to the ship. And what might happen to them because of it.

They'd got half way up the ladder when someone called, 'Excuse me,' from the bottom, and Standish turned to see deckhands Bronson and Falls staring up at him.

'Have you seen Chippie anywhere around, sir?' Falls asked. 'Down aft or anythin'?'

'Sorry, no.'

The boy felt pleased all over again, but a bit embarrassed as well. He never quite got used to being called 'sir', although he couldn't help noticing when some of them pointedly avoided using the term, especially the older hands. But Bronson and Falls were pretty new to the sea, with even less time in than Standish had.

'Why, what's happened?' he asked, noticing the uneasy glance that passed between the two seamen.

So they told him – about the collision, and the way they'd run aft without waiting for Chippie and Bosun Skinner – and there was no attempt to pretend they'd been anything but scared witless. But then they told him about the look on the bosun's face as he'd passed by them in the alleyway . . . and the unsettled feeling they'd got regarding the carpenter's absence.

'Bose looked a bit . . . well . . . peculiar,' Bronson finished.
'You know . . . like he was shocked or somethin'?'

'Could Chippie be trapped, d'you think,' the boy said
anxiously. 'And Bosun Skinner's gone to get help?'

'Excep' that we were still there,' Falls pointed out logically.
'*We* could've helped, couldn't we?'

'I thought for a minute he was goin' to kill us,' Bronson
muttered apprehensively. 'Jesus but he did look queer!'

The boy, Standish, hesitated, frowning doubtfully down at
the dog which seemed to nuzzle against his leg as if trying to
get as close to him as possible. But dogs couldn't help, though.
You couldn't share responsibility with a dog, not even a sea dog.

'I think we'd better go forr'ad and look for Chippie,' he said,
suddenly making his mind up. It was really his first experience
of command, in a way, so the only thing he could use as a
guideline was what he hoped others would do for him if *he* was
missing.

Perhaps it was because Standish was so young and innocent
that it never occurred to him that he also had a responsibility
towards the safety of the two equally inexperienced seamen he
found himself so unexpectedly commanding. And that to
venture on to the exposed forward decks of a possibly sinking
ship was a formidable task even for men like Skinner and
McRae, who knew the sort of things which could happen when
a ship lost its natural buoyancy, and consequently would at
least be aware of the danger signs.

And would get out of it, fast. Perhaps with even enough time
left to stay alive. For a little while longer, at least.

They were halfway along the centrecastle alleyway leading
to the foredeck – the apprentice, the two young deckhands and
the bright-eyed sea dog – when the great brass siren on
*Lycomedes'* high funnel began to blare in short, resonant blasts
which totally overwhelmed the crash of the seas and the howl
of the wind.

85

Only the ship wasn't screaming any more. Now she could only bellow in helpless anguish. A futile, melancholic dirge.

An experienced seaman might have suggested she was trying to warn them . . .

Fourth Engineer Chisholme, still finely balanced on the razor's edge between life and death down at the bottom of the ship, didn't hear the siren telling him there was an emergency.

I mean – who needed *telling*, f'r Chrissakes . . .

And certainly not when you're waist deep in water one moment – doggedly clawing your way through a monstrous swirl of floating rubbish, icy-cold North Sea and twelve-year-old bilge deposits – then suddenly the tide's come in again and everything's gurgling, compressing horror swamping up over your ears like an express lift and floating your hair vertically while all you can do is screw your eyes tight with the fear of it, and retch and suffocate an' cling like a petrified barnacle to the one slender length of steel tube that still anchors you to the world of the more-or-less living . . .

And swear blasphemously and pray, all at the same time. Though praying needs a bit of concentration to do it properly while swearing seems to come that bit easier during the periods when you're actually drowning . . . if you forget to hold your breath, anyway, which means the drowning comes just that little bit quicker while spiritual salvation's slipped a few more spluttering blasphemies further away . . .

Then there was another thing Bert Chisholme couldn't understand – apart from why the bloody sea had been filling the boat up for the last three minutes – or was it three hours – of the voyage? And that had been the expression on Third Engineer Bowman's face as he'd obligingly absolved Bert of any responsibility for saving him by spiralling neatly out of arm's length on the crest of the flood.

Because Bowman undoubtedly *had* looked pleased about

something. And sort of triumphant. Which wasn't really the kind of demeanour you'd normally expect from a flotsam shipmate with a broken back and only the latter half of death to go . . .

But then the bottom of the ladder was right in front of him, gleaming softly like one of those water-diffused lovers' visions in a romantic movie, only Bert had never, ever imagined anything so beautiful, so incredibly desirable, as that geometrically ascending invitation to live a little longer under a clear and open sky.

Not even during all those times before. When he'd been seasick.

So he took a firm grip on himself. Deliberately forcing his mind clear of the web of hysteria threatening to overwhelm him at the last crucial moment, trying desperately to focus oil and salt-blurred eyes on that vaguely determined point where the catwalk became ladder and the chequered steel plates converted to soaring rungs.

Then *Lycomedes* hesitated, seemingly not quite certain of which way to roll, and Bert reached a cool, calculated decision. Let go . . . smooth, calmly evaluated dive from here to there while the ship maintained her fractional bonus of stability . . . one clutch at the handrail of the ladder, and it would be up, up and away for Bert Chisholme, Indestructible Man!

So stop debating the issue, Bert. An' bloody well *GOooooo!*

And he very nearly made it, at that. Oh, it wasn't so much a nonchalant, flowing swoop – more a wild-eyed, floundering lunge of desperation, really – but he did manage to wallow and splutter across most of the swirling mess between him and the stairway to paradise. His fingers even brushed the ladder, felt it firm and reassuring and, above all, leading above him . . .

Until something soft and yielding wrapped itself around his submerged legs, interrupting his forward motion with an insistent embrace. Something which didn't feel at all like the

87

kind of obstacle normally found blocking the catwalk of ships' enginerooms.

But it wasn't a normal ship's engineroom any more, and there *was* something there which definitely shouldn't have been, so Fourth Engineer Chisholme missed his last chance of salvation by the thickness of a skin of paint and submerged instead in a splash of flailing arms, protruding eyes and an aggrieved conviction that this was definitely the last bloody STRAW . . .

He also managed the first few syllables of an agonised 'Oh *God* but there shouldn't've *been* . . . '

Though there wasn't really any way of telling whether it was a prayer for sanity, or a run-of-the-mill blasphemy.

Yet, even then, one useful snippet of information did emerge from that sudden traumatic immersion. As Bert disbelievingly went under, still with his eyes wide open and staring.

Because he finally discovered *why* Third Engineer Bowman had looked so pleased with himself. Even during the last tortured milliseconds of his existence . . .

Captain's Steward Huang Pi-wu slept on.

Certainly the slight contemptuous curl to his lips had gone now, to be replaced by the merest shadow of concern. But it wasn't because he'd heard *Lycomedes*' emergency signal blaring over and through every nook and cranny of the accommodation – it was simply because Huang was a superlative lover, a positive maestro in the art of wooing as he played on the uncertainties of Yeh Chun's feminism as others would the strings of some delicate instrument.

Therefore his expressed concern was a carefully weighed balm, a simple, kindly gesture to neutralize the distress revealed in the despondent eyes of the adoring woman kneeling over him as she suffered indescribable torment through the belief that she had, in some way, failed and disappointed him.

While now, having breached her last defences, he would reveal the true generosity hidden within his heart and the forgiveness which could only be endowed by a man of supreme tolerance – because he would actually *touch* her! Allow her to revel thankfully in the euphoria his caress would bestow. Enable Yeh Chun to writhe with sensual gratification under the magical rewards offered by his expertise . . .

Huang continued to sleep. Happily, and resolutely.

While the ship continued – equally resolutely – to sink!

Resolution, on the other hand, was far from being the order of the day in other parts of the stricken ship by three minutes past the Cataclysm.

Such as in the galley, immediately abaft the officers' saloon.

Where, still kneeling in the lukewarm swirl of soup, roasting fat and sickness which covered the tiled deck, Stan Young continued to stare uncertainly at the empty doorway – empty since Eddie had so abruptly departed in search of help for Chief Cook Dempster.

But had he . . . ? Gone for assistance, that was. Or had Ferguson really used it as an excuse to get out on deck where he at least stood a little more chance of surviving than the two chefs would, surrounded as they were by steel bulkheads which might suddenly transform into gyrating decks and deckheads instead as *Lycomedes* rolled over and began her final plunge to the bottom.

Which would, in its turn, convert her galley into a revolving butter-churn of death for its occupants, with Second Cook Young and Chief Cook Dempster all mixed up with seven hundred company-crested china plates, twenty-one stainless steel teapots, eighteen bottles of tomato sauce, a ten pound tin of dishwasher soap powder, one partly-cooked leg of lamb with a fork stuck in it and, maybe, two tons of other culinary and assorted missiles.

Stan closed his eyes tight for a moment and tried to swallow, only there was a lump of fear in his throat which wouldn't go away no matter how hard he tried to convince himself that the ship was OK, and that she'd just lie there a while and roll her guts out before the Old Man and Chief Barraclough sorted things out and got her under way again.

He couldn't, though. Oh, admittedly the lights were still on, and the steady hum of the blowers and the galley extractor fan all showed that *Lycomedes'* power supply was functioning normally. The main engine was still running, too, but that wasn't quite so reassuring – the way it seemed to be racing a lot higher than usual, with the vibration dancing all the cups and pans on their hooks like a row of chattering teeth, and producing a steady background tintinnabulation from the cutlery drawers.

But she definitely felt heavier, more disinclined to rise to the seas. Which was bloody ridiculous, really, seeing they hadn't been stopped for more than three or four minutes in actual fact, and surely a ship like *Lycomedes* couldn't take *that* much water in her in such a short time. Not unless she had a big hole right below the plimsoll line. A very big hole . . .

Dempster began to whimper again while his hands opened and closed in vague, clutching gestures. A single glistening tear squeezed through the corner of one eyelid and trickled slowly down the lobster-red cheekbone. Stan squealed an involuntary and panic-stricken '*Eddie*' before he realized that Eddie had gone and there wasn't anyone to help at all now, so he dropped his voice to a whisper in case he woke Chief Cook Dempster up properly, and urged, 'Easy, now. Take it easy now, Chief, an' we'll see you right . . . '

He felt so lonely. He'd never felt so lonely before in all his life. Or so inadequate.

But they would be going again soon, wouldn't they? Even if the ship was quite badly damaged she still couldn't actually sink or anything. Ships as big as *Lycomedes* just didn't sink. Not just like that, in the middle of the sea.

Not ordinary, average sort of ships.

Stan sat back and felt a little better. It was all a question of logic, really. And commonsense. Though he didn't know what they would do about dinner tonight, not with the roast and veg all churned up on the deck along with the Old Man's favourite Mulligatawny. While he didn't have a hope in hell now of preparing the apple crumble they'd planned as an alternative to the *Glace à la Framboise* already waiting in the deep freeze.

Logic. That was what was needed instead of getting panicky about a bit of a bump which would naturally make them want to stop and see everything was still all right. And he could always fix a cold meal with potato salad and tinned ham, even with old Dempster being out of action for a while. Come to that there was probably enough time in hand for a bit of grilled steak or chops, and French frieds. Or fish, perhaps?

Logic. Like stop worrying, Stanley boy. I mean, if there *was* an emergency they'd be soundin' the emergency signal f'r a start, wouldn't they then . . . ?

Which brought Second Cook Young's reasoned appreciation of the situation to that precise moment in time when *Lycomedes*' siren abruptly drowned the humming blowers, the whimpering of the burned man and the fidgety chatter of knives, forks and spoons.

Rather suggesting it *was* shaping up to prove a totally illogical day after all.

Hermann still had his beady, malignant little eye fixed expectantly on the open door of the chief engineer's cabin.

He'd hardly said anything at all since the chief and second had departed so abruptly at the first indications of the Cataclysm. But perhaps, to Hermann, that was as illogical as the pattern of events seemed to Stan Young in the galley – because Mister Barraclough would never normally have considered leaving without at least a passing and cheery farewell to his repulsive, half-plucked bird.

Like 'Bloody parrot!'

Or, 'Go on, then. Go on an' pull 'em *all* out. Then you can bloody freeze to death . . . '

Which was the absolute stuff of life to Hermann. The peak of ornithological happiness. The ultimate in malevolent togetherness. Man and Bird locked in uninhibited, total war . . .

But parrots don't think logical things, so *Lycomedes'* emergency warning didn't cause more than a ruffle of the few feathers left on Hermann's breast. Then he sidled interestedly along his perch until he was leaning casually against the bars surrounding him.

Still watching the door hopefully, though. Holding himself at instant readiness to deliver a vitriolic squawk of abuse the very moment his arch-enemy hove in sight.

Particularly if accompanied by the second engineer. Now Hermann the Parrot *really* hated the second engineer . . .

AAA . . . AAA . . . AAAA . . . !

Kemp keyed the urgency call prefix and then waited, still hunched over the operator's desk.

The second sparks watched expectantly. His hands were still trembling but otherwise Bentine seemed to have calmed down considerably since the first shock of the impact.

Kemp muttered irritably, 'C'mon . . . c'mON, somebody,' and Bentine started to say, 'Trigger the auto-alarm an' wake the bastar . . . ' then the chief operator suddenly tensed, one hand still on the key while the other adjusted the headphones around his neck.

Then he started to write, frowning slightly in concentration.

Anxiously Bentine gazed over the chief's shoulder.

Before muttering, in a vaguely apprehensive voice. 'I never really thought about that before . . . about being rescued. By a Russian.'

## CATACLYSM PLUS FOUR MINUTES

By the time Chief Officer McRae had finished sounding the seven short and final long blasts of the general emergency signal, nobody aboard *Lycomedes* was left in any doubt whatever that the situation was already critical.

Apart from Huang Pi-wu, of course. About to transport his enraptured Yeh Chun to the very heights of the Seventh Happiness with one fantasy caress.

And Hermann. The bloody parrot.

Though to a great many men the siren didn't make any real difference. To the radio operators, the two senior engineers, those already on the bridge – because they were already at their posts and actively responding to the Cataclysm.

To others it was merely an additional burden on already overstretched nerves. They were the members of *Lycomedes'* complement who, by pressure of circumstances, were unable to conform immediately to the urgent demand to assemble at their muster station. Men like Second Cook Young, waiting apprehensively for Eddie Ferguson to return with a rescue party for the burned Dempster. Or like Oggie Donaldson, who'd suddenly found himself presented with a smashed-up Greaser Halliday at the engine room entrance, and told to 'Do what he could', f'r crying out loud. Him – Oggie – who'd normally avoid the responsibility of even deciding what to have for dinner if possible.

Then there was the self-appointed search party. Apprentice Standish, deckhands Bronson and Falls, and Seadog, all of whom were about to embark with naïve heroism on the foredeck

93

of the foundering ship in conscientious quest of a mislaid carpenter.

And Fourth Engineer Chisholme. Currently approaching the end of a long session of drowning . . .

But in general the previously dispersed majority of *Lycomedes'* crewmen were – during the fourth minute of the Cataclysm – beginning to assemble in a white-faced but ordered group on the boat deck.

Many eyes were fixed questioningly on the now deserted bridge wings, waiting apprehensively for authority to appear from the wheelhouse and either reassure, or commit them irrevocably to the next stage of disaster.

Some eyes were still shocked. Almost apathetic. And they seemed to be the eyes which gazed most constantly outboard.

Staring numbly into the tempest. At the fury of the sea.

By the time Bosun Skinner reached the boat deck it would have been very difficult to tell precisely what he was feeling. That awesome, undeviating passage which so unsettled Bronson and Falls had now eased to the unhurried progress of a man well able to cope with the stress of the moment.

Until you looked closely into Skinner's eyes. And then you might have wondered uncomfortably. Because there was an agony there which should have warned you to stand back a little, or even leave the bosun's presence altogether if you were a particularly perceptive man. While there was also something more – a sort of introspective resignation. And if you'd peered that deeply into Bosun Skinner's soul then you might also have asked yourself exactly how many men *did* die four minutes ago down there on the forward deck when *Lycomedes* rolled and snapped an old sailorman's neck.

But being an ordinary, average man you probably wouldn't have noticed anything odd about Skinner at all. Because you, like everyone around you, would have been more preoccupied with your determination to conceal from your neighbour the grisly apprehensions within your own mind, rather than speculate too deeply on the private horror within his.

Consequently nobody realized that stolid old Bosun Skinner had already become a temporary victim of the Cataclysm. And that the merest added pressure could tip the largest man aboard *Lycomedes* towards a macabre and implacable determination.

To see justice done. Like it said in the Bible.

An eye for an eye . . .

When Eddie Ferguson left Stan looking after the burned cook in the galley he'd headed straight for the open air in the shape of the starboard centrecastle alleyway.

Having arrived there he hesitated, however, leaning back for a moment against the cold steel housing and feeling wave after wave of relief swamping over him that, at last, he was finally clear of the trap. And slowly the claustrophobic fear began to leave him, replacing itself instead with sick apprehension about what really had gone wrong with the ship, and what he was going to do next.

Because Eddie couldn't shake that last appealing look of Stan's from his mind. And the uncertain, almost doubting plea of – 'You will *come* back, Eddie. Promise me you will, eh . . . ?'

Not that he had. Actually promised, or anything. Though naturally he fully intended to. No bloke worth calling himself a man would dream of leaving his mates inside a sinking ship – if she *was* sinking, of course, because that bloody frightening emergency siren that had just stopped blaring could simply mean they were only being cautious up there on the bridge . . .

. . . and if she didn't sink, Stan and Chief Cook Dempster would be OK anyway an' they could all laugh about it later over a glass or two of beer . . . Then Eddie suddenly imagined the chief cook's charred hands wrapped around an icy-cold glass, and shuddered at the very thought of it. Which, in its turn, made him think about the reality of the situation. Like the fact that Dempster could very well die of shock from his injuries anyway – while Stan Young didn't *have* to stay inside the galley with him, did he? All said an' done Stan had more or less volunteered to act as nursemaid, but just because one bloke takes a decision to be a hero it shouldn't mean that everyone else has to follow suit, does it? And Stanley Young was perfectly able to just get up and head for the boat deck in search of assistance without expecting him – Eddie – to . . .

'*Christ!*'

Which involuntary comment marked the precise moment in time when Officers' Steward Ferguson actually became aware of the conditions prevailing outside the secluded little world of the catering branch. Until then he'd been so preoccupied with the pros and cons of how to be a responsible shipmate and a guaranteed survivor all at the same time, that he'd not actually viewed the surrounding seascape through the eyes of a chap threatened with the distinct possibility of, very shortly, being not so much on it as . . . well . . . *in* it.

Because the sea, from centrecastle deck level, seemed to have ceased being a reassuringly buoyant entity surrounding *Lycomedes*. Now the ship appeared isolated, marooned in a shrieking maelstrom of hurtling white spume with no identifiable surface to it but only a smothering grue in which a man – even supported by a bright orange lifejacket – would still only breathe in five per cent air and, for the last few seconds of consciousness, nineteen times the volume of storm-suspended water droplets.

And Stan Young reckoned the chief *cook* had survival problems . . . ?

'Ohhhh, *Chri*st!' Steward Ferguson sobbed again, totally shattered.

He began to run towards the ladder to the upper decks, his

sole reaction being to put as much altitude between him and that nightmare smother as possible.

It never really occurred to Eddie that he was engaged on a somewhat foredoomed exercise.

Considering *Lycomedes* herself was inexorably settling lower and lower into the North Sea, even as Eddie climbed.

Chief Engineer Barraclough, on the other hand, was descending faster than Steward Ferguson was rising. And Chief Barraclough was already below the surface of the water.

Academically speaking, of course, the sea level being outside *Lycomedes'* hull while the chief was inside – though even from the point where he and the doggedly trailing second stared over the ladder rail and down to the bottom of the engineroom itself, it was obvious that the little bit of the North Sea already inside the ship would very shortly catch up with the level of its surrounding matriarch.

Then there was the noise. Stunning, overwhelming by its intensity, even to ears accustomed to a lifetime of captive and concentrated tumult . . . the thunder of the imploding deluge, the cacophony of the still-racing *Pielstick*, the surge and boom of waves battering against the hull plating as if driven by an implacable determination to cut short even the few minutes left before they, too, could enter *Lycomedes'* ruptured corpse . . .

Barraclough skidded to a halt, swinging round and gazing up at his assistant with his bald pate reflecting the glare of the overhead lights and his eyes bleak with the concern and the hopelessness in them. His mouth moved spasmodically, roaring apparently unavailing against the volume of the Cataclysm. But ship's engineers are unusually versatile men with extraordinary powers to communicate despite overwhelming odds, and the second understood Barraclough's facial convulsions as clearly as if they'd been chatting over a quiet pint in a dockside bar.

D

'Who's down below?' the chief bellowed. 'Bowman an' who else?'

The second leaned forward, placing his mouth alongside Barraclough's ear. 'Fourth engineer, and the watchkeepin' greaser . . . Black! Carbon Black!'

'I'm going down. You kill that bloody main engine, and fast!'

'I'm coming *with* you, f'r God's sake.'

Barraclough shook his head furiously, determinedly. 'Do what you're told an' kill that ENGINE. Then check an' see both auxiliaries are switched into the line . . . We'll need all the power we can get until . . . until . . . '

But Barraclough couldn't finish saying what was in his mind, so he just threw one last, slightly hoarse imperative which brooked no argument whatsoever.

'Jus' DO it, Charlie. Then get out of it an' take Donaldson an' whatsisname with you.'

And he was gone. Sliding easily down with his hands gripping the smooth oily rails and his feet raised slightly above the ladder treads like he'd done a thousand times before, descending into the belly of his beloved *Lycomedes* . . . Only this would be the last time. The very last time for Chief Barraclough.

Because after him would come the fish. And the bug-eyed sea creatures and the sidling crustaceans and the sinuous apodes and the molluscs. Then the ooze would gradually begin to occupy *Lycomedes'* silent, macabre engine spaces, while the slime and the insidious algae would flourish and multiply over every shiny brass pipe and polished steel facet . . .

. . . until, finally, she would cease to be recognizable as a ship. Cease to be anything at all other than a mouldering, fragmenting excrescence on the bed of the North Sea.

An eroding necropolis, entombing the bones of those men who had already died within her, and the ones who would shortly join them.

A SHIP IS DYING

Perhaps even the mortal remains of Chief Engineer William Barraclough himself.

Doomed, until the very end of time, to be accompanied by a skeletal and eternally reproachful parrot called Hermann.

# Chapter Six

Alone, alone, all, all alone,
Alone on a wide, wide sea!
*S. T. Coleridge*

## CATACLYSM plus FIVE MINUTES

A ship is, basically, an elongated steel box.

That ship-box is constructed of many individual members, bonded together to act in concert against the stresses imposed on the whole. While those stresses, in themselves, are many and varied.

For instance there are the transverse stresses, caused by the ship's rolling motion, tending to distort the cross-corners of the steel box, racking and straining to fracture the 'knees' or brackets connecting the deck beams to the vertical frames.

Then there are the collapsing stresses – caused both by the sea pressing inwards over the submerged areas of the ship while increasing by a steady crushing rate of 64 pounds per square foot for each foot depth of water, and also by the vertical deadweight of the cargo within her holds, all of which tends to draw the two sides of the ship inwards and together – a factor evidenced in the days of the sailing ship when, after loading, all rigging frequently slackened to the extent that it had to be taken up on the shroud and backstay screws . . . whereupon already harassed chief officers suffered nightmares at the possible consequence of forgetting to ease them off again before the ship finally discharged.

There are the local stresses imposed on our ship-box. Such

as on the weaker sections of her frame formed by openings in the deck for hatches and superstructure. Or the strains inflicted by masts and swinging derricks, or winches, deck cargo, the windlass itself . . . and all these apart from the equally disconcerting complications of the *vertical* stresses, where her more buoyant compartments, such as her engine space, tend to create an upward pressure, while the loaded cargo holds exert a downward force right next door . . .

But there is yet another form of stress which can cause a ship to cry out abruptly, then break, and finally founder. A form of stress which leaves her particularly vulnerable to the assault of the Cataclysm.

The longitudinal stress. The Achilles Heel of many a vessel in hazard . . .

Take a length of flexible plastic. A fairly long length – of about the same proportions as an ocean-going cargo ship. And then balance it on your finger. And what happens . . . ? It tends to droop at each end. So you support your little plastic facsimile of an ocean-going ship with a finger at each end instead – and all of a sudden it's collapsing in the middle.

Now, increase the size of your piece of plastic until it *is* a proper ship – only built of steel now, with all its frames and stringers, beams, beam knees, plates, pillars . . . and, instead of your fingers, support your ship by high waves – the sort you get in, say, the North Sea.

And it still tends to collapse in the middle when your wave-fingers support her at each end. While her bow and stern will still want to droop downwards as soon as one of those waves passes along her length to lift only her middle section.

Seamen call the condition *hogging* and *sagging*. It exerts a constantly varying strain on a ship hundreds, perhaps even thousands of times a day in severe weather. But she doesn't normally break in half because of it, even then. That was why they built her with all those skilfully connected strengthening members in the first place. Like the keel and keelsons, longitudinals and margin plates, stringers . . .

Only a lot of those component parts weren't tied together any more in the ruptured underwater structure of the Motor Vessel *Lycomedes*. Not after the Cataclysm had overwhelmed her.

But she still kept on hogging, though.

And sagging.

Captain Graham Shaw was also under constantly changing forms of stress as the Cataclysm entered its fifth minute.

Just like *Lycomedes*.

Except that the strains suffered by the captain weren't inflicted through any physical origin – or only indirectly – but more by the psychological pressures exerted on all who command in time of adversity. Those lonely, demanding and unavoidable dilemmas of supreme responsibility.

While the master of a ship in distress, totally isolated from the world over the horizon, is perhaps confronted by the ultimate and most awesome responsibility of all . . . to weigh his duty to save his vessel and cargo against the even greater priorities of his passengers and crew.

Certainly *Lycomedes* carried no passengers. Not apart from a dog – and Hermann the Parrot, of course – who'd never really been so much a passenger as an unshakable encumbrance, anyway.

Which factor did ease, to some small extent, the burden on Captain Shaw.

He'd never really found himself under much pressure to attempt to save *Lycomedes* either, come to that. Or her cargo, furnishings and fittings. Because he'd known she was going to die thirty seconds before she'd even spitted herself on the seacliff – that surge of bitter hopelessness he'd endured while she was still turning, still a whole ship, had predicted the end as surely as the explosion of a mine or the white-hot blast of a torpedo in her racing flank.

While now – as the Cataclysm entered its fifth minute of actuality – any lingering optimism in the captain's heart was irrevocably dashed as he stared silently ahead through the streaming wheelhouse windows.

Because already her forward deck was permanently submerged under a seething, crashing hysteria with only the rearing black silhouette of the fo'c'slehead struggling to remain above the constantly driving seas. And in the centre of it all, precisely where the exploded maw of number one hold should have been, was a great whirlpooling hole in the water with straw mats and dunnage and splintered hatchboards and a hundred bright new-wood packing cases all spiralling and circling round and round the vortex before being sucked into the belly of the dying ship . . .

. . . whereupon they were spewed yet again into the hushed, underwater vastness below to express gleefully to the surface once more, like little boys on a playground shute, to hurry round and round and round . . .

But, even with the inevitability of *Lycomedes*' foundering, Shaw still faced perhaps the most critical decision of all. To select that precise moment in time to give the order . . . *Abandon ship*.

For, if he gave it too soon, while the sheltered decks still afforded a safe haven, then the unnecessarily extended minutes of exposure before rescue could destroy many of those men who weren't already doomed to drown.

Yet if he miscalculated – delayed even one micro-second too long – *Lycomedes* herself would kill them all instead.

And keep them aboard for ever. A ghoulish, bobbing crew of phantom sailormen . . .

'. . . do now, sir?'

The captain blinked, dragging his eyes away from the scene through the wheelhouse windows. Chief Officer McRae was standing behind him, eyes anxiously searching Shaw's face. Shaw suddenly realized he was still pressing the call button on the engineroom phone and allowed his hand to drop with a surge of futility.

'They're not answering,' he said quietly. 'The chief engineer – all the engineers . . . they must be down there but they're not answering.'

Second Mate Fuller hurried from the chartroom waving his usual piece of paper. 'The Decca's still operating and I've laid off a bearing and distance from the Vyl Light, sir . . . forty-six miles.'

Shaw nodded. 'Thank you, Mister Fuller. Now see if you can raise anybody on the bridge VHF. I'll speak to Kemp in the radio room myself.'

The second mate bit his lip. 'You want me to put out a Mayday, sir. Or an urgency Pan?'

'Mayday. And . . . Mister Fuller?'

'Sir?'

'Ask them to come quickly. Please.'

Fuller muttered, 'Yessir,' very emphatically, unable to prevent his glance from straying through the open wheelhouse door to where the sea spat hissing fingers of greed towards the bridge. McRae noticed absently that it was starting to snow now, fluffy white flakes gusting in little whorls, chasing each other round and round the gale-torn corners of the wings. 'Like those flotsam packing cases are doing,' he thought. 'Around the hole in the sea where there should've been ship . . . Like *I* might be doing in all too short a time, for pity's sake. Just floating. Face down and aimlessly. Round and round, an' bloody well *round* . . . '

'I'd like to start mustering the crew as soon as possible, sir,' he said calmly.

Shaw knuckled his forehead savagely, massaging the corners of his eyes. McRae knew why – understood the enormity of the captain's dilemma better than anyone else aboard *Lycomedes*, and was grateful in a selfish sort of way that his wasn't the decision of when the dying must begin.

'She's rolling heavily,' the Old Man muttered. 'We won't get all the boats safely away with her working like this, David.'

McRae shrugged imperceptibly. 'If she develops a sudden list we won't get any of them away.

The captain looked at him. 'Have you ever seen men trying to launch boats in this kind of weather?'

'Not apart from in a nightmare.'

'I did. Once. She'd been torpedoed. We were very close to them, but it didn't make any difference. Not in the end . . . ' Shaw seemed to brace himself abruptly, lifting his chin. He had taken his decision.

'We'll stay with the ship. For the moment anyway . . . '

He fixed McRae with a steady, almost a defiant glare. 'Have the liferafts cleared away, Mister. And lower the boats to embarkation level then bowse them well in against the movement. But no man . . . I repeat – no single man . . . is to board until I give the order. Do you understand?'

*Lycomedes'* chief officer nodded. 'Aye, aye, sir!'

Before glancing forward involuntarily, to where there didn't seem to be very much of a ship left to stay with any more.

And hoped that those apprehensive men waiting anxiously on the boat deck would understand as well.

Oddly enough Fourth Engineer Chisholme – currently involved in the process of drowning during the fifth minute of the Cataclysm – *was* finally beginning to understand.

Oh, not about why the captain had decided to keep his crew aboard instead of immediately abandoning ship or something. In fact, to be brutally honest, the particular Lobster Quadrille

form of quandary facing the bridge – the *Will we; Won't we;*
*Will we; Won't we . . . Ha WILL we launch the boats?* – hardly
seemed a matter of pressing urgency to Bert right at the
moment, what with him being highly unlikely to participate
either way.

No. It was simply that Fourth Engineer Chisholme's sub-
merging flash of comprehension had finally explained that
oddly satisfied expression mellowing Bowman's death-mask.
The triumphant look which had caused Bert such perplexity
on the last occasion in which he'd observed the third engineer
passaging aimlessly by his little generator-island.

Even more – because Bert's final involuntary immersion also
revealed the identity of the misplaced thing which had pre-
vented him from reaching those tantalising ladders . . . *and* it
provided the added bonus of keeping him up to date on the
outcome of Greaser Carbon Black's earlier and somewhat self-
centred dash towards survival.

Which didn't seem to have been terribly successful. Or not
any more so than most of the other things Carbon Black had
ever attempted, judging by the underwater evidence which met
Bert Chisholme's popping eyes . . .

The dirty, billowing overalls – they were very much Carbon
Black, for a start. And the hair. Long, unkempt . . . and now
floating above the nodding head like waving tentacles – that
could very well have been Carbon Black, too. And the button
nose, distorted by the refraction of the swirling flood but still
vaguely recognizable. Then there were the ears . . . the pallid
hands . . .

. . . but it was the sagging, vacant jaw which finally caused
Bert to identify the man floating so placidly under the water,
one leg jammed irretrievably under the bottom step of the
ladder where someone – perhaps an already doomed and
broken third engineer – had forced it.

The jaw, and the open mouth. The gaping, toothless cavity

of a mouth . . . Now that was *definitely* Black! Pure, original Carbon Black, lately of the severely distressed Motor Vessel *Lycomedes* . . .

. . . but then a hand reached out. A shimmering, clutching hand . . . Carbon Black's dead yet still blindly moving hand *feeling* for him. An invitation from a sodden corpse, urging him to join the silent band of cadavers at the bottom of the sea . . .

Bert Chisholme began to shriek a long spiralling cloud of bubbles. Totally submerged and half way through drowning, yet he still managed quite a lot of a scream.

There didn't really seem much else to do. Not under the circumstances.

Bentine glanced apprehensively up at the radio room clock. It said they'd hit whatever it was they'd hit five minutes ago, yet there was still no further word from the bridge. No *Mayday* position, no indication of how badly they were damaged. Not even a rough estimate of how long they'd got left . . .

Kemp muttered '*Shit!*' in a frustrated growl and keyed a blunt GET OFF THIS FREQUENCY. DISTRESS TRANSMISSION PENDING.

'Bloody Liberian. Wants to send a revised ETA to his owners.'

'How many've we raised up to now, Chief?'

Kemp sent another ACKNOWLEDGED. STAND BY then transmitted the urgency signal groups again. XXX . . . XXX . . . XXX . . .

'Four including the Yankee warship,' he said flatly. 'But only the Russian seems close enough to give assistance otherwise.'

'How close is close?'

'Hour, hour and a half . . . they'll confirm when they get our final position. Otherwise I'll give them a DF bearing on our transmission.'

Bentine nodded and smiled weakly, hopefully. 'That's not too long, eh? We'll be OK till then . . . '

*Lycomedes* rolled heavily, swinging right over to starboard so that the second operator had to grab for the edge of the desk with a muffled squeak. Gradually she started to come back, but only in a tired sort of way. Kemp looked up into Bentine's white face, then dropped his eyes so the kid wouldn't see the sudden fright in them.

'Yeah,' he said reassuringly. 'Yeah, we'll be eating Borsche for dinner . . . With vodka!'

THIS IS LYCOMEDES . . . URGENT . . . XXX . . . XXX . . . XXX . . .

Well over half of *Lycomedes*' crew had already reached the boat deck by the time Bosun Skinner's grim-faced course brought him to the bottom of the starboard bridge ladder.

Now they were standing in desultory groups, huddled along the lee side of the radio room and officers' accommodation and talking in low, almost conspiratorial voices. The majority of the seamen already wore their life-jackets, mostly with self-conscious embarrassment – bright orange and hugely bulky; tousled heads framed against the upstanding padding of the flotation collars – but some still held theirs in a defiantly casual way, dangling loosely by the recovery webs as if loath to accept that this was anything other than just another bloody drill . . .

'Get them on,' Skinner snapped, hesitating for the first time. 'Jus' get them on an' stop playin' silly buggers!'

Someone said worriedly, 'What's happening then?' and a peevish voice muttered, 'Christ but you don't expec' the bridge to tell *us*, do you.'

Feeny, one of the older AB's, offered knowledgeably, 'We oughter be swinging out the boats, Bosun. She's flooding in the engine space . . . me an' Harry was below an' we heard it. The water an' that.'

'Yeah,' affirmed Harry, constantly checking with anxious fingers to make sure his life-jacket tapes were secured. Then he tugged the plastic whistle from its little pocket and blew it tentatively, experimentally.

'You blow that again an' I'll shove it down your bloody throat,' a greaser snarled nervously. 'A whistle blast means "Abandon ship" you stupid sod!'

'She *is* floodin' though . . . I'n't she, Harry?' Feeny urged doggedly.

'Yeah, Feen,' Harry confirmed again, this time removing the water-activated battery of his survival light from *its* pocket and shaking it doubtfully. But everyone knew Harry was a great talker.

Skinner stared grimly at Feeny. 'You sure, Feeny. That she's flooding the engineroom?'

'Chief engineer's down there now. And the second. An' Oggie Donaldson an' that greaser whatsisname . . . Halliday. Second told us to get the hell out've it – me an' Harry. Din't he, Harry?'

Harry went back to checking his lifejacket tapes. 'Yeah, Feen,' he rejoined. After a bit of consideration.

The peevish voice from the back asked, 'So what *do* we do then?'

'Nothing.' Skinner turned away, towards the bridge ladder. 'Don't do nothin' until you get an order. Savvy?'

'But Feeny says we're *sinking*, for Christ's sake!'

'Yeah,' Harry confirmed predictably. Then he saw that everyone was looking at him so he got flustered and added, with uncharacteristic eloquence, ' . . . She's . . . er . . . sinking. Sort of.'

'Well she can't sink, see? Not 'til the captain says so.'

Somebody giggled. It was an involuntary, nervous giggle but it seemed to ease the tension in the group huddled by *Lyco-*

*medes'* starboard lifeboats. Skinner shook his head and began to climb the ladder.

'I'll be back,' he promised the sea of orange life-jackets warningly. 'Nobody do nothin' until I come back.'

The peevish voice from the middle of the crowd started to sing '*Whyyyy are we waiting . . . Why are we waaaaaiting . . .* '

Then others took up the chant. But there was no malice there, only good natured resignation. With, perhaps, a dash of forced bonhomie to camouflage the fear.

' *. . . Oh, whyyyyy are we waaaaaitinnnnnng . . .* '

Because even now – five minutes after the Cataclysm and the ship well down by the head – nobody really believed *Lycomedes* was going to sink. Not actually *sink*, anyway.

It just didn't happen like that. On your ordinary, average sort of voyage.


Probably one of the strangest things about the Cataclysm was that – apart from Bosun Skinner – nobody else aboard *Lycomedes* had yet realized that Chippie *was* dead.

Deckhands Bronson and Falls – they'd been too busy running for their lives to see what had happened behind them on the forward centrecastle deck. While first-trip Apprentice Rupert Cassiday, the only other person to be leaning over the bridge rail and actually see the accident, had almost immediately forgotten it again with the shock of the actual collision itself. Anyway, even if he had remembered, he'd never have imagined that the carpenter's fall had been anything more than a nasty tumble followed by appropriate assistance from that obviously capable demi-God, Bosun Skinner himself.

Yet every pair of eyes on *Lycomedes*' bridge had been staring ahead almost constantly during the last five minutes, grimly watching the advance of the sea and the maelstrom smothering her number one hatch. So why hadn't *they* seen a dead man lying trapped under a winch barrel, literally thirty feet below their noses . . . ?

Well, try it for yourself. Stand in *Lycomedes'* wheelhouse alongside Shaw and McRae and Second Mate Fuller, and look out. Or, if you don't happen to have a foundering ship's bridge handy, stand at a second floor window instead and try to imagine the winter North Sea stretching all around you. And the thirty foot waves and the scream of the gale, and the spume and the emptiness and the grey, lunatic hysteria of it all . . .

. . . but you still won't be able to see Chippie. Because even if you press your nose flat against the glass he'll still be concealed in that narrow strip of deck directly below, out of your arc of vision. In the hidden ground.

The *dead* ground . . .

Which was why only Skinner still knew about the Cataclysm's first victim – but he was still dazed, still unsettlingly quiet under the shock of it, and nobody could have realized that either. Not right then.

And it was why three unwary young men and a dog were stubbornly sheltering in the lee of the centrecastle alleyway, preparing to face the lethal menace threatened by a ship which was inexorably hogging and sagging towards breaking point in a Force Ten nightmare.

Just to search fruitlessly for a perfectly unconcerned corpse.

After Chief Barraclough had disappeared into the flooding glare of the engineroom, the second engineer began to run towards the control room door with mixed feelings – all of them unpleasant.

The telephone from the bridge was buzzing steadily, as if someone up top had pressed their finger on the button and just kept it there – which wasn't really surprising, under the circumstances. Reflex action made the second hesitate momentarily, hand half outstretched to grasp the receiver, then the clamour of the *Pielstick* claimed hysterical priority so he lunged for the main engine cut-off instead.

Until slowly, very slowly, the mechanical thunder died away for the last time. But it didn't bring silence to *Lycomedes'* engine spaces – a few more minutes would bring that – because there was still the tumult of the imploding flood and the softer, muffled boom of the jostling North Sea against her steel sides to remind him of the quickly decreasing safety margin remaining before *Lycomedes* changed from ship to plummeting charnel house.

The deckhead lights flickered, grew dim as the main engine alternator failed, then came on again with full brilliance when the first auxiliary generator automatically cut in. Glancing up the second noticed the pointer of the bridge telegraph standing at twelve-o-clock high . . . STOP ENGINE.

Feeling a bit sick he wondered just how close to answering that remote command Bowman had managed to get before he died – because the second had no doubt whatsoever in his mind that everyone on watch below at the moment of the Cataclysm *was* already dead and past human help . . .

. . . which reminded him of Chief Barraclough again, all alone down there with less chance of getting out if the ship went suddenly than any other man aboard – which meant absolutely no chance at all.

The bridge phone stopped ringing abruptly, disconcertingly mute, as if nobody on deck had time to worry about missing engineers any more.

Then a dishevelled figure appeared in the control room doorway and the second whirled with the abrupt shock of it and, at the same time, a fleeting hope that maybe – just maybe – he'd been wrong and that Bowman or Fourth Chisholme or even Carbon Black had miraculously survived the deluge.

Until he saw it wasn't a miracle at all, merely an agitated

Oggie Donaldson who immediately began to tug frantically at the leather straps securing the Robertson stretcher to the bulkhead while gabbling over and over again, 'His face, Second ... Halliday's face, all smashed in an' ... Christ but his *face*, Second ... '

'Easy,' the second blurted, coldly aware of the panic rising within his own mind. 'Take it easy, Oggie, an' we'll see him right.'

'He'll die. In a boat out in that weather ... 'E'll *die* f'r cryin' out ...

The stretcher fell off the bulkhead with a crash. Donaldson said hysterically, 'Oh dear ... Oh dear God ... ' and snatched it up, bumbling haphazardly towards the door. The stretcher jammed crosswise and the little greaser started to sob, still struggling to push it horizontally through the narrow exit. The second roared, 'You stupid BASTard!' in a sudden fit of keyed-up rage, then dragged his voice to a barely-controlled level and added tightly, 'Easy, Oggie lad. Up an' down with it, then get out and start strapping Halliday in. I'll be along in a minute ... OK?'

*Lycomedes* lurched sickeningly, lying right over to starboard then coming slowly back. The rumbling surge of water from below carried into the control room like a peal of distant thunder.

Donaldson squealed, 'Oh *God*!' again and went through the door like a bullet from a gun, stretcher levelled in front of him in an ungainly, charging sort of motion.

'Take it EASY!' the second bawled, feeling shame and anger and a terrible resentment all mixed up with the sick fear in his belly. Nightmares like this just didn't *happen* to a bloke. Not to your ordinary, average sort've bloke ...

He hesitated, listening with growing agitation to the flood below and wondering what superhuman driving force had enabled Chief Barraclough to go down to meet it.

Then, quite deliberately, the second engineer turned and went back into the control room, heading for the bridge telephone even as *Lycomedes* began to carry over to port, maybe for the very last time.

But he had gold rings on his sleeve, as well – only one less than Barraclough. And they wouldn't allow him to leave the flooding engineroom before his duty was done either.

To the remaining members of *Lycomedes*' crew – those not actually doing anything other than waiting for orders or for help – the fifth minute of the Cataclysm passed in much the same way as the preceding four.

Agonizingly slowly. With far too much time to think, and imagine, and to become more and more apprehensive. Especially in the case of Second Cook Stanley Young, still committed to voluntary confinement with his injured senior by the intangible bonds of friendship, yet also becoming more and more uncomfortably aware that even the strongest bonds can fray under constant chafing.

And finally break. Like a man's nerve . . . Like Stanley's very nearly did when someone down below stopped the main engine and all of a sudden the familiar and reassuring galley sounds stopped too, with the cutlery drawers now only emitting an occasional clink as the ship reached the extremity of a roll instead of their earlier, persistent rattle, while the rumbling solidity of the *Pielstick* itself faded for the very first time since they'd sailed.

Leaving only the chilling, distant moan of the storm outside, allied with the soft percussion of the sea against *Lycomedes*' flank, to provide a background dirge for the alien skitter of unsecured utensils rolling across the fouled deck and the gut-wrenching whimpers of the unconscious man.

Suddenly Stan let out a sob, covering his ears with his hands to shut out the fear of it all.

'Hurry, Eddie . . . ' he whimpered towards the empty galley door. 'Oh *please* hurry an' come back . . . '

Which was precisely what Eddie Ferguson *was* doing – hurrying. Towards the boat deck. Though that earlier, unsuspecting glimpse of the mountainous seas threatening *Lycomedes* hadn't left very much space in the steward's reeling mind for thinking about the second part of Stan Young's lonely appeal right at that moment.

The 'going back' part . . .

Hermann crooned a thoughtful, carefully selected obscenity then – gripping the vertical bars of the cage with his beak – began to pull himself up like a tattered monkey on a fairground stick.

Having reached the top he cautiously revolved until he was suspended upside down, and asked the empty cabin, 'OO'se a bloody wonder . . . Oo'se a bloody wonder?'

Never once, during the whole gymnastic operation, did Hermann's expectant, reptilian eye leave the open doorway. It was almost as if he didn't want to waste invaluable slanging time from the very moment of Chief Barraclough's return to the fray.

Which the chief undoubtedly would. Hermann the parrot didn't have any doubts at all about that. But then Hermann was the only living creature left aboard *Lycomedes* who still didn't have any fears about anything.

Except for Huang, of course. Still offering indescribable pleasures to his dream lover by the gentle river in the Perfume Garden of Kwangsi Chuang. Sleeping without a care in the world, secure in the knowledge that – apart from Yeh Chun's devotion – his life savings of one thousand, three hundred and sixteen pounds in the little tin box under his bunk were as safe as . . . well, nearly as safe as *Lycomedes* herself.

The search party ventured timidly on to the blizzard-swept

foredeck in the closing seconds of the fifth minute.

Bosun Skinner reached the bridge wing and impassively turned to face the open wheelhouse door. Oggie Donaldson reached Greaser Halliday and dubiously placed his hands under the groaning ex-hero's shoulders, trying to roll him into the stretcher without actually looking too closely at how badly a man could be injured by a puff of air.

Fourth Engineer Chisholme sensed Carbon Black's floating spectral hand close around his overalls with inexorable finality.

And Captain Graham Shaw replaced the radio room telephone on its hook with a heavy heart. He had just admitted to the world that he had lost his ship.

That there was no more hope for *Lycomedes* . . .

# Chapter Seven

O hear us when we cry to thee
For those in peril on the sea.
                    *William Whiting*

## CATACLYSM plus SIX MINUTES

SOS . . . SOS . . . SOS DE LYCOMEDES GBYD . . . HAVE
STRUCK SUBMERGED OBJECT POSITION 55 10 18N 06
12 50E FORWARD HOLDS AND POSSIBLE ENGINEROOM
FLOODING . . . ANTICIPATE ABANDONING WITHIN
THIRTY MINUTES . . . IMMEDIATE ASSISTANCE REQUIRED
SOS . . . SOS . . . SOS DE LYCOMEDES GBYD . . .

LYCOMEDES GBYD DE UNITED STATES WARSHIP FORDON
COUNTY . . . PROCEEDING FULL SPEED YOUR ASSISTANCE.
MY ETA 1605 ZULU . . . YOUR TRANSMISSION RELAYED
TO AREA SAR COORDINATOR . . . WILL MAINTAIN
LISTENING WATCH THIS FREQUENCY . . . GOOD LUCK.

ALL SHIPS DE . . . ID SOMEONE TRANSMI . . . TRESS
CALL. MY RADIO EQUIP . . . ALFUNCTIONING.

UNKNOWN SHIP DE LYCOMEDES GBYD . . . GET OFF
THE LINE. DISTRESS WORKING THIS FREQUENCY.

WARSHIP FORDON COUNTY DE TUG SEA DIAMOND . . .
AM ENGAGED IN TOW ENE ECKO FISK OIL FIELD BUT
WILL SLIP AND PROCEED LYCOMEDES IF REQUIRED

. . . EARLIEST ETA CASUALTY 1740 GMT . . . CONFIRM.

SEA DIAMOND DE UNITED STATES WARSHIP FORDON COUNTY . . . STICK WITH THE JOB IN HAND BUT OFFER APPRECIATED.

SOS . . . SOS . . . SOS DE LYCOMEDES GBYD . . .

LYCOMEDES GBYD DE SOVETSKOGO SOYUZA URFT . . . AM IN HASTE TO YOUR AID. MY ETA 1555 GMT AND BEFORE AMERICAN WARSHIP . . . ALL HAPPINESS AND GOOD STRENGTH TO YOUR SAD CREW.

COMNAVFORCE EUROPE DE USS FORDON COUNTY . . . NATO SECRET IMMEDIATE . . . SUSPECT SOVIET VESSEL INTENDS USING LYCOMEDES INCIDENT AS PROPAGANDA EXERCISE.

USS FORDON COUNTY DE COMNAVFORCE EUROPE . . . NATO SECRET IMMEDIATE . . . AFFIRMATIVE YOUR UNCHARITABLE CONCLUSION. MAKE EVERY EFFORT TO UPSTAGE HIM BUT STRESS PRIORITY TO SAVE LIFE.

SOVETSKOGO SOYUZA DE UNITED STATES WARSHIP FORDON COUNTY . . . PROPOSE LOCAL LYCOMEDES RESCUE EFFORT BE COORDINATED THROUGH ME IN JOINT OPERATION.

FORDON COUNTY DE SOVETSKOGO SOYUZA . . . PROPOSAL REJECTED. SOVIET INTEREST ONLY TO PRESERVE LIFE AT SEA AND NOT POLITICAL FACE OF UNITED STATES FORCES OF AGGRESSION.

SOVETSKOGO SOYUZA DE INFORMATION MINISTRY OF

USSR . . . SECRET IMMEDIATE . . . POLITICALLY
ADVANTAGEOUS YOU EFFECT RESCUE SURVIVORS
BRITISH MERCHANTMAN LYCOMEDES BEFORE ARRIVAL
NATO ALLIANCE VESSEL AND IN ACCORDANCE FINEST
TRADITIONS SOVIET MARITIME FLEET . . . STRESS
YOU ALSO ENSURE SUITABLE PHOTOGRAPHIC RECORDS
ARE RETAINED FOR DISTRIBUTION WORLD PRESS.

SOVETSKOGO SOYUZA DE UNITED STATES WARSHIP
FORDON COUNTY . . . YOUR REJECTION MY PROPOSAL
FOR INCREASING RESCUE CAPABILITY OF LYCOMEDES
MERCY FLEET DULY NOTED AND RELAYED TO
APPROPRIATE PRESS AGENCIES . . .

. . . but nobody aboard *Lycomedes* gave a damn about all that.

Still, whatever happened, from now on the ship wouldn't die
secretly, mysteriously, as so many vessels before her. Through
the electronic medium of Kemp's rattling morse key every
radiotelegraph-equipped vessel in the North Sea – every
continually listening shore station – would know of the *Lycomedes* Cataclysm, while every suddenly alerted operator would
feel an uneasy sympathy and be only too aware that 'There, but
for the grace of God, go I . . . '

The ship was shouting with a human voice too, Second
Officer Fuller's tightly controlled tones being transmitted
through her bridge radiotelephone to any ear tuned to VHF
Channel 16 – the International calling and safety frequency.
Only there wouldn't be any real hope of an answer at such
short range. *Lycomedes'* still scanning radar would have shown
the presence of anything close enough to effect immediate
assistance – even a fisherman – while all the glowing PPI
revealed were those eternally shifting legions of identical
mini-blips.

But Fuller tried, though. Six minutes ago that same screen

hadn't shown anything either – yet they'd still impaled themselves on a cathedral in the middle of the sea!

'Mayday, Mayday, Mayday . . . This is Golf Bravo Yankee
Delta *Lycomedes* . . . Golf Bravo Yankee Delta *Lycomedes* . . . '

Science and modern technology had made it all so sophisti-
cated. But it still meant the same as the inverted ensign in the
rigging, the red flare in the sky or the burning tar barrel on
deck.

'For God's sake help us. *Please* . . . '

'This place is getting more like a railway station every minute,'
McRae reflected bleakly, gazing at the sudden influx of people
into the wheelhouse.

First a bloody-faced Third Mate Wise, now fully dressed
complete with duffle jacket, still looking vaguely bewildered
yet striving anxiously to give the impression of the classic,
steely-eyed seaman in adversity – until you noticed the tips of
fluffy red carpet slippers peeping from under his trouser
bottoms.

Then Apprentice Cassiday, even more confused and out of
his element but now with a bravely resolute set to the schoolboy
features. The initial shock had passed in Rupert's case – already
this was the great adventure he'd wistfully imagined ever since
he'd first felt the insistent tug of the sea and from ships.

The fear would come again to Rupert. But it would be a little
while yet. As *Lycomedes* settled lower and lower, and a boy's
romanticism degenerated into nightmarish reality.

And finally the predictably resentful reappearance of
Quartermaster Clements, struggling through from the chartroom while balancing a big plastic canister against the roll of
the ship and muttering darkly, 'Distress flares, no less . . .
Christ, but how basic c'n you *get*?'

Suddenly McRae noticed that the main engine had stopped.

Just as the telephone from the engineroom rang.

Captain and chief officer both lunged for the receiver until Shaw won the race, snatching the handset from its cradle while Mickey Wise, totally unaware that they'd suddenly heard a cry from what had seemed an already sealed grave, asked petulantly, 'Did we hit something or what. And what's happening now, then?'

'*Bridge*. What's happening below . . . ?'

'What d'you want me to do now, sir?' from Apprentice Cassiday. Keenly.

'Oh yeah, we hit somethin', Mister Wise. Christ but did we *hit* somethin' . . . ' Ernie Clements. Accusingly.

The captain again, gripping the phone with unconcealed anxiety. ' . . . then where's Mister Barraclough? . . . Below? But who's with him, man . . . ?'

'Mayday, Mayday, Mayday. This is Golf Bravo Yankee Delta *Lycomedes* . . . '

'Oh Jesus! Three hundred feet long!' Third Mate Wise. Finally shattered. Staring at the *Navwarn* file he'd just picked up from the deck.

'I think the ship's a little bit down by the head, sir.' Apprentice Cassiday once more. Being tentatively helpful now.

' . . . Vyl Light Vessel bearing zero seven fife true, range forty six . . . four sixer miles . . . Forward holds flooding fast . . . '

' . . . me? Oh, I'm just the bloody quartermaster. Jus' A B Clements, so don't ask *me* what's happen . . . *HOW* big did you say f'r cryin' out loud?'

'NO one got out? What are you telling me, Mister . . . ? That *nobody* got out of the engineroom, for God's sake . . . ?'

McRae turned away quickly, slipping through the starboard door and out on to the snow flurried wing. He'd heard enough to explain both the lack of response from the engineroom until now and also to underline the need for urgency. For if they were that badly holed then *Lycomedes* herself could very well take the decision of whether to stay or leave out of Shaw's hands – by shortly abandoning her crew, instead.

Once clear of the wheelhouse the still-increasing wind clawed at him with appalling ferocity, every battering gust a frozen lance spearing through clothing with sadistic precision, already hunching him in reflex submission while at the same time snatching spitefully under the lapels of his reefer to flail cheekbones in a vicious tattoo of pain.

'Please stop it. Wind . . . ' a distant voice screamed from somewhere deep down within him. '. . . stop it, stop it STOP IT!'

And then he himself halted abruptly, uncertainly, one hand clutching his fluttering lapels while the other shielded the fat, skimming snowflakes from his eyes as he saw a man standing sombrely at the head of the ladder, simply standing there waiting for him as if they had all the time in the world left to freeze to death. Until he recognized Bosun Skinner and felt a tremendous surge of relief, for Skinner's experience and stolid professionalism was the one factor which might help to tip the odds in their favour.

He didn't particularly notice the emptiness in Skinner's eyes, so his relief remained undiminished. He didn't query Chippie's absence right away either because he assumed the carpenter would still be taking soundings, confirming the inevitable. Just like the Department of Trade and Industry, Sea Transport Branch, would have expected of a properly responsible ship's carpenter.

So McRae just said, 'Afternoon, Bose,' and felt silly as soon as he'd mouthed the words, but Skinner didn't smile at the formal absurdity.

'They say she's floodin' the engineroom.'

'Captain's talking to them now. Second engineer's switched in the auxiliaries. It's bad, though, Willie . . . '

'*Bad?*' Skinner snarled brutally. 'She's bloody finished,

Mister . . . We got radar, electric navigators, echo sounders, DF – everythin' a ship could ever need, yet she's still finished. An' all because some brassbound bloody college kid can't use the eyes God gave 'im.'

The mate stepped back, blinking in shocked disbelief. This wasn't Skinner, surely. Or certainly not the Skinner he'd known before, anyway . . . And then a resentful anger surged under all the doubts and fears, temporarily overcoming the misery of his own keenly-felt inadequacy.

Before he could stop himself he retorted viciously, 'Just belay that, Skinner. You're not the only one scared gutless, so get on with your bloody job an' leave the recriminations till later. D'you read me loud and clear, Bosun?'

For what seemed a very long time the two men glared wildly at each other across the wing of the dying ship, momentarily unaware of the driving snow and the shriek of the storm and the black, hissing seas piling outboard. And then suddenly – with disconcerting calm – Skinner scratched the side of his nose with a wet, dirty finger.

Before remarking, almost absently, 'It's chilly. Shouldn't you go an' slip into some foul weather gear while you got the chance?'

The mate frowned, thrown off course a second time by Skinner's attitude, but he still didn't read any more into the old man's opening accusation than a perhaps understandable and momentary bitterness against deck officers in general.

He also felt himself shaking violently, chilled to the marrow under the cutting edge of the wind. 'I . . . There's no time. Perhaps someone could get it from my cabin . . . ' He looked at the bosun searchingly. 'Well . . . ? Can we get the crowd away. Four boats to launch, in these seas?'

'What does the captain say?'

'We wait. Swing them out, then . . . wait.'

Skinner nodded expressionlessly. 'It's good sense. Don't leave the ship till the ship leaves you.'

The bosun turned away, placing one foot on the rung of the ladder to the boat deck. Then he hesitated and looked up at the mate.

'I'm not scared, Mister McRae,' he said quietly. 'Not f'r myself, anyroad.'

'I'm glad.' The cold dragged the corner of McRae's mouth into a wry travesty of a grin. 'Because personally I'm bloody terrified . . . and does that answer my question, Willie?'

'Question?'

'Whether you think we've a snowball's chance in hell of launching the boats safely. In this?'

*Lycomedes* fell away into a trough, mastheads gyrating enormously against the snow-flecked overcast. The tumbling crest of the passing wave sighed majestically to leeward, nearly level with the bridge. And the bridge itself was almost sixty feet above the waterline.

'No!' Skinner said, oddly dispassionate. 'But it'll help take their minds off what's happenin' to them, won't it . . . Jus' trying to.'

Fourth Engineer Chisholme, involved in sinking, screaming and drowning at the bottom of the engineroom, already had his mind fully occupied.

In fact in Bert's case there had been very little time for calculated diversions from that moment when he felt the clutch of the dead Greaser Black begin to drag him through the water, hauling him undeviatingly through liquid silence towards the gaping maw of the cadaver bobbing in company with him.

And that was the moment when Bert finally did give up hope. Chucked in the towel for the first time since the bottom had fallen out of his oil-hot, ordered little mechanical world. Oh, he'd fought – by *God* but he'd fought for survival – against nausea and shock, and the unbelievable violence of the deluge itself, but this really was the bloody end. This submarine assault from a water-powered zombie in a gyrating tomb where dying men smiled cleverly and corpses beamed in toothless welcome . . .

'Get it over with . . . ' he shrieked. Noiselessly, because there wasn't any breath left in his lungs to scream in any other way. 'Jus' get it over with an' let me die, then . . . '

Those eyes! So close to him now that he could detect the bitter resentment of the already-dead. And that mouth . . . crimson-blue against the pallor. Swollen-tongued and monstrously distorted . . .

'NOOOOOOooooo . . . ' Bert gagged, twisting convulsively.

'Come *on*, lad. Easy does it.' Carbon Black snarled.

Bert flailed hysterically at the vice-grip on his collar, each arm restrained by leaden fatigue.

'Pack it *in* . . . Jus' getta GRIP've yourself, laddie!' the Ghoul bellowed. Then queried with diabolical cunning, 'Where's Bowman . . . You seen Bowman down there?'

Chisholme giggled weakly, triumphantly. 'Third's had it . . . ' He retched, dribbling a stream of oil and sea water and listening distantly to the thunder of the flood. ' . . . Third's laughin' at you, Zombie! Laughin' hisself sick, you sepulchral bastard, 'cause he's already dead an' past anythin' you can . . . '

But Bert suddenly stopped gabbling, abruptly aware of the fact that he *was* able to hear the tumult raging in *Lycomedes*' engine space once again. Which did seem pretty odd, really, seeing Carbon Black's world had only gurgled and bubbled and not been at all noticeable in an audible sense.

Which was the point where the phantom lifted him vertically, then shook him like a rag doll with his head lolling idiotically and the hysteria a sick, uncontrollable mockery . . .

. . . until his eyes snapped wide open.

Whereupon Chief Barraclough – who wasn't in any way an optical illusion – stopped shaking and roared instead, ' . . . sure? You *sure* Bowman's dead, laddie . . . ? And the greaser. What about Black?'

'Thank you, Chief,' Bert whispered. 'Oh thank you very, very much indee . . . '

'*BLACK*, dammit!'

Bert collapsed on the ladder, legs still dangling uselessly in the whirlpooling scum already mounting steadily, rung by rung, to capture him again.

'Dead, too,' he panted, feeling, at the same time, an uneasy relief that Greaser Black *was* dead after all. Because Bert could never have lived with the knowledge of a drowned sailor who still beckoned seductively from the grave. And now he knew for certain it had only been the hand of Chief Engineer Barraclough reaching out towards him below the surface.

And it *had* been, dammit.

. . . hadn't it?

The chief gripped his arm, pulling him upright again. For a moment longer they gazed bleakly over the maelstrom which concealed *Lycomedes'* bedplates. Even Bert's little generator-island had sunk below the rising spate. Now only the silent bulk of the fourteen cylinder *Pielstick* still reared defiantly towards the glaring deckhead lights.

While, directly abaft the main engine, a swelling excrescence roared and bubbled, transmitting eddies which bumbled excitedly through every corner and secret space, constantly stirring the vague white shape still faintly detectable below the ladder it had once tried so desperately to climb.

Barraclough looked old, suddenly. Old and small, and not at all powerful any more.

'Go on up, Bert,' he said tiredly. 'There's nothing more for us down here.'

They turned away and slowly, almost unhurriedly, began to

climb the long shiny path towards the deck. And towards the full fury of the storm, which was why Chief Barraclough wasn't hurrying, while Fourth Engineer Chisholme – in six minutes of time – had done all the hurrying he ever intended to do again.

Behind them, in the abandoned engineroom, Third Engineer Bowman cruised into view from the lee of the *Pielstick*. Spread-eagled on his back in the ultimate relaxation he seemed to follow Bert's stumbling retreat with cynical, unblinking amusement. He was still smiling, too, in that enigmatic, very secretive way.

But perhaps that was because Third Engineer Bowman really knew what had happened to Bert down there, underneath the water. When a dead man clutched at him with necrophiliac anticipation.

Unless, of course, it had been a still barely-alive man.

Simply appealing for help . . . ?

Unlike the chief's and fourth engineer's controlled retreat, Eddie Ferguson had shot up his particular ladders to the boat deck like a distress rocket, having once assessed the true state of the weather outwith the confines of *Lycomedes*' galley area.

It was only when he finally arrived, and found that nobody really seemed to be doing anything more urgent than self-consciously testing lifejacket lights or tugging at already tightened securing tapes, that Eddie began to wonder if he hadn't made a bit of a fool of himself. Privately, of course, with no one around to see, which didn't make it quite so bad.

Even the chief officer, McRae, was simply standing talking to the bosun at the head of the bridge ladder and, while they both looked pretty unchuffed about the situation, neither of them appeared particularly anxious to launch boats or institute any similar operation which suggested *Lycomedes* might have to be abandoned in the immediate future.

Reassured, he began to think about Stan Young again, and the burned chef, and scanned the groups of men waiting under the boat station signs for someone to report to. The chief steward preferably, or even a deck officer for that matter, because they'd know about the morphine Dempster would need before any attempt could be made to move him.

As he searched, eyes narrowed against the whipping snow-flakes, old Feeny came past, accompanied as ever by his personal echo, Harry Whatsit. The AB stopped and eyed him with benign severity.

'You gotta lifejacket, mate? You gotta have a lifejacket on . . . i'n't that right, Harry?'

'Yeah, Feen,' Harry agreed, staring at Eddie with matching disapproval.

'Seen the chief steward, Feeny?' Eddie asked anxiously, but Feeny wasn't to be so easily diverted from his self-appointed task of seein' the lads was OK.

'You oughter getta lifejacket on, son. Skinner'll 'ave your guts f'r a lifeline if he sees you without a . . . '

' . . . lifejacket?' Harry blurted, inspired to tentative oratory. Then shuffled uncomfortably as Feeny turned with awesome dignity and fixed him with a reprimanding glare.

' . . . without a *life*jacket!' Feeny completed pointedly. Harry simply continued to shuffle, overwhelmed at his own temerity in trying to upstage his friend and mentor. Then he hauled out his whistle yet again before remembering that, if he tested it one more time, there was a pretty fair chance everyone on *Lycomedes*' boat deck would simultaneously jump over the side, so he shoved *that* back hastily and positively danced in total confusion.

'Except I haven't *got* a lifejacket, Feeny,' Eddie blurted nervously, 'It's in my cabin . . . What's the chief steward's boat station?'

Feeny blinked in shocked outrage. ' 'E won't give you *his*

now, will 'e? It's not reasonable to expec' a man to give up 'is lifejacket . . . is it, Harry boy?'

Harry didn't dare actually to say anything. He just shook his head. Very, very quietly.

'Christ!' Eddie thought desperately. 'This isn't getting me anywhere. An' if we need lifejackets, then why isn't somebody *doing* something to try an' prevent us having to use them for real. Like letting us get in the boats so's we don't have to bloody swim home . . . '

But he was another one who couldn't really believe *Lycomedes* was sinking. And anyway, he'd always thought of ships' life-boats as being virtually infallible things which floated in seas big enough to overwhelm a ship of *Lycomedes*' size. After all – a light bulb can survive a typhoon, can't it?

Besides, the chances were that Huang would have brought his up for him, seeing both jackets were stowed casually in the bottom of the wardrobe they shared. And the little Chinese was bound to have been in the cabin when they hit. He always was at this time of day. Head down, snoring contentedly . . . and with that inevitable, and highly intriguing smile on his Oriental features. Eddie had often wondered about that smile, come to think of it.

He decided to leave the lifejacket for a little longer and find the chief steward. Obviously nothing was going to happen to the ship in the next few minutes, while the quicker they could get poor bloody Dempster topside and fixed up with a shot of pain-killer the better.

It never occurred to Steward Eddie Ferguson that he had temporarily succumbed to the same strange lethargy which seemed to have gripped many of *Lycomedes*' crew in that sixth minute.

The feeling that now the initial panic was over, there wasn't any immediate danger, any real threat.

Because while she was down a bit by the head she was still

E

stable, considering the seas running. That even though the main engine had stopped, the lights remained on, which meant the auxiliaries were still running like sewing machines. That the boats were still in their chocks, while they'd've been swung out by now if the captain had any real doubts about the situation . . .

And, above all, that things like major disasters just didn't happen nowadays. Not where vessels were 'Lost with all hands' or 'Sunk with appalling loss of life!'

Not to ordinary blokes, anyway.

Aboard an ordinary ship. Like *Lycomedes*.

But by this time things really did seem to be looking a little better, a little less bleak, for many people.

For Bert Chisholme, for instance. Saved for the present if nothing else, while any future had to be more hopeful than the one Bert appeared to face thirty seconds before. Then there were the men on the bridge – at least they *had* finally heard from the engineroom, and now knew that the combined expertise of Barraclough and the second were available to try and ease, if not prevent, the onrush of the flood. Hope, if not optimism, springs eternal.

In the radio room Kemp and Bentine had received positive proof that there *were* other ships in the North Sea, and even that was reassuring in a situation where loneliness can assume outrageous proportions.

Nothing more had happened to Stan Young in the galley during the past minute or so, and sixty seconds of non-event had to be good news in his particular nightmare. Chief Officer McRae had got Skinner's apparent solidity behind him in a period when he needed every boost he could get to his own self-confidence. Huang Pi-wu was getting rather more than a morale booster from his fantasy lover by this time – and he was still about as lethargic as you can get while your boat's sinking.

Hermann the parrot had suddenly caught sight of a minute scrap of peanut in the bottom of his cage which probably cheered him up no end, Hermann being nothing if not an opportunist bird.

Even the prospects for the badly damaged Greaser Halliday were brighter. At least Oggie Donaldson had managed to get his stretcher through the control room door, which meant that the first hurdle delaying his long-overdue passage to the boat deck had been overcome.

So it was ironic, but perhaps equally typical of the Cataclysm's perversity, that everything suddenly started to go . . . well . . . wrong from that moment on.

Relatively speaking, of course.

It all began with a noise.

A rather obscure, hard-to-place noise. Almost as if coming from somewhere deep inside *Lycomedes* . . .

## CATACLYSM plus SEVEN MINUTES

Apprentice Standish, deckhands Bronson and Falls, and Seadog were just abreast of number three hatch still on the higher level of the forward centrecastle deck, when Falls first heard it.

They were also very close to Chippie, only he'd broken his neck under the port side winch so the remarkably small corpse was still hidden from the search party by the raised coaming of the hold. But even in life Chippie always had tended to be a quiet, introspective man – other than with Bosun Skinner, at least. His death had simply made him still more elusive, still more insignificant, even clad in yellow oilskins against an open ship's deck.

And anyway, it was the noise which caught the young deckhand's attention at that moment. A distant, apparently subterranean rumble only vaguely heard. Or *was* it a rumble from below, within the ship? Or did it simply come from the play of the wind . . . from the snow-obscured horizon where the elements, having already offered many variations on a theme of violence, were now preparing a crescendo based on lightning, out of thunder.

Falls halted abruptly, head cocked apprehensively to one side and swivelling slowly, concentratedly. 'What's that?'

The boy looked back at him while Bronson stopped, too, eyeing the turmoil a mere few feet away from him over the bulwark and trying to convince himself it was all a nightmare. Not really happening at all.

'Come on!' Standish called urgently. All of a sudden he'd started to wish they hadn't ventured out here either, but he still felt it was his duty to check on Chippie's safety because he knew that the old carpenter – or the bosun or Mister McRae for that matter – would have done precisely the same thing for him.

'There's something moving. Down below us . . . There it is again!'

The three of them stared hard at the deck, willing whatever it was to occur again so's they could pinpoint and identify it. Seadog sat in the middle of the ring, wagged his tail and looked pleased. But he thought they were all paying close attention to him.

Nothing happened though. Things never do when you want them to. Like car brakes that squeal for months, then remain mutely conformist while the mechanic's sceptical ear listens – and screech like banshees at the first halt sign past the garage.

'Nothing's happening,' Standish said. Sceptically.

'Aw, let's get it over with, Archie,' Bronson muttered, still sparing half his concentration for what was happening outwith the ship's rail.

'But I *heard* it. A sort of . . . I dunno . . . a noise of some kind,' Falls struggled for descriptive inspiration a moment longer then capitulated weakly. 'I think we oughter go back, sir. That's what the siren was for. An' there's the dog to consider.'

The apprentice hesitated before lifting his head critically. 'The wind's dropped quite a lot . . . Look, I'm just going to nip forward as far as the break of the well deck while there's a lull. You two hang on here, OK?'

The wind hadn't, of course. It was simply that the mean wave height was now well above the level of *Lycomedes'* lower decks, protecting them slightly in the lee of their crests. It was Standish's second mistake.

'Here,' he urged, holding out Seadog's lead. 'Hang on to him – in case I have to dodge a lump of water or something!'

'Go on – I'll come with you,' Bronson said grudgingly. It wasn't that he felt any strong desire to do the right thing, simply that it seemed one way to clear his yardarm with Bosun Skinner after his earlier panic. For when all this was over, and people started to remember things. Especially big, irritable people.

'Oh leave the bloody dog an' I'll come too,' Falls snapped, suddenly finding himself outnumbered. 'Jus' let's get there an' back quick, eh?'

But in Falls's case there didn't seem much alternative. He wasn't quite scared enough yet to run away a second time, but he certainly didn't have the courage to wait, all alone, on that nerve-racking stretch of deck and listen to the sound of something monstrous happening right underneath his feet.

Because the noise *would* come again, somehow he knew that without any doubt at all. Just as soon as they moved farther forward. Farther away from the illusory safety of the superstructure.

Standish nodded encouragingly and knelt down, passing Seadog's lead under the red-painted seawater pipe running along the scuppers. He felt quite pleased in a way that the two seamen had volunteered to follow him under what were,

133

admittedly, rather unsettling conditions. It sort of endorsed his own secret conviction that he was the kind of chap who would automatically lead in time of crisis. A good officer. Commanding by personality rather than rank . . .

The dog sat, suspiciously watching as he finished tying the clove hitch in its lead. He stood up, patting the velvety brown head and murmuring, 'Good dog . . . Stay, now. You stay.'

The dog whined suddenly, crying for the first time since they'd left the kennel on the poopdeck. Oh, it was highly unlikely that it realized the danger in being firmly tethered to a seven thousand ton potential anchor – no more than Hermann the parrot, currently imprisoned in a steel cage in Chief Barraclough's cabin, could appreciate *his* somewhat restricted prospects for survival. Yet Seadog had already proved that he had an animal's sense of awareness, an uncanny anticipation of impending threat.

'Stay,' the boy emphasized as he turned to leave. Commandingly, of course.

Whereupon Seadog started to howl mournfully, nose uplifted and pointing forward, following the three departing figures grimly struggling to make headway against the roll of the ship.

It was a penetrating, distracting lament. Added to the existing tumult of the wind and the seas pummelling *Lycomedes'* flank, and the steady rumble of freely cascading water swilling across her forward well deck, it completely drowned the next vitally important warning when it finally came . . .

Chief Engineer Barraclough became aware of it when he and Bert Chisholme had climbed half way up the ladder from the flooding engineroom.

He stopped abruptly, head angled downwards, the earlier despair suddenly replaced by a scowling concentration. Two treads above him the fourth just sank to his knees and held grimly to the rail, gagging convulsively as nausea swept over him in great shuddering waves. But Bert had long passed the stage of awareness. Now there was only a suspended fuzz of exhaustion, made even harder to endure by the uneasy feeling that he was simply dragging himself out of the frying pan to drop into the fire.

Or the North Sea. If there *was* still any of it actually left outside the bloody ship.

'You hear that?' the chief called urgently. 'A noise . . . Somethin' not right?'

Bert took one glance backwards, down to where the black swirl gurgled and the gusher roared white foam, and the great mass of water swilled from side to side in a rumbling torrent every time the ship rolled . . .

. . . and whispered, 'Christ but you got to be jokin', Chief!'

Barraclough didn't move for a moment longer, still listening, with that inquisitorial glare probing every dark corner of the pandemonium below, then his grip on the rail tightened convulsively, knuckles white against oil-smeared hands.

'*There!* Like metal, laddie . . . Not the water itself.'

And Bert Chisholme heard it that time, too. A distant, hollow sound. Almost a scream, magnified and distorted by the volume of the cavern around them. He felt the hairs on the back of his neck begin to rise and the drowned, distorted face of Greaser Black hung before him as before, only now with the vacant mouth wide and baying . . .

'Christ!' he whimpered again, 'You were dead, Carbon. I *know* you were dea . . . '

But then Chief Barraclough swung him violently around, hit him hard across the face and, despite the pity in the older man's eyes, snarled savagely, 'Snap out've it, Chisholme! I said METAL . . . steel against *steel*, dammit. Not ghouls an' dead men, d'you hear?'

It came again. Still ghastly, still blood-chilling . . . but only the sound of the Cataclysm now, even to Bert. So Bert nodded.

And smiled, just a little. Because some things – even terrible things – are infinitely preferable to others.

Which was the precise moment when the chief did the oddest thing and overtook him in a great hurry, squeezing his bulk against the opposite rail. 'Keep going, son,' he shouted. 'But the bridge . . . I'll need to tell 'em. Time . . . they don't have much time . . . '

And he was gone.

Bert looked down again. He saw Bowman floating on his back a long way below and it was hard to tell for sure but the third didn't seem to be grinning any more. He didn't seem to be doing anything particularly frightening, for that matter. But dead men couldn't, could they?

It was the one thing Bert had felt reasonably certain of for the very first time in seven long minutes.

He didn't try and climb any farther. Not now he'd heard what was happening to the ship.

Because the sea would get him anyway. And he was far too tired to go to a lot of trouble, simply trying to avoid the inevitable.

Stan Young became aware of something monstrously wrong at almost the same instant as Chief Barraclough, only in the second cook's case there wasn't quite the same cool reaction.

In fact he just heard the screech from forward, froze in terror until the second, longer drawn-out rumble followed, then whirled towards the galley door and yelled, 'Eddie . . . ! F'r God's sake, EDDIE . . . !'

An appeal which Eddie Ferguson completely missed, the officer's steward being currently engaged in freezing to the marrow under a barrage of snowflakes, two decks above the galley, still searching anxiously for someone who would listen to him.

Stan swung back, skidded awkwardly in the congealed fat

mess on the deck, slammed down on one knee with a sob of
agony then, galvanized by yet another distant squeal of rending
metal, kept right on crawling towards the inert body of Chief
Cook Dempster.

'Out! We gotter get out, Norrie . . . Sinking. She's started
sinking, Norrie, an' we gotter get out . . . '

He grabbed the red-and-fungus-grey arm but the burned
man writhed hideously, drawing away with a high pitched,
almost animal whine. Near hysteria, Stan lunged for the arm
again and screamed, 'Goddam you but I'm tryin' to HELP,
you stupid bast . . . '

Only Dempster rolled completely over this time, curling into
a foetal, pleading bundle with the gravy and the soap powder
and the thick brown soup sliding down and over his limbs until
he looked -- to Stanley's bulging eyes – just like a basted,
recalcitrant mummy.

The ship boomed again, Stan snatched again . . . and the
chief cook roared again. And so it went on, a desperate game of
catch-as-catch-can in that shambolic madhouse with crested
plates whirling across the deck astern of tumbling, bouncing
tureens and tinkling, twinkling silver spoons . . .

. . . until Stan Young stopped in mid-lunge and just let
his head sink into the ooze, and started to cry with all the
pathos that fear and frustration and a total inadequacy could
bring.

The cooked man lay, too, whimpering softly. His eyes were
open now, staring up at the deckhead with an expression of
hurt incomprehension as he tried to understand what had
happened to him and – perhaps even more inexplicably – *why* it
had.

Stanley's eyes were tightly closed in defeat. A tear squeezed
from each corner and ran down his face, tracking erratically
through the dirt and the sweat. He realized now that he could
never hope to get Norrie out on deck unaided, yet he also knew

beyond any doubt that he could never bring himself to leave his friend all alone.

He was a failure. All his bloody life he'd been a failure, an' now he couldn't even look after himself, never mind Norrie Dempster. Slowly his hand reached out and ever so gently closed around the chief cook's leg. Where it wasn't burned.

'It's OK, Norrie,' he whispered. 'I'm not going, so's you won't be lonely. An' Eddie'll be back soon, with help . . . '

He didn't think of it in any other way. But the simple gesture had established Second Cook Stanley Young as possibly the bravest failure aboard *Lycomedes* on that hopeless winter's day.

A quite extraordinary man indeed . . .

All of which created a curious parallel with the current situation beside the internal engineroom access, where Greaser Halliday's equally simple gesture of opening a door despite Chief Barra-clough's warning had converted him – Greaser Halliday – into *Lycomedes'* most failed failure of the Cataclysm.

But there the comparison ceased. For one thing Halliday was still unconscious, which meant that for the first time in his life he couldn't protest to anyone about anything. Secondly, there were enough people available to assist in carrying him topsides towards the somewhat temporary safety of the boat deck. And also there was a proper immobilizing stretcher handy which, while it wouldn't exactly add lustre to his swimming ability, could at least ensure passage above with minimum aggravation to his injuries.

Unfortunately every silver lining had its cloud which, in Halliday's case, hovered above him in the shape of Oggie Donaldson, involuntary first-aidsman. And Oggie's bumbling efforts to shovel his accident-prone mate aboard the stretcher were doing nearly as much damage to Halliday's chances of survival as the steel door itself had in the first place.

'Oh God . . . ' he kept repeating, straining to lift the inert patient. 'Oh dear *God* . . . '

Halliday slopped over and lay neatly in the cradle of the Robertson. Face down.

'Oh dear, oh dear . . . ' Oggie stuttered, still trying to keep his eyes averted while fumbling to get a better grip on the dormant greaser's shoulders. Despairingly he sort of heaved and twisted all at the same time just as Chief Engineer Barraclough stormed up the last few treads of the ladder, whereupon Halliday rolled clean over the edge of the stretcher to slump – totally uncooperatively – two feet from where he'd started off.

'Gerrimo*nn*it!' Barraclough snarled urgently, still running.

'I'm . . . sir . . . I can't . . . '

'GerrimONNIT, Donaldson, an' stop messing about!' the chief roared, altering course towards the control room door with uncompromising disregard for the roll of the ship.

' 'E keeps fallin' *off've* it, f'r Christ's sake!' Oggie screamed back hysterically. Only the chief had gone by then, diving through the doorway, and the little greaser was once again a lonely Samaritan. And that was the moment when he, too, heard the noise. That muffled, spine-chilling rending sound from down below.

'Oh dear . . . ' said Oggie, frantically scrambling across the stretcher towards his insensible charge. 'Oh dear, oh *dear*, oh dear . . . !'

Meanwhile, just round the corner, in the control room itself, the second engineer whirled as Barraclough entered. The chief noticed the phone still gripped in the second's hand and, crossing the space between them in two long strides, snapped, 'Bridge on there, Charlie?'

The second nodded, holding it towards him. 'Captain's at the other end.'

Barraclough grabbed it, then hesitated for the first time since he'd heard the noise. Maybe it was the appeal in his deputy's anxious stare. He said bleakly. 'One . . . Bert Chisholme. Bowman and the greaser are dead . . . '

Bringing the receiver up he barked, 'Barraclough here.'

Watching him numbly the second couldn't shake the sudden thought of Bowman's wife out of his mind, and the look he knew would be in her eyes when she found Bowman was dead and he was still alive . . . until for the first time *he* heard the screeching from forward of the engineroom bulkhead – unnoticed until then because he'd been on the phone – and realized with sick apprehension that Julie's eyes might only be full of sadness, without any reproach at all, because he, too, could very well be staying down here with Bowman from the next moment onwards.

The chief was speaking again. Urgently. 'Two dead so far, plus one seriously injured, one badly shocked . . . Yes . . . yes, we'll get them up ourselves, Captain, but hang on – how does she look forward from where you are?'

He listened, nodding abruptly, then, meeting the second's eye, covered the mouthpiece. 'Bring the fourth up that ladder quick, Charlie. Then try an' organize Donaldson and Halliday. Get everyone the hell out've here . . .

The second swung round, heading for the door. Even as he did so a further tearing, hideously threatening, carried above the constant rumble of flooding seawater. He felt the ship lie over, shuddering in every plate as the sea which had caught her passed aft along the hull, booming and sighing and only separated from him by a thin steel skin.

' . . . well it sounds bad from down here, dammit. She's tearing somewhere forr'ad . . . No – structural, not cargo . . . Negative again, Captain! We need more hands down here like we need a fourteen foot step ladder an' a three piece bloody band . . . '

The bedlam roar of the Cataclysm struck the second an almost physical blow as he stepped from the sound-proofed control room on to the high catwalk. Staring downwards he could see only water, jet black under the glare from the lights but studded with flotsam battens and swirling rubbish and bright yellow oil drums until, with a clutch of horror, he made out the shape of a tiny white man revolving slowly, round and round and round in the middle of the pool.

There was also a second white man sitting quite unconcernedly on the treads of the ladder below him – not so tiny this time, because he wasn't very far away, and not particularly white either, come to that. More an oily, soaking grey, really – but the dirty white man seemed to be just watching the clean white tiny man and not making any attempt whatsoever to get out himself.

'BERT!' the second roared, starting to move towards the top of the ladder and hating Chisholme passionately for making him descend even a little way into that floodlit crypt.

Behind him in the control room Chief Barraclough was still shouting urgently into the phone.

' . . . sounds like one and two already flooded. And if she's breaking up forr'ad've number three bulkhead an' *that* collapses . . . God, Graham, but she'll go down like a bloody sounding lead . . . '

Seven minutes had now passed since the extraordinary part of the afternoon had begun.

It was also the end of the period of lethargy.

# Chapter Eight

No man will be a sailor who has
contrivance enough to get himself
into a jail; for being in a ship is
being in a jail, with the chance of
being drowned . . .
              *Dr Samuel Johnson*


## CATACLYSM plus EIGHT MINUTES

Within the enclosed spaces of a ship – as with any other
structure – sound is magnified, usually easier to detect, isolate
and identify. Especially to ears already subconsciously attuned
to danger.

So it wasn't really strange that those people still below decks
in *Lycomedes* had been first to sense the impending and final
assault of the Cataclysm – apart from that momentary flash of
intuition suffered by deckhand Falls as he stood uneasily
listening on the storm-ravaged centrecastle. And Falls was too
inexperienced to heed the warning anyway.

For it *was* a warning.

Because *Lycomedes* was beginning to break in half. Very
quickly.

Certainly viewing her from above – from the bridge and
wheelhouse – any observer would still have been totally
unaware that the ship was dividing. In fact even under close
scrutiny from a lower level, such as from where the search
party stood, it was virtually impossible to detect the still-hairline
fracture which zig-zagged outboard to port across her seething

well deck, or the slightest suggestion of a compensatory buckle in her starboard deck plates.

And there was no possible way in which one could see the port outer side of the dying ship. Where from her bulwarks downwards, following a nearly vertical path towards the surface of the sea, that hairline crack had already become an unmistakable rent in *Lycomedes'* hull – a steadily opening and closing fissure as the North Sea hinged the ship up, and down, and up again.

For within minutes of the Cataclysm a great number of her plates and longitudinal members had abruptly parted, some under the initial impact of the sea-cliff, others through the subsequent working of the weakened frame while, as each successive longitudinal gave way, the strain on the remainder proportionately increased.

Fatiguing. Bending while at the same time twisting fractionally as *Lycomedes'* bow section forced to starboard of her centreline. Rupturing . . . and finally shearing.

As, with unremitting persistence, she continued to hog. And sag.

And tear herself in half.

The captain reacted instantaneously to Barraclough's warning from the engineroom. He'd known the chief for a very long time and was grimly aware that *Lycomedes'* senior engineer was not given to overstatement. Also Barraclough was in the best position to assess the danger, and Shaw valued the chief engineer's judgement as highly as his own.

Other than when it came to choosing parrots, at least.

So when Barraclough gave his flat, considered opinion on the imminent prospect threatening the ship Shaw simply snapped, 'Right! Then get everyone out of there . . . and that goes for you, too.'

Just for a moment he wondered – almost wishfully, in a way

– if the chief would argue, because that would have indicated a hope that, perhaps, some little respite could be gained by the engineers remaining below. But Barraclough's distant voice, muffled by an unsettling background rumble, came through with unmistakable determination.

'Damn right I will. And . . . Graham?'

'Yes?'

'What's it like up there?'

Shaw didn't need to look. His eyes had never left the grey, screaming seascape filling the wheelhouse windows. *Lycomedes* seemed totally isolated now, encompassed by a half-mile circle of sucking troughs and rearing, fragmenting crests while, outside that periphery . . . nothing. Only a never ending grue of impenetrable snow-fog devouring even the long, sliding North Sea rollers.

'Not good, Bill,' he answered calmly. 'It isn't very good at all.'

Then he hung the engineroom receiver back on its hook for the last time ever, swung round to face the watching eyes of the men grouped in the wheelhouse, and said, 'Mister Wise. Please go down to the boat deck. Advise the mate that time appears to be running short and I'd be grateful if he could have the boats readied as soon as possible . . . '

He hesitated, glancing involuntarily outboard as a huge foaming crest lifted above the level of the bridge wing as if anxious to impose on even the few minutes of time left under his control, then swept astern with a gleeful hiss. *Lycomedes* rolled to ten . . . twenty . . . twenty-five degrees, before starting her return journey to the vertical.

' . . . but my earlier instruction still stands, tell him. No one is to embark unless I give the order. You stay to assist, and ask Mister McRae to come and see me as soon as he's ready.'

The third mate gulped, nodded violently, and disappeared at the double. The outrageously red carpet slippers made an odd *pitter-pattering* sound as he careered through the starboard door. Like a nervous heart beat. Very fast.

Like the pace was becoming aboard *Lycomedes*, for that matter. Seven minutes already gone – an incredibly precious but totally unpredictable number left.

'Mister Fuller.'

The second mate looked up from the radio. 'Sir?'

Shaw eyed him closely. Appraisingly. Certainly the young officer's face had lost that earliest bitterness. The dazed guilt had smoothed away, too, but the captain – perhaps better than any other man aboard – could sense the anguish still gnawing at Fuller's mind.

'Have you raised anyone within VHF range?'

'Only strength two, sir. Too faint to understand, though I think they said "Warship".'

A momentary hope glowed within Shaw. It was only a very small hope. 'In that case Kemp will have called them so we'll know shortly . . . Secure from the set now, I want you to take charge of preparing the liferafts. Clear away the lashings and have ladders, knotted ropes, canvas hoses – anything suitable for boarding – rigged. As many as possible. But you will not launch until you either hear the "Abandon Ship" signal or the ship appears to be in imminent danger of foundering without warning . . . Just use your own judgement, Mister Fuller.'

Fuller pushed the R/T handset back into its clip and seemed to gaze for an unnecessarily long time at the radio. Then he turned back to face the captain. His expression was bitter again, almost cynical.

'*My* judgement, sir?'

Shaw didn't hesitate. 'Why not? Personally I have complete confidence in it. And in your ability.'

Fuller stared at him for a moment, blinking hard, then nodded abruptly and swung towards the door. Then he stopped and looked back. 'I'm sorry. I can't describe it any better . . . about the ship.'

'On you go! Just see that everyone with you wears a life-jacket, and that includes yourself.'

The captain watched him leave, slipping through the port door into the swirl of snow, then caught sight of a small, hesitant figure waiting silently behind him – Apprentice Cassiday, still flushed and anxious to be a part of the Great Adventure.

The boy said timidly, 'Can I help, sir?'

Shaw chewed his lip. If the ship went quickly, none of them stood much chance wherever they were. If she gave enough warning, the youngster would have adequate time to leave. And he sensed it was terribly important to Rupert to feel he was participating in the battle, even if only to prevent him dwelling on what could happen in the very near future.

'Thank you, Mister Cassiday,' he answered gravely. 'I believe the radar is still operating. You keep watch on the screen and inform me as soon as you see anything at all . . . What range is it set at? The little window in the top right hand corner will tell you.'

The youngster craned over, looking very determined. 'Twenty miles, sir.'

'Good.'

The captain stared out of the window again, not really seeing the storm, or the waves, or the smash of the seas over *Lycomedes*' forward decks. It didn't matter what the radar range was – other than that twenty miles would be the maximum distance even a warship could hope to steam in one hour under those conditions, probably much less – but his mind was turning over and over incessantly. He had to make a decision very quickly now . . . *two* decisions, in fact.

The first on when to abandon *Lycomedes* – that hairline calculation which, if made unnecessary minutes too early or one split second too late could kill them all – and secondly, perhaps even more difficult, on *how* to abandon her.

In the boats, for instance . . . ? Where boarding from upper-deck level would be simple, especially for the injured, but the launching would be a horrific task . . . Or alternatively by inflatable liferaft? Where the threat from exposure would be considerably lessened while they huddled together under the protective canopies to benefit from mutually generated body heat – but the actual embarkation, with the rafts running amok in those monstrous seas and men trying to leap aboard from trailing ropes and bucketing ladders . . . ?

'*You* don't have one, do you?'

Shaw emerged abruptly from his reverie. Quartermaster Clements, blissfully overlooked under the pressure of the past few minutes, was eyeing him with an all too familiar stare of accusation.

'Have one what?' the captain queried, momentarily off balance.

'A lifejacket . . . sir. "See that everyone wears a lifejacket" you told the second mate – an' you don't 'ave one yourself.'

'You're relieved from duty, Clements,' Shaw murmured wearily. 'Just go to your boat station and wait for orders.'

The recalcitrant helmsman glanced meaningfully at the view from the bridge. 'Not much point, is there? I been at sea long enough to know what chance we go . . . '

'Enough *said*, man!'

The captain glanced pointedly at the listening apprentice and Clements shut up immediately. Just before starting on a new, openly petulant tack.

'Well, who's goin' to *get* your jacket, then. An' who's goin' to pass messages an' that while you're doin' the commanding, Captin . . . An' fire off the flares an' answer the phone an' . . . '

Shaw couldn't help it. He started to laugh as he picked up

the radio room telephone. Eight horrific minutes into the Cataclysm and he actually started to laugh.

'Ernest Clements,' he chuckled, still totally disbelieving. 'By God but are you trying to tell me you're actually *volunteering* for something . . . Of your own free will . . . ?'

Chief Operator Kemp held the transmitter key down for two fifteen-second periods to assist confirmation of *Lycomedes'* position by listening direction finders, then rattled the station call sign once more and sat back, arching his back uncomfortably.

'That's it then,' he said calmly. 'Anyone else nearer than the Yank or that Soviet job either has to be asleep or bloody deaf.'

Bentine looked at the signal pad doubtfully. 'ETA sixteen oh five for the warship. They should arrive at about the same time – them and the Russians.'

'Fifth Cavalry versus the Cossacks,' Kemp grinned. 'Right now I'm not the slightest bit biased. I'd be happy to talk politics nicely to a communist . . . '

He stopped talking abruptly, listening. Bentine eyed him nervously. 'What's wrong, Chief?'

Kemp's grin had faded so he freshened it a bit for the kid's benefit and said casually, 'Nothing. It's for some other station.'

But it wasn't. It wasn't even a call he'd heard, it was a noise from deep down in the ship – almost as though someone was tearing a strip of paper. Only Kemp knew it wasn't paper.

'Met a bloke once who said they carry seventeen different flavours of ice cream,' he continued, watching Bentine surreptitiously as *Lycomedes* fell away before a big beam sea and rolled way over to port. He felt a bit more reassured when the second operator steadied himself automatically and frowned after only a moment's anxiety.

'The Yanks? Thought you reckoned it'd be Borsche an' vodka tonight?'

'Who's fussy. Either way I enjoy eating foreign.'

148

The phone from the bridge started to ring. Kemp couldn't stop himself grabbing for it just a little too quickly.

Behind him Bentine blurted suddenly, 'God but I'm scared.'

'Which shows it won't take much,' the chief operator thought savagely. 'To start a general panic that could drown the whole bloody lot of us . . . '

Every face on the boat deck had turned towards McRae and Bosun Skinner as they slid down the ladder from the bridge. They all looked the same, those expectant faces – deliberately expressionless, tightly controlled so the bloke next to you wouldn't sense the sickness in your gut – but the eyes revealed the real apprehension, the real prayer that all the mate was going to say would be, 'It's OK, boys. No sweat . . . the flap's over . . . back to routine 'cause she'll float till the bottom rusts out've her . . . '

Only he didn't.

He simply snapped, 'Swing out the boats. Lower them to embarkation level . . . Two hands in each boat and no more for the moment. Mister Skinner will take charge of two and four port side. Seaman rates man the luffing handles and winch brakes . . . Quickly now!'

Someone muttered, 'Christ!' in sudden fright. The greaser beside him retorted shakily, '*HE* can go to the back of the queue f'r a start, mate. 'E's the only one doesn't need a bloody boat to get ashore.'

But this time nobody laughed. Not even for show.

Nobody moved, either. Not for a moment. Until Skinner stepped forward, stuck out his jaw, and roared hugely, 'All of them who doesn't agree – take your lifejackets off an' get back down below. There'll be a union meeting in the mess room in five minutes.'

And that ended the period of lethargy on *Lycomedes*' boat deck.

Mickey Wise arrived from the wheelhouse just as the crowd broke into a hubbub of activity, Skinner's voice still carrying above the clamour. ' . . . an' number off like you been taught. Six men to each station while the rest jus' shut up an wait . . . '

The faces around McRae were animated now, the nervousness and disbelief that this was really happening clearly apparent. Yet there was another quality, too . . . a sense of purpose, almost relief that something positive was finally being done even if it meant they were one step closer to abandoning *Lycomedes*.

Of course every man on deck felt secure in the belief that, while the prospects for his shipmates looked pretty grim at the best, *he* would make it OK. That his own personal survival was assured no matter what happened to everyone else.

Each and every one of them – with perhaps the exception of McRae and Skinner – knew that much with the certainty that has kept man fighting against overwhelming odds ever since the beginning of time.

But there again, most of them had known with equal certainty that an ordinary ship like *Lycomedes* couldn't possibly sink in the first place.

Right up to a few seconds ago, anyway . . .

Certainly Chief officer McRae's mind had slammed into top gear under the adrenaline of positive action. Even after Third Mate Wise had somewhat breathlessly passed the captain's warning to speed the preparations McRae remained cool, his earlier sense of inadequacy overwhelmed by the pace of events.

'Right. Skinner's gone round to the port side. You look after number three boat . . . ' He hesitated, wondering whether to say anything about the third mate's rather inappropriately fluffy footwear, then decided not to – Mickey needed all the confidence he could get. 'But deck level only, remember . . . Chop, chop, Three Oh!'

Mickey Wise, looking every inch the rugged seaman – from

the ankles up – swung away hurriedly, bumped into someone wearing a white jacket, said, 'Oh I'm *terribly* sorry', then disappeared into the milling crowd yelling, 'Number three boat's crew over here . . . well, over there . . . At the BOAT, dammit . . .'

The newcomer in the white mess jacket looked flustered, even more so than most of the others in that cutting wind which flailed them unendingly. 'Sir,' he appealed desperately. 'Sir, I've gotter get help . . .'

But Steward Eddie Ferguson – who didn't have a lifejacket and who'd no sooner convinced himself that the ship wasn't sinking when he'd found it probably was after all – Eddie was possibly as highly qualified to look flustered as anybody aboard *Lycomedes* at that moment. Especially seeing he'd spent two completely logical minutes in convincing himself he didn't have any special responsibility towards Stan Young and Chef Dempster.

Just before sticking his neck right out anyway, for the mate to wield the axe.

Which McRae did. Unhesitantly. As soon as Eddie had finished revealing the dilemma of the Cooked Man in the galley.

'So get back down there, Ferguson. Take Feeny and Harry Whatsisname . . . Use the stretcher from the locker in the port alleyway and get Dempster up here fast!'

'What about morphine or somethin'?' Eddie blurted, starting to feel sick again at the prospect of returning to that nightmare shambles below. 'Chef's in bloody agony. We daren't touch him without pain killers.'

*Lycomedes* began the big roll to port. McRae watched bleakly as the lifeboat grablines, becketed around the gunwale, moved steadily away from the vertical. Ten . . . fifteen . . . twenty degrees and still leaning out towards him.

'I'm sorry, Ferguson. You might not have time . . . Certainly not to wait until they take effect. Just get him on deck no matter what, but if you hear the "Abandon ship" signal . . .'

151

This time McRae did hesitate significantly. Then he continued flatly, ' . . . leave Dempster. Just get clear of the accommodation and go like hell for your nearest liferaft stowage.'

The mate glanced anxiously over the steward's shoulder. There were fifty other men in hazard. All of them with problems. 'Come *on*, Lindsay, into the boat. And you, Stocks . . . '

Eddie turned away blindly, all the old doubts and claustrophobic fears flooding back. Only they were worse now, because this time he really was committed. From now on his only way to leave *Lycomedes* had to be via the galley. He would have to jump into the frying pan before he could even get back into the fire . . .

Suddenly he realized he was wasting precious seconds of survival time and started to run wildly aft, searching for Feeny.

Behind him the pressure of the Cataclysm was steadily erupting in a series of barked commands.

' . . . clear those lifelines, dammit!'

'Slack away gripes now. Handsomely does it, boys . . . '

'Those bloody spreaders, Jock – ditch them. *An*' the cover . . . '

Already-numbed hands fumbling with unfamiliar lashings. Shins slamming into unsuspected thwarts. Bulky lifejackets hooking over projections with malevolent persistence. Oh, they'd done it all before, aboard *Lycomedes* – statutory boat drill as laid down by the Board of Trade, an' a bloody bind at that. But never for real . . . never under pressure . . .

' . . . and pass that painter forr'ad . . . OUTBOARD've the davit, Stocks. Now the bottom plug . . . Easy, Lindsay, don't panic lad . . . '

On the forward centrecastle deck Seadog maintained his mournful soliloquy until the search party had disappeared from sight behind the contactor house above the break of the well deck.

Then the dog stopped whimpering abruptly and licked his lips, eyes still fixed unblinkingly on the spot where his companions had vanished. He didn't try to pull at the lead which secured him to the sinking ship, in fact the only sign of movement now was from the velvety brown ears which continued to flicker alertly for no apparent reason.

But there was a reason, all the same. Because Seadog could hear sounds inside *Lycomedes* which were still inaudible to human senses. And the frequency of those alien noises was rapidly increasing, especially during that eighth minute of the Cataclysm.

Just as the tempo of tightly controlled desperation was increasing in every part of the ship.

Or nearly every part . . .

For instance Hermann wasn't at all desperate. Parrots can't be. Parrots are pretty bird-brained creatures by definition, which means they aren't really capable of any depths of feeling in the human sense of the word.

And anyway – even if Hermann *was* able to show true feeling, it would only have been impatience in his case. Combined with a strong dash of malevolent forward planning.

Boy, but was Hermann gonna launch one helluva preemptive verbal strike on Chief Engineer William Barraclough, incompetent parrot fancier extraordinary, just as soon as he reappeared in that still-open doorway.

Hermann slid sideways down the bars to the bottom of the cage and sidled towards the peanut he'd spotted. He didn't eat it right away, even a parrot's entitled to a little pleasurable anticipation.

Instead he started to warm up for the coming fray, pugnaciously ruffling what few dilapidated feathers he'd got left, back-kicking the sand under his reptilian claws.

'Mummy's gotta fancy man . . . ' he crooned, somewhat obscurely. 'Mummy's gooooooooooo . . . tafancyman.'

But you surely don't expect logic, do you? Not from a bloody *parrot*?

Huang Pi-wu wasn't the slightest bit desperate either.

But on the other hand he wasn't quite as securely settled in his escapist dream world as he had been, either.

Perhaps it was the fact that *Lycomedes* just didn't feel like a ship any more, the way she yielded so sullenly – so totally – to the seas sweeping down on her. Or because her main engine was silent, its subconsciously reassuring beat replaced now by the rumble of flooding water. Perhaps Huang was also becoming distantly aware of the sounds of her disintegration, penetrating even the bulwark of sleep.

Whatever it was the image of Yeh Chun was inexorably fading. Slowly, ever so slowly, his love was beginning to dissolve. Her wondrous beauty still remained to fill his heart with longing, but it was only a memory now. Without substance. Without true happiness . . .

Huang's ethereal fantasy was about to explode into nightmare reality.

Either just before – or at the precise moment when – his cradle of ecstasy finally sank.

Along with his one thousand three hundred and sixteen pounds. Sterling.

UNITED STATES WARSHIP FORDON COUNTY DE AREA SAR CONTROL . . . IMMEDIATE UNCLASSIFIED . . . REGRET NEGATIVE YOUR 1427 ZULU REQUESTING HELICOPTER ASSISTANCE LYCOMEDES CASUALTY . . . ADVISE STAND-BY MERCY FLIGHT AVAILABLE IMMEDIATELY WEATHER MODERATES WITHIN MINIMUM OPERATIONAL REQUIREMENTS . . .

## CATACLYSM plus NINE MINUTES

Chief Engineer Barraclough had slammed the phone on to its hook after his final abrupt conversation with the captain and whirled to face the control panel.

Auxiliary generator temperatures . . . ? OK Oil! pressures . . . ? Check. Revolutions . . . ? Steady as a dead man's stare. Amps . . . volts . . . load . . ! He swung towards the door and started to run. *Lycomedes'* auxiliaries would run sweet as a nut for as long as they were likely to be required. There wasn't a gauge or an instrument invented which could tell him precisely how long that would be, though. Only the feel of the ship and the steady thunder of the flood could guide him in assessing that.

And the numb sensation in the pit of his ample stomach.

Because there were the noises, too. Louder now and increasing in frequency. A man didn't need an electronic panel and four gold rings on his cuff to estimate that, whatever was happening to *Lycomedes*, it was going to happen very, very soon . . .

Little Donaldson was still in the alleyway, Greaser Halliday still sprawling in gruesome disarray beside the stretcher. Barraclough skidded to a furious halt and snarled, 'Where's the second . . . an' I told you to get Halliday *on* that, laddie.'

Oggie stared up, blinking back the tears of frustrated rage. 'I dunno – an' I bin bloody well *tryin'* to since . . . '

'What d'you mean – you don't know?'

'Him, *Halliday*! I keeps shovin' him on an' 'e keeps fallin' OFF've it, Mister Barraclough. I been tryin' to *tell* you tha . . . '

'I mean the second engineer. And the fourth, dammit. Haven't they come out of the engineroom yet?'

'Yes . . . No . . . I dunno, sir. I dunno anythin' any more . . . What's them noises about. We're goin' to sink, aren't we, sir . . . '

'Great God *Almighty* . . . ' the chief snarled, heading back into the engineroom with the anger building into a tightly welded knot deep inside him. But there was fear there, too, now. Fear and a terrible apprehension based on forty years of knowing ships, and knowing what ships could do when they finally stopped fighting.

'And gerrimONIT NOW' he roared over his shoulder so hugely that the stentorian bellow seemed to remain hanging in the air even after the chief's physical presence had evaporated in a downward direction again.

And then it finally happened. Something vital snapped. Not only deep inside the ship but also inside the mind of a man . . .

*Lycomedes* lay over before an avalanching sea. This time the screech of rupturing steel carried from forward to obliterate even the pandemonium of the Cataclysm and the helpless fury of Chief Engineer Barraclough.

It also obliterated the last traces of Oggie Donaldson's already shredded courage. He abandoned Halliday and started to scramble frantically aft, heading for the open door leading to the deck.

'She's going . . . !' he shrieked, eyes bulging convulsively. 'Get clear . . . Gotter get clear of the ship . . . '

He stumbled out on deck through the door at the after end of the accommodation just as *Lycomedes* reached the culmination of her roll, masts angled to twenty-five . . . thirty degrees from the vertical and the poop deck thrown high into the air as the wave passed under and astern.

To starboard – above him – there was only the line of canting rails and the sky with its crazy procession of scudding, wind-slashed clouds. Below, at the bottom of the hill, Oggie could only see water . . . great yawning crevasses opening in grisly welcome, quite literally underneath his feet.

He became disoriented. There was no horizon, no datum line to establish the true limits of his topsy-turvy environment. He was a man in a rotating barrel at some bedlam carnival, just waiting for the whole bloody world to overbalance and squash him . . .

Oggie started to claw his way uphill, shrieking in desperation, arms outstretched imploringly towards the rail in a terror-crazed effort to get out from under . . . Anything. Anything rather than to be trapped below the ship as she finally capsized . . .

He swung himself over the rail and launched his body outwards. With grim irony *Lycomedes* herself assisted him . . . she started to recover from that sickening roll at the precise moment when Oggie needed all the help he could get to overcome her inertia.

It was also the moment when Oggie finally realized he'd made a mistake. Even through the blind hysteria of total panic Oggie sensed *that* much. He screamed his resentment all the way towards the sea, bouncing and tumbling down the angled ship's side in a ragged cartwheel of arms, legs and whipping shirt tails . . .

His lungs were completely empty by the time he hit the water. Without any reserve of buoyancy he just kept on going down, down, all the way down to the bottom of the sea.

It was very dark, and very cold, and very, very frightening. But only for quite a short time . . .

And no one ever did discover what had happened to poor bumbling little Oggie Donaldson. All because – for the first time in his life – he'd actually taken a decision. And more or less stuck to it.

Senior Apprentice Standish, leading the search party on the forward centrecastle deck, had stuck resolutely to his decision, too. They'd struggled as far as they could go, right to the break of the well deck and in a splendid position to view every possible corner where Chippie might have been delayed or even trapped.

Except for the space under the port cargo winch, of course. But that was behind them by that time.

And it was then that Michael really began to have doubts. As they clung to the rail, staring down in utter disbelief at the force of waves which tumbled inboard in solid green cataracts to smash headlong into one another before climbing skywards in clutching arcs of spindrift . . .

. . . and all around, the cargo. Boxes, battens, splintered hatch boards, half a score of bobbing yellow custard tins . . . gaily printed tea towels, three rubber tyres in impeccable line ahead formation, blackly projecting humps cruising like some North Sea mini-monster . . .

Falls whispered, 'Holy Mother've God!' while deckhand Bronson just gazed open-mouthed at the whirlpool marking *Lycomedes'* forward hold, and out over the uproar of swirling foam breaking thunderously across the almost submerged fo'c'slehead itself.

The boy shouted nervously, 'He's not here. We'd better get ba . . . '

Then he stopped shouting abruptly and simply stared in disbelief.

Because yet another sea had begun to throw *Lycomedes* over to port – which was perfectly understandable under the circumstances. As was the way the water already pouring across her bowed foredeck began to rumble and swirl even more turbulently, fighting to retain the ground it had already won as the ship tried to rise to the sea, attempted – no matter how sluggishly – to free herself of the weight smothering her head . . .

. . . but the phenomenon which really shattered Senior Apprentice Standish was the sudden realization that water was also exploding *upwards* – and almost directly below them, at that – in a wide, fountaining curtain through a crack which seemed to run from the centre of the deck outboard and right along that angle formed by the forward end of the centrecastle and the flat plane of the well deck itself.

Which was quite ridiculous, of course. The only thing that could cause *that* to happen was that the whole ship was breaking into two parts . . .

And then the sound itself came, reverberating until the hubbub of the storm was completely overwhelmed by the grating of steel upon steel, overstressed by pressures greater than any human agency could even begin to conceive. Discordant, clamorous . . . a stridency of horror filling the air . . .

'Get BACK!' the boy screamed.

The curtain of water disintegrated as a roaring sea smashed through it, swamped through and over the rail before them and picked Falls up as casually as a tin of custard powder. It carried him outboard, over the port line of the bulwark and into the massive grue of foam which surrounded the heeling *Lycomedes* before he'd even had time to shout.

He was – had been – a religious man. He'd been taken just as he crossed himself with one hand instead of hanging on to the rail with both as stark terror had caused Bronson and the boy to do.

Even then Bronson nearly went as well, on the crest of that first wave, but Standish lunged desperately for the howling deckhand's collar. He clutched, held, started to sob appealingly, 'Help yourself . . . Getta *grip*, Brons . . . ' then the next flood overtook them, slammed them down under its green, crushing violence, and propelled them in a helter skelter bundle of togetherness aft along the deck.

To Standish it seemed a very long passage underwater. He found it wasn't so frightening as he'd imagined – being drowned – and even had time to think about his mother, and the way he'd messed everything up with his first command . . . and Seadog. He wondered sadly about Seadog over on the starboard side because he knew the sea that was killing him must have overwhelmed the captive animal as well . . .

Something hard struck him agonizingly in the small of his back. He felt Bronson's collar rip away leaving only a thin strip of material clutched in his fist . . . Something else was impeding his progress aft, too, now. Something soft and yielding and a lot more comfortable than the first immovable barrier . . . The water was turning from a dark green to a lighter, more opaque green . . . Gurgling . . . draining away . . .

'I'm alive!' Michael thought, feeling quite surprised and enormously pleased all at the same time. 'I really am still *alive* . . . '

He blinked owlishly up at the sky and saw that the bridge was almost directly above him. He'd been swept right aft before being left like a stranded fish alongside the dripping steel coaming of number three hatch. It seemed that one of the cargo winches had actually halted his involuntary progress.

Someone was leaning over the bridge wing high overhead. The chap appeared to be shouting and waving his arms furiously so Michael tried to sit up but nothing happened – only a pain which really did hurt, and a funny, dead feeling in his legs.

The tiredness began to swamp over him in languorous waves. He started to worry about Seadog again . . . and Falls and Bronson . . . until a strange thing happened. His mother came and knelt beside him, and took his hand gently in hers, and Michael felt an enormous happiness warming him, making him feel all cosy and safe inside.

Gradually his head fell to one side. A man lay beside him, wearing bright yellow oilskins and simply gazing at him with a rather odd, completely empty expression.

'Hello, Chippie,' Michael whispered, 'I knew we'd find you somewhere . . . '

He died then. Feeling happy in the knowledge that he'd carried out his duty.

His spinal cord had been severed by the impact of his striking Chippie's winch. Deckhand Bronson – for it was Bronson and not his mother kneeling beside him on that storm-torn open deck – felt the young boy's hand relax ever so gradually.

And began to cry.

The captain had still been smiling about Ernie Clements's new-found philosophy of voluntary service when Kemp's voice came through over the phone.

'Radio room.'

The chief operator's reply sounded flat, almost matter-of-fact. Shaw wondered how much of it was deliberate. 'Captain. What acknowledgements to our SOS so far?'

'Two, sir. Within an hour's range . . . an American warship and a Russian.'

Shaw stopped smiling as the despondency came over him again. It wasn't a surprise – he'd already seen the empty radar screen – but somehow the confirmation emphasized his hopelessness. 'Nothing else . . . No one closer?'

'No, sir. The warship keeps relaying but . . . '

Kemp's voice trailed off. They both knew the odds against anyone else coming in after three minutes of distress working. Shaw asked sharply, 'Are you ready to go over to emergency power if we lose the generators?'

'Aye. RP supply's satisfactory. And Bentine's checked the reserve transmitter as well.'

'What about Bentine. Do you need him with you, in view of the situation?'

Kemp's tone was dry. 'What *is* the situation?'

'Bad! She may go very quickly when she does, Mister Kemp.'

There was a brief hesitation. Then the chief operator said calmly, 'Do you mind leaving that with us, sir?'

'The decision's up to you. And Bentine . . . Got that pencil

F                                                                161 of yours handy? I want you to send an "All stations" immediately . . . '

It was only as Shaw finished dictating his up-date on *Lycomedes*' condition that the wave took the ship on the bow, and the discord of steel against steel carried clearly up to the bridge itself.

Whirling in shock the captain caught one brief image of Clements frozen in the act of handing a lifejacket to him, only now the quartermaster's mouth sagged dumbly – not at all the expression of mild reproof which Ernie had originally planned to go with the presentation.

Shaw dropped the telephone, roared, 'Out've the WAY, man!' and flung himself through the port door and on to the bridge wing.

Ignoring the whiplash of snow he peered desperately ahead, gripping the teak rail convulsively with both hands. He saw the fountain of water rising from the after end of the well deck . . . watched it falter and crumble as the incoming sea rolled across it . . . stared transfixed as a struggling flotsam seaman appeared from behind the contactor house and rode the roaring water clean over *Lycomedes*' bulwark to be swallowed immediately in the maelstrom along her side . . .

'Oh my *God*!' the captain muttered, still not believing what he'd just seen because it had all happened so quickly, and there shouldn't have *been* any men on that nightmare forward end in the first place.

He believed even more firmly in Chief Engineer Barraclough's prediction, though – about what could happen to his ship. The rumble of fracturing plates and the curtaining water simply confirmed that *Lycomedes* really was breaking apart . . . but he still didn't accept that hallucinatory voyager who'd flitted so briefly across the stage of the Cataclysm.

Not until two *more* semi-submerged men swamped into view from the same impossible source, bowling up the canting deck

towards him in an inextricable welter of flailing limbs . . .
except that, when the receding sea had finally left them, Shaw's
incredulous eyes could suddenly make out . . . *three?*

He leaned out over the rail and began to shout a totally
unnecessary warning – presumably they'd already gathered it
was bloody dangerous down there – but fear for his crew was
beginning to sap the captain's ability to remain detached, to
concentrate on the priorities for survival of the greatest number.

Until he realized the futility of his action and he swung away
from the rail to where Clements was now eyeing him with
wary apprehension.

The agony of *Lycomedes* from forward again. Impatient in
its promise. Shaw knew they had very little time left.

'Get your lifejacket on quickly,' he urged. 'Then see what
can be done to help those poor devils down there . . . '

The wind seemed to die away. Just for a moment.

From below, carried only faintly, there came the sound of a
man. Crying.

Huang Pi-wu's left eye flickered open and the last lingering
image of Yeh Chun was erased from his subconscious.

He screwed the eye tightly shut again, struggling to recapture
even a fragment of that spell-binding dream garden where
everything was possible and there was no sadness, no ugliness
. . .

Until the strange noise came once more.

He opened both eyes. Very quickly.

Somehow he knew almost immediately that the ship was
sinking. But Huang was a very switched-on Oriental. He'd felt
that same wary desire for self-preservation once before – that
time when he'd performed a high speed retreat from the place
of his birth, the advancing Red Menace and the real,
in-the-flesh version of Missee Yeh Chun, all in one neat
move.

You see, it hadn't been just a dream – about Yeh Chun and the Gate of a Thousand Happy Lovers, and the perch in the river and all that stuff. It had been more of a reminiscence in a way . . . while Huang's motivation for his Hong Kong pierhead jump hadn't really been purely political either.

They could get pretty physical about babies born out of wedlock in Huang's part of China – especially with the unfortunate boy friend – no matter which government's bigot happened to be administering a lesson on morality in the local execution square . . .

Huang Pi-wu sighed philosophically. It was better now, making love in his dream garden. Yeh Chun looked much prettier than for real. And she never grew any older, or any less desirable. And she never, ever got pregnant.

He swung his legs over the side of the bunk and stood up. *Lycomedes* rolled back to the nearly vertical and he lifted his head critically, feeling the ship. Then he nodded. He still had a little time.

And he was a fatalist anyway. It was much more practical than being brave. Methodically he began to prepare himself for the coming struggle.

Firstly he lifted Eddie Ferguson's bright orange lifejacket out of the wardrobe. Next he produced a knife and, ever so carefully, cut the pristine white-rope ties from the jacket, laying them neatly beside it on the bunk.

Then he dug into his already open clothing drawer and withdrew a brand new pair of underpants wrapped in a plastic bag. Removing the pants from the bag he folded them tidily and laid both articles – pants and bag – beside the vivisected lifejacket.

Then he went back to the wardrobe and unhooked the hanger supporting his best shoreside suit. Slipping the leather belt from the trouser loops he added those items to his growing survival kit on the bunk . . .

Actually it all seemed a pretty inscrutable thing to do.

Even for a . . . well . . . a chap from the autonomous region of Kwangsi-Chuang, for instance?

'Fuck it!' Steward Ferguson snarled nervously. 'I still don't have my lifejacket.'

'Told you!' Feeny remarked, totally vindicated at last. 'Din't I tell 'im 'e shoulda gotta lifejacket, Harry boy?'

'Yeah, Feen,' Harry confirmed, faithful as ever. 'You did tell 'im 'e shoulda gotta . . . '

'Belt UP f'r Chrissakes!' Eddie blurted, grabbing frantically for the stretcher.

But Eddie was more than a little distraught by then. It seemed they'd no sooner reached the stretcher stowage than *Lycomedes* emitted that blood-curdling screech – or maybe it had been Oggie Donaldson secretly going over the wall that they'd actually heard from where they now stood, outside the alleyway door leading to the saloon and galley.

Either way, the chilling lament suggested their remaining survival time had just been severely curtailed.

Yet oddly enough, despite the noise and the spray which hissed in long, ominous spatters down the alleyway, and the dread of having to look once again at the agonies of Chief Cook Dempster, Eddie Ferguson was more grimly determined than ever to see his self-imposed mission through.

It wasn't courage – certainly not courage as far as he was concerned, being scared out of his mind at the prospect. No, it was more of an unavoidable necessity really . . . in that Eddie had suddenly realized, much to his disgust, that he couldn't leave *Lycomedes* without his mates. He simply couldn't just shrug off his responsibilities no matter how hard he tried to be logical about it.

It made Eddie just like Stanley Young, in the galley. It also made Chief Cook Dempster a very fortunate man.

Comparatively speaking. In a rather grisly, illogical sort of way.

The steward swore as he felt a nail split, tugging too hastily at the straps. Feeny sucked a hollow tooth pointedly and took over, brows creased in a laborious frown. Eddie stood there eyeing his two unperturbed shipmates with growing agitation – almost outright fury – at the way neither of them seemed even aware that the bloody boat had a hole in it.

But old Feeny had been at sea even longer than Bosun Skinner, and Feeny had already composed himself to being taken eventually by that sea. It had provided him with a good life. He didn't have any fears that it wouldn't also offer an equally satisfying death whenever it came.

While *Harry* . . . ? 'Christ!' Eddie brooded bitterly, 'He wouldn't even know he was drownin' unless you wrote it on a board an' bloody well showed it to him under water.'

Which was a bit unfair, really. And a bit impractical. Harry couldn't read, either . . .

The stretcher came away in Feeny's hands and he nodded appreciatively. 'These is 'andy things,' he said, looking at it with a nostalgic eye. 'We use ter use these on the convoy rescue ships, I remember. Back in the last lot've bother.'

'Yeah,' Harry agreed. Then his face lit up with a brief flash of inspiration. ' . . . for *carryin'* people with.'

'Come ON,' Eddie howled over his shoulder, already running towards the galley.

But Steward Ferguson's apprehension was perfectly understandable. Now even his imagination was starting to play tricks on him.

He could have sworn that, just for a moment as he leapt over the entrance coaming, he'd seen that young deckhand, Archie Falls, pass by.

White as a ghost. Reaching up from the water along *Lycomedes'* side.

*

Kemp had heard the captain drop the radio room phone just as *Lycomedes* began to heel under the onslaught of that last sea. He wasn't aware that three more men were dying in those few seconds but he did understand the meaning of the noise which came from forward.

It suggested that the message he'd just received for transmission was already being overtaken by events. Such was the speed at which the Cataclysm was escalating that even plans made by Shaw during the ninth minute could well be obsolete – totally impracticable – by the end of the tenth.

Automatic reflexes made him jam one knee under the desk recess, leaning rigidly over to starboard in his chair to compensate for the angle of roll, yet even as he did so he was aware of a numbed realization that this could be *it*, by God . . . that she could be going already . . .

Then *Lycomedes* hesitated . . . stopped heeling . . . and began to return to whatever passed as vertical on that madhouse afternoon.

Bentine let out a pent-up breath behind him and Kemp turned to see the kid – eyes screwed tightly shut – clinging to the book shelf. Even after the ship levelled the second operator's knuckles stayed white as parchment.

Kemp said quickly, warily, 'The Old Man says you can go to your boat station if you want to, Johnny . . . OK?'

Bentine kept his eyes shut. 'What's the word. It's bad, isn't it?'

'Not too good.'

The second took a deep breath, seemed to hold it for a moment, then exhaled again and opened his eyes. It gave him strength, somehow. Almost as if he'd just won a battle.

'I'll hang around a while,' he said calmly. Then he grinned. It was only a little bit shaky. 'F'r a start you never did tell me, did you . . . About that Ingrid bird in Copenhagen?'

Kemp felt a dull pain in his leg and became aware that he was still jamming it hard against the underside of the desk. He eased it, quickly changed the uncomfortable expression on his face to a reciprocal smile, and reached for the key.

'Hasn't anyone ever told you,' he retorted severely, 'that sex is only supposed to be man's *second* strongest instinct . . . ?'

ALL STATIONS DE LYCOMEDES GBYD . . . HULL FRACTURE NOW SUSPECTED FORWARD OF BRIDGE . . . MAY HAVE TO ABANDON IMMEDIATELY SHOULD NUMBER THREE BULKHEAD COLLAPSE OTHERWISE INTEND STAYING WITH SHIP AS LONG AS POSSIBLE . . . PRESENT CASUALTIES TWO DEAD . . . TOTAL SURVIVORS REMAINING FIGURES FIVE ONE . . . REPEAT FIGURES FIVE ONE INCLUDING MASTER . . .

But as Chief Radio Operator Kemp had already reflected – that signal had been drafted nearly one minute ago.

And a minute was a very long time. Almost a tenth of a Cataclysm.

# Chapter Nine

Theirs was the giant race,
before the flood.
               *John Dryden*


## CATACLYSM PLUS TEN MINUTES

Before *Lycomedes'* bow section began to break away, the stresses
acting on the bulkhead separating her intact number three and
the flooding number two hold had been increasing at a fairly
constant rate.

Enough air was trapped in number two to ensure sufficient
reserve buoyancy to slow the ship's rate of sinking. Only as this
air was forced out – and *Lycomedes'* head descended into the
sea – did the water pressure mount against the steel partition.

Captain Shaw had been able to form at least an educated
assessment of the time left before that flood-generated stress
would overcome the bulkhead's structural resistance – and
*Lycomedes'* final defence be breached.

Consequently, even erring on the cautious side, he had
anticipated a reprieve of at least thirty minutes in which to
prepare for abandoning. It was a calculated risk based on logic,
the captain's intimate knowledge of his command and, perhaps
more intangibly, the feel of the ship herself . . . a seaman's sense.

Until the noise came. And that hanging curtain of water
which betrayed the transverse split already wrenched across her
deck, revealing that the trapped air pocket in number two hold
was suddenly venting free . . . allowing the displaced air to be
replaced by water . . . adding a crazily escalating momentum

to the forces acting against that last resisting bulkhead . . .

It meant *Lycomedes*' remaining life-span was no longer a calculable factor.

Shaw knew that her original thirty minute stay of execution could now be reduced to five.

Or three.

Or even – as *Lycomedes* lay over before the next advancing sea – to no more time at all . . .

'Leggo gripes. Wind out together now . . . '

'Rudder! Gie's a hand wi' this bastard *rudder*, Jimmie . . . '

' . . . so CUT the lashing ye stupid fu . . . '

'This is no good,' McRae thought bleakly. 'This is no bloody good at all . . . '

A seaman abruptly started to clamber out of number one boat, eyes round with terror. 'I'm gettin' out've this. Launch the rafts, f'r Christ's sake, Mister. Rafts we at least got a chance with . . . '

'Get back aboard,' McRae snarled. 'Just you get back aboard that boat, Lindsay, an' see those lifelines clear . . . NOW, laddie!'

Lindsay was right. Of course he was right about the boats, but the mate knew he was watching the first symptom of blind panic. And panic was contagious. It would flash through the men on that wallowing deck with the speed of a forest fire.

*Lycomedes* ponderously began her next roll, Lindsay, awkward in the girth of his orange lifejacket, teetered indecisively on the edge of the gunwale, then, with a shrill screech of fright, overbalanced and fell.

He landed on outstretched hands. Nearly every man on the starboard side heard the crack as the young seaman's right forearm shattered. He lay whimpering, 'Jeeze . . . Oh jeeze my arm somebody . . . '

'See to him, one of you,' the mate snapped, sympathy only

barely detectable in his bleak gaze. 'And you instead, Hennessy – into the boat . . . '

'Mister *McRae*!'

The mate swung, homing on the shout. The captain stood at the top of the bridge ladder looking down. The urgency in his expression caused McRae to break into a run, taking the treads three at a time.

'Sir?'

'Secure from swinging out the boats!'

'Aye, aye, sir! Secure from swi . . . '

The mate stopped the automatic response abruptly. Blankly. ' . . . eh?'

'You'll probably not have time to prepare for lowering safely now. Especially not under these conditions. I've sent young Cassiday to instruct the second mate to launch all liferafts along the lee side. Muster the crew and have them go down there. Immediately if you please, Mister.'

McRae noticed irrelevantly that Shaw still retained that old fashioned formality, even despite the circumstances. He also felt conscious of a growing disbelief that the situation had deteriorated so quickly in the two or three minutes since he'd left the bridge.

He glanced at his watch, then back up at the captain. 'Ten minutes? Surely to God she can't be *that* badly holed . . . '

'She's breaking in two, dammit! You can see from the bridge . . . Please hurry them along.'

'Is this an order to abandon, sir? I saw the radar . . . there was nothing on the PPI. We'll be a long time in the water before anything gets here.'

'An hour. But by boarding now we at least have the best chance of avoiding panic when she does start to go. I intend to remain on the bridge. Tell them it's a precautionary embarkation, but if you hear me sounding the signal . . . '

McRae nodded grimly. There was no need to wait for

clarification. Other than on one inescapable reality. 'What about the injured? We're trying to bring the chief cook up from the galley. Ferguson says he's badly burned . . . Even lowering him to sea level could kill him. Certainly lying for an hour immersed in a waterlogged liferaft will.'

'What do you suggest? The chief engineer has at least one seriously injured man as well. And Clements has gone to help some poor devils forward . . . They'll all have to be embarked the same way.'

McRae took a deep breath. That little voice was back, screaming inside him, 'You fool . . . you absolute bloody fool . . .'

'Say I try launching one boat? Port side forward . . . it'll give me a lee. It'll also give Dempster a chance. And the others.'

'It'll give you no chance at all, Mister. Neither you nor Dempster, nor any of your boat's cre . . .'

Which was the moment when *Lycomedes* herself took all the responsibility, all the decision-taking off Captain Shaw's over-burdened shoulders. And proved that even minute by minute changes of plan were no longer flexible enough to keep pace with the Cataclysm.

Because this time she didn't simply offer temporary submission to the next sea which creamed into, and under her wallowing near-corpse. This time it felt different from the very start, even as the ship began that lurching, reeling oscillation . . .

. . . for she was bellowing unrestrainedly now. Thundering constantly from forward in a paroxysm of ripping steel and displacing cargo and exploding air pressure . . .

Ten degrees . . . fifteen . . . twenty . . . Oh, they'd already counted it a hundred heart-stopping times in the last ten minutes aboard *Lycomedes*. Only this really was an exclusive nightmare . . . Twenty-five degrees an' *still* bloody toppling downhill . . . Nobody moving a petrified muscle. Gripping. Staring with dull eyes . . .

Please, God, please God, don't *don't* doNNNNN'T!

McRae rigidly gaping up at the captain . . . and behind Shaw, the line of the bridge rail. But even behind *that* – the sea! Which meant he wasn't looking *up* any more but simply along a horizontal plane . . . and that *Lycomedes* was now plummeting forward as well as sideways f'r cryin' out LOUD . . .

Suddenly Mickey Wise from aft. Feverishly. The only man-made sound from that angling deck during those few paralysed seconds of the tenth minute.

' . . . clear it, Bellamy! Clear that bloody outboard *chock* . . . '

Not that it mattered any more. Mickey's boat was on the high side, at the top of the hill. It couldn't possibly be launched from that angle, even to a sea like polished glass.

But Third Mate Wise was still trying frantically to catch up with plans changing from minute to minute, not second to successive terrifying second.

*Lycomedes* gave a great shuddering tremor.

Still gazing hypnotically over the captain's shoulder, Chief Officer McRae actually saw her forward part – complete with fo'c'slehead, well deck, numbers one and two hatches and the whole arcing length of her foremast . . .

. . . he actually watched it break clean away.

And disappear. Like a two thousand ton rabbit, into a hole in the sea . . .

Sitting as calmly as you like on the engineroom ladder, Bert Chisholme had simply glanced up when the second clattered down to him, and said, 'I'm not moving another bloody inch till I've had a rest, Charlie. So shove off!'

The second had ground to a disconcerted halt and just glared at the bedraggled fourth engineer with a mixture of disbelief and plain, unconcealed fury. The rage was for having been forced to make this unnecessary descent in the first place – the disbelief because no one could understand that Bert had already gone way past the stage of fear. As far as he was concerned he was already dead. Only the technical completion of the act was left to be tidied up.

So the second had grabbed Bert's collar and hauled and shouted at the same time, 'GERRUP, Chis'um! Jus' get the hell out on deck, will you . . . '

But Bert, being utterly fed up by then with people snatching for him – dead or alive – had clung doggedly to the ladder stanchion, closed his eyes and snarled dangerously, 'Sod off, pal! Unless you want a rest, too . . . a thousand bloody *years* rest . . . '

The sound had followed then. The sound and the first lurch to port which had encouraged Oggie Donaldson's decision to commit involuntary suicide . . . Another clattering of feet rushing down the ladder, and Chief Engineer Barraclough arrived looking equally furious and breathing heavily.

The second stared up at his senior wildly. Still hauling. 'He's crazy! Won't go, he won't . . . Bloody nutter an' always was . . . '

Barraclough stopped, opened his mouth to roar a futile order, then, just as abruptly, closed it again. Instead he scratched his head for a moment, eyeing Bert speculatively, then gave a sort of a shrug.

And sat down on the ladder. Pulling out his pipe in a most leisurely manner.

But Chief Barraclough was very wise. He'd learnt a long time ago that there were more ways than one to arrive at any objective. Nobody watching could ever have guessed at the effort of will this simple gesture was costing him as he listened expressionlessly to the rumble of *Lycomedes* breaking in half just ahead of that engineroom bulkhead . . .

'Stop pulling at him like that, Charlie,' he said remonstrative-ly. 'You go on up and see Donaldson right with Halliday, then take 'em both up to the boat deck.'

Unseen by Bert he jerked his head urgently at the second,

who saw the warning look in the chief's eyes before hesitating then, unwillingly, beginning the long run back to the top. Barraclough sniffed, patted his pockets vaguely until he found his tobacco pouch, and started to fill his pipe.

The fourth engineer watched him. There was a trace of anxiety on Bert's face for the first time. 'She's sinking, Chief,' he offered tentatively. 'You do *know* that, don't you?'

'Aye.'

Barraclough dropped a strand of tobacco. With great concentration he picked it from his knee and crammed it back into the pipe bowl. A long way below them Bowman's body submerged in a welter of piling water as *Lycomedes* reached the end of her roll. It was also that precise moment in time when two more men died on the foredeck and Oggie disappeared over the wall from aft.

Bert's grip on the stanchion relaxed. He asked doubtfully, 'So why are you sittin' here, then. If she's sinking?'

Barraclough lit a match then lifted an eyebrow, puffing hugely. 'Same reason as you, Bert. I'm bloody fed up.'

The fourth hauled himself upright with a sigh. His eyes still looked like black marbles in the snow but there was animation there too, now. The apathy had gone.

'You're a blackmailing old bastard, aren't you . . . sir?' he stated. Quite succinctly.

'Yes,' the chief agreed and then, pointedly, 'An' if you'd get your finger out, laddie, I'd stand a better chance've gettin' to be an even older one.'

The sea had almost covered the cylinder head of the main engine while the racket from forward had fused into one long, echoing tumult as they finally started up the ladder together. The old and the young. The bloody-minded and the dogged.

They reached the top just as the second rolled Halliday neatly on to the stretcher. Barraclough had only time to snap, 'Where's Donaldson, Charlie?' while the second had yelled back, 'Christ knows but I don't figure on hangin' round any long . . . '

Just before *Lycomedes* had begun that second horrendous stagger to port.

And her bow fell off.


Quartermaster Clements, en route to the foredeck from the bridge and obeying orders unquestioningly for what was perhaps the first time in his life, reached deckhand Bronson kneeling by the winch in record time.

But seeing Ernie Clements had virtually fallen down most of the ladders in his haste to get there and back to safety, that wasn't particularly surprising.

Bronson looked up and the quartermaster saw with embarrassment that there were tears streaming down the deckhand's face.

'They're dead,' Bronson cried. 'Both dead, an' Falls gone over the side, Ernie . . . '

'C'mon, mate! She's going too fast ter waste . . . '

Then the roll. And the bedlam of rending steel, ear-splitting at such close proximity. A solid wall of seawater suddenly racing round the contactor house and roaring up the canting deck towards them. Clements just lunged for Bronson's arm and dragged him bodily aft in blind panic . . .

Bronson screamed, 'We can't leave them . . . We can't just leave them, Ernie . . . '

'Bloody TRY me . . . '

Then the foremast started to tumble towards them . . .


In the galley Stan Young finally discovered he was going insane.

It wasn't all that much of a surprise. For ten minutes now he'd been in the company of a scalded untouchable man aboard a ship which had turned into a reeling, clanging coffin.

Oh, he'd kept his eyes closed ever since that last hopeless effort to get Chief Cook Dempster out of the galley. He'd kept his hands pressed tightly over his ears, too, but he still

couldn't deaden the bedlam of skittering cutlery and runaway
equipment and bits which seemed to keep breaking from the
ship . . .

. . . and then the strangest thing of all happened. The thing
which finally convinced him he'd really blown his lid.

When something licked him. A great, wet lick. Right up the
side of his face!

He squealed in fright at that, certainly – eyes snapping open
in stark terror. It was the biggest shock he'd had for a whole
two minutes at least.

The dog didn't seem to be particularly frightened though. It
just sat there, pink tongue lolling and big brown eyes gazing at
Stan with mournful curiosity.

It was a very bedraggled-looking dog. Not really the sort of
dog you'd expect to see when you went mad – that kind should
have been all bared fangs and red, snarling jaws and foam-flecks
like Sherlock Holmes had tracked down in *The Hound of the
Baskervilles*.

This one just looked ordinary, apart from the wet. It had a
soft, silky muzzle and huge paws and big floppy ears which
seemed to be moving alertly all the time. There was a chain
around its neck, too, with what looked like a frayed bit of
lead attached to it as if it had broken away from somewhere . . .

. . . only there aren't many places you can tie dogs to in the
middle of the North Sea, even on a calm day.

So Stanley reckoned that proved he was definitely going mad.
It was a bit like believing you'd found a whale tied to a tree in
Hyde Park, say. Or a polar bear in your bath . . .

Which brought him to the moment when *Lycomedes* began
to fall over. He knew she was doing that because Chief Cook
Dempster screamed again and slid to port, out of his sight,
leaving a long polished track of clean tiles across the fouled
deck.

Then the impossible dog went, sideways and still sitting like in a slow motion cartoon – with an uncomfortable, surprised sort of look on its face.

'At least nothin' *else* can happen,' Stan reflected numbly as he, too, commenced to follow the chief cook, the odd dog and the leg o' lamb dinner down the angled – and still angling – skating rink.

Which all went to prove what a crazy day it was in the North Sea.

Because almost immediately three wierd apparitions appeared in the open galley doorway – now above Stan's head – and bore down on him with flailing arms and wide, staring eyes . . .

'The Angels of Death,' Stan thought gloomily, not at all surprised by now. For one thing he was seeing visions anyway, and apart from that he was just about to die – which one would assume was certainly a pretty logical time to meet an angel . . . *three* angels.

Only thing was – they were all swearing and snarling very un-Christian phrases, which did seem a bit unusual really.

Even for a mad bloke like him to imagine.

Hermann didn't see any angels. Though even if he had done, and they were as sulphurously profane as Stan's appeared to be, he would probably have been delighted. Hermann had never been a bird to refuse a vituperative challenge.

He didn't have any cause to doubt the ship's stability either – Hermann was incarcerated in a hanging cage, which meant he was now the only creature aboard *Lycomedes* who still lived in a horizontal world.

Chief Barraclough's dressing gown suspended from its hook on the back of the door seemed to fascinate Hermann, though, the way it kept on lifting farther and farther away from the vertical. So much so that he even forgot about the peanut for a moment.

178

But perhaps even parrots can be impressed by a really faultless display of levitation . . .

*Lycomedes* carried six twenty-person liferafts – four on the after end of the centrecastle deck, two on her poop.

Second Officer Fuller and three seamen had managed to manhandle both starboard midships rafts – still in their fibre-glass containers – over to the port rails, ready for launching from the lee side when the order came from the bridge.

Or, as Shaw had said, whenever Fuller's judgement demanded that the moment had come.

Each liferaft was attached to the ship by a painter which also acted as the operating cord. Ideally the container would be jettisoned complete, one sharp tug on the painter – and the raft would inflate automatically, bursting free from its container as it did so.

Fuller felt the ship lying over. He closed his eyes for a moment, trying very hard to pray. Then he snapped them open . . . she was still rolling . . .

'Let GO!' he bellowed.

The first liferaft hit the water and immediately began to inflate.

It was the very last second of the tenth minute since Second Officer Michael Fuller had driven *Lycomedes*, at full speed, right into a bloody cathedral.


## CATACLYSM plus ELEVEN MINUTES

If you stand an oblong block of wood on end, tilt it just a few degrees to one side, then let go – it will return to the vertical. It would have been released while in stable equilibrium.

Tilt it again . . . but through, say, sixty to seventy degrees this time . . . and let go. Being an oblong block, with a base considerably narrower than its height, it will continue to fall sideways. And that demonstrates a block of wood in a state of unstable equilibrium.

If that block of wood had been a ship, forcibly inclined to a similar angle of heel, it would have capsized just as surely as the block itself did.

So if it had been *Lycomedes* – and *Lycomedes* had continued to tilt like that block of wood – then neither Captain Shaw nor Chief Barraclough nor Hermann the parrot nor anyone else aboard her would have lived to see the end of that eleventh minute.

But she didn't. She stopped falling over and just lay there in the water . . . only this time she didn't fall upright again, either.

Because there is a further condition of stability which applies equally to blocks of wood or to ships with people in them . . .

Try and balance your block on one edge. Jugglers do it all the time, and sea lions, so it must be possible . . . and when you, too, have succeeded you will immediately appreciate that it could theoretically remain in that curious attitude for ever – unless someone, or something, pushes it just the tiniest bit one way or another.

But, while it teeters briefly on edge, it is in what is known as the state of *neutral* equilibrium.

Yet, loaded as she was on leaving Swansea, *Lycomedes* should not have reached that critical condition before she'd been heeled to some seventy odd degrees.

And she actually hesitated in that nerve-racking roll before she'd even reached forty degrees from the vertical. Under normal circumstances she was still well within her calculated range of stability . . .

. . . only these were no longer ordinary circumstances. While *Lycomedes* was no longer an ordinary ship.

It was rather as if someone had pressed a heavy piece of lead into the downward-facing side of that tentatively poised block of wood, throwing it totally out of balance.

Because she was now simply a part-ship. Her bow section had sunk immediately leaving only a giant whirlpool in the sea which filled, grew fresh waves, and commenced to smash unrestrictedly at the fragile bulkhead which now formed her foremost point.

Her cargo had also begun to shift. Tractors once secured firmly in her tween decks with chains and wire ropes were now free and running amok . . . Steel bars originally shored and wedged to withstand anything less than a Cataclysm gradually rumbled and crushed their way to port . . . Cases of cigarettes and whisky compressed to matchwood under heavier cargo, increasing the free space, allowing the adjacent weight to rampage even more unrestrictedly. Tons adding to tons of juggernauting imbalance as *Lycomedes* lay over under the continuous seas bearing down on her . . .

. . . as well as the water already inside her. Piling more and more readily to one side of her flooding engineroom . . . taking advantage of every added degree of list to consolidate its attack on her failing stability . . .

Which meant that *Lycomedes* had already reached that condition of neutral equilibrium.

Only nothing could ever push her back to the vertical.

While it now needed only a progressive sequence of additional forces – an even higher than usual wave, a further shift of cargo, a few more roller-coastering tractors – to tip her right over until her propeller saw the sky.

And *that* was known as the condition of capsizing.

Not that she necessarily would, of course.

For instance if her number three hold bulkhead went first, she wouldn't have enough time to turn right over before she sank . . .

The captain was the first man to move on *Lycomedes'* upper deck after the period of The List.

He'd watched the mainmast incline steadily towards that critical angle of heel, then hesitate like a doubtful finger still pointing to the sky before finally slewing to a halt.

Or more accurately – as the captain knew only too well – to a temporary rest.

He felt, rather than saw, the bow section break away. Whirling he caught one chilling image of *Lycomedes'* fo'c'slehead rearing out of the sea ahead . . . her foremast arcing downwards and backwards all at the same time with the whipping flail of her triatic stay zipping overhead like some gargantuan fisherman's cast . . . a snow white plume of atomizing spray climbing in a *swoosh* of compressed air . . . the starboard cable leaping clear of the inverting windlass with its anchor booming and crashing vertically as it smashed seaward . . .

'It's gone,' McRae whispered disbelievingly. 'The whole bloody forr'ad end gone.'

Shaw clung to the rail and fought to turn himself aft again, trying desperately to overcome the inertia of their suddenly chaotic environment. The mate ashen-faced below him, still standing upright on the ladder yet leaning diagonally across it at the same time . . . some men on the boat deck skidding and tumbling to bring up frantically against the now drunken line of the deck housing, others frozen to lifeboat grab-lines, embracing stanchions, hanging with the clutch of utter despair . . .

Lindsay, the seaman who'd broken his arm a minute before, shouting in a high, pleading voice from the inverted vee on the deck where he'd rolled.

'Help me someone! My arm . . . Help me *up* for God's sake.'

A sudden movement among the statues at the after end. Somebody running abruptly for the ladder to the lower deck. It acted as a trigger. Men began to mill almost aimlessly under a rising hubbub of near-hysteria.

'She's going, lads . . . Save yourselves.'

'Archie . . . Where *are* you, Archie f'r . . . !'

'Port boats! We c'n still use the port boats.'

'Gerrout the bloody way, Stenhouse, or I'll split ye . . . '

Shaw roared savagely, 'Stand fast, damn you! There's still time . . . '

Below him McRae suddenly swung and clattered down the ladder. 'Do what you're told . . . Leave the boats, make your way to the liferaft stations an' WALK, DON'T RUN!'

But the wind tore at the mate's urgent commands, shredding them unintelligibly under the general clamour. Still only a few men totally out of control but the rest of the crew eyeing that ladder-head with increasing anxiety, every last one of them fearful of being left at the rear of the survival queue.

Someone else forcing his way through the mob, pushing frenziedly. 'Hurry up! Hurry *up* damn it 'cause she's capsizing . . . '

McRae grabbing him, swinging him round and against the side of the boat with a crash. 'Try that on again an' I'll put you right over the wall, laddie.'

Shaw backed away from the scene and began to run downhill, through the wheelhouse doors and into the empty, silent space. He could also hear them on the port side from there – the same hoarse warnings of doom. One voice yelling, 'Into the boat an' the hell wi' the officers!' Another, cracking with fear, 'My lifejacket . . . Leggo my bloody lifejacket, you bastard!'

And Bosun Skinner. More dominant even than the storm. 'First man to touch that brake handle gets 'is SKULL opened!'

The abandoned wheel . . . the silent telegraph pointing forlornly to 'Stop Engine!' The glow of the radar screen, still operating even now it only had a half-ship to see from; streaming, snow-encrusted windows staring emptily forward over . . . over nothing at all except sea. A cylindrical flare pack rolling slowly downwards against the ledge . . . A dirty orange lifejacket . . . The radio room telephone receiver hanging diagonally away from its cradle . . . A sodden, discarded piece of message form, now only barely legible.

. . . THREE HUNDRED FOOT LONG . . . PARTED TOW IN . . . ESSELS IN IMMEDIATE AREA ADVISED TO KEEP CLOSE WATCH . . .

The captain lunged for the siren lanyard.

And *Lycomedes*' deep-throated whistle blared from the canting funnel, shocking men's voices into dazed silence, over-powering even the cry of the wind and the rage of the sea . . .

Somewhat perversely, perhaps, very little panic was displayed by many of those men still below decks when *Lycomedes* listed so abruptly, then struggled to retain that tenuous stability which everybody sensed could only last a little longer.

The engineers, for example. Still at the end of a long corridor before the open deck, and saddled with a millstone round their collective necks in the recumbent form of Greaser Halliday.

The second had just announced bluntly that he didn't intend to wait around any longer, not for the curiously vanished Oggie Donaldson or any other bloody reason, when the whole ship started to hang, rather than roll, and they all fell heavily against the passage bulkhead.

No one uttered a sound for a moment, each waiting almost resignedly for the end. Until the chief muttered tightly, 'She's stopped. Give me a hand with Halliday . . . steady the stretcher, Charlie.'

Bert swallowed and eyed the tiny rectangle of grey sky at the far end of the alleyway. A few minutes ago he'd already given up any hope of even seeing that much of the outside world ever again. He still didn't reckon he was a lot better off now.

Feeling almost vindicated he said, 'You'd've been better off leaving me. I did tell you, din't I?'

Barraclough didn't waste time looking at him. 'Go back down if you want to – but you call me 'sir' before you do, Chisholme . . . Get his head. Gently now.'

'Aye, aye,' the fourth engineer retorted in a hurt tone. He'd only been trying to show a little selflessness. '*Sir*.'

Then Bert really looked closely at Halliday for the first time and began to feel that recurring nausea creeping up on him all over again.

'He could die if we move him,' he muttered uneasily.

Barraclough listened to the rumbling below their feet, and the thunder of the sea against *Lycomedes*' side, and felt the ship moving restlessly, uncertainly, as she prepared for her final going.

'Just lift him,' he requested coldly. 'And don't be so *bloody* silly . . . '

They'd nearly reached the grey rectangle at the end of the alleyway, staggering and skidding in mounting apprehension, Bert carrying one side of the Robertson, the second on his right, when the older man stopped.

Dead.

Which wasn't an entirely surprising reaction. Especially after the mystery surrounding the missing Oggie Donaldson.

Because all of a sudden the second had realized that Chief Engineer Barraclough had disappeared as well . . .

Stan Young wasn't panic-stricken. Not any more.

Not even when the three glissading angels slammed uncontrollably into the downhill ship's side next to himself, Chief Cook Dempster, the totally ruined dinner and that curious, impossible dog.

Stan said, 'Hello, Eddie,' with just a slight trace of disappointment.

But he'd really felt that Angels of Death would have been much more dramatic under the circumstances, having now

185

firmly resigned himself to going down with the ship. Apart from which Eddie Ferguson and the two blaspheming new-comers . . . Feeny, was it? An' Harry Whatsisname . . . Well, they wouldn't stand much chance now either because Stan still retained enough of a grip on reality to appreciate the impossi-bility of climbing back up a heaving, grease-smeared slope of nearly forty degrees . . .

Still, he didn't want to appear too unappreciative. He turned and touched the chief cook gently, reassuringly.

'Eddie's come back, Norrie,' he murmured. 'You'll be OK now that Eddie's come back . . . '

But Norrie didn't seem particularly bothered either. He just stared back unblinkingly from under the congealing skin of slime.

Suddenly Harry said wonderingly, ' 'Ere, Feen. Look at that, then.'

And stuck his leg out. The bone seemed very white where it projected from the wound of the compound fracture caused by the big seaman's fall . . .

Meanwhile Stan had started to giggle as he looked at the Burned Man. Then he stopped giggling abruptly and looked solemn instead. It was a very solemn moment.

'Chef's dead,' he announced, contemplating with some awe the glorious irony of it all. 'Norrie Dempster's gone an' died. So there was really no need for any of us to ever have been here at all . . . '

Somewhere remotely above them *Lycomedes*' siren began to blare a final warning. 'We've got to get out!' Eddie Ferguson blurted frantically, looking about him with wild eyes.

But Feeny only eyed Harry's smashed leg in disgust. 'You do know you gone an' buggered us up f'r gettin' out of here, don't you?'

Harry's eyebrows drew together in an effort of concentration. 'Yeah, Feen.'

The old seaman settled back comfortably. It never occurred to him to leave Harry – they'd sailed together for too long to do a pointless thing like that – and anyway, he'd had a bad chest for years. He didn't go much on his chance in a liferaft in that mess . . . and the dying would be bloody hard.

He felt the ship sigh a little. 'It won't be long, mates,' Feeny said. 'Gotta fag, Harry boy?'

But Harry was still trying hard to catch up with the reality of breaking his leg, never mind staying aboard *Lycomedes* for ever and ever. Death would come more as a surprise to Harry than a horror.

'You mean f'r smoking, Feen?' he queried vaguely.

'You're mad,' Eddie Ferguson whispered, staring at them wildly. 'You're stark ravin' mad, the whole soddin' lot of you . . .'

Seadog whimpered suddenly, allowing its ears to fall close back against its head. Stan patted it cautiously. He didn't want to get bitten or anything, not at the last minute.

'Nice dog,' he murmured tentatively. 'Nice dog, take it easy, eh?'

'Help me Mother of God . . . ' Eddie shrieked, lunging forward and upward at the same time. 'Please *help* meeeeeee . . .'

He got nearly half way up to the galley door before his outstretched hands lost their grip on the grease-smeared oven side. Eddie never even noticed that the oven was still on. And hot enough to cook a leg of lamb. Or a chief cook.

He roared a terrible resentment as he slid helplessly, all the way back down to the bottom of the grave . . .

Second Officer Fuller snapped, 'Next one.'

He watched as the second liferaft splashed over the side and some ten feet below him. The seaman beside him jerked the painter sharply and immediately the container burst open while the orange canopy of the raft itself uncurled, flopping over in a hiss of compressed air.

'Mister Fuller, sir.'

Fuller glanced up anxiously. Young Apprentice Cassiday was running towards him. 'Captain says you're to launch the rafts, sir . . . '

The second mate almost smiled, jerking his head at the two already in the water. At least it proved he still had *some* judgement left, and that was terribly important to him.


The toppling foremast missed the fleeing Ernie Clements and deckhand Bronson by a very long way. Clements never even knew whether it had finally struck what was left of *Lycomedes'* forward end or simply crashed harmlessly into the sea alongside.

The recoiling lash of the triatic stay didn't, though – that originally tightly stretched wire between the two masts. It took Bronson obliquely, dissecting him from shoulder to hip before he was even aware he had died.

Quartermaster Clements, still clutching a part of Bronson, continued to struggle for a few more steps bawling, 'I'm a *volunteer*, f'r God's sake . . . You can't do this to me when I'm a volun . . . !'

And then a pink wave finally overtook him, smothering his ultimate aggrievment for ever and ever.

When it had gone there was nothing at all left by number three hatch cover.

Apart from a torn, bright yellow oilskin. Still trapped under a perfectly ordinary cargo winch.


Kemp had felt the radio room going over and snapped, 'Get out've it, Johnny,' then, without even waiting for word from the bridge, he'd lunged for the transmitter key.

ALL SHIPS ALL SHIPS ALL SHIPS DE LYCOMEDES

GBYD . . . DEVELOPED SUDDEN LIST. I THINK WE ARE
SINK . . .

'Christ!' Bentine shouted. 'There's no aerial current on the
meter . . . You're not trans*mitt*ing, Chief.'

The chief operator felt the ship hesitate, then stop capsizing,
and whispered shakily, 'Oh thank you, wherever you are . . . '
He swung in the chair and saw Bentine staring at him white-
faced. Desperately he tried to think . . .

'Mast,' the second sparks blurted. 'Maybe the mast's gone an'
we've lost the HT aerial.'

'Switch over to the reserve set . . . '

Above them the siren began to bellow, drowning the sound
of running feet from the boat deck outside.

Kemp hunched over the key again. He'd never felt really
scared before. Not like this.

' . . . then do as I say, Johnny, an' get OUT!'

Captain Shaw released the siren lanyard. During that time he'd
closed his eyes and, though he wasn't a particularly religious
man, said a sort of prayer.

It hadn't been a prayer for himself. It had simply been a
prayer for his crew.

And when he'd finished he forced himself to walk calmly
back up the sloping deck towards the head of the bridge ladder.

No one was running any more, or clinging quite so desperately.
He would never know whether it was the prayer or the shock
of the siren, or the combined power of both acts, but as he
looked down over the faces of those men in hazard he felt sad,
yet also very proud indeed.

'Lead the way to the liferaft boarding point, Mister McRae,'
he called gruffly. 'At least ten men in each for warmth. Stream
drogues as quickly as possible and connect the painters in order
to keep us together . . .

He hesitated. Around him the sound of the Cataclysm bellowed in fury, but it had finally lost a little bit of the battle. For the very first time it had been defeated. There would be no more mass panic aboard *Lycomedes*.

'Abandon ship!' The captain said, 'And may God go with you all . . .'

# Chapter Ten

Lord, Lord! methought what pain it was to drown!
What dreadful noise of water in mine ears!
What sights of ugly death within mine eyes . . . !
*William Shakespeare*

## CATACLYSM plus TWELVE MINUTES

The Cataclysm had struck so suddenly, so devastatingly, that the majority of *Lycomedes'* crewmen – other than those injured by direct contact with the ship's structure – were still perfectly fit and able in a physical sense.

Yet each one of them had already ceased to be an ordinary man. Just as surely as *Lycomedes* had ceased to be an ordinary ship, bound on an average voyage.

Their body chemistry had now changed. The immediate threat presented by the sea-cliff had activated the hormone called adrenalin within each individual. Blood pressure and heart rates increased dramatically; sugar content in blood streams had risen; men's body heat soared as blood vessels in the skin constricted, insulating against heat loss; muscles retained more of that blood and therefore became excited, less easily fatigued . . .

It was a dangerous time. Men became more liable to panic, as had already occurred on the boat deck, and to the drowned Carbon Black in the engineroom. Men also made foolish mistakes, as did Oggie Donaldson, who'd abandoned ship at the wrong time and died because of it – or Greaser Halliday, who'd opened a door without thinking. Or Apprentice Standish who'd earnestly guided Bronson and Falls to their end, as well as killing Quartermaster Clements half way through his voluntary mission of mercy . . .

In the extreme men would become suicidal, like poor, confused Stan Young, now patting a dog in the galley and waiting quite cheerfully for the ship to sink. Or even homicidal . . . though only Bosun Skinner might have given any cause to wonder what might eventually happen there. Oh, he'd done a stolid, unbending job of keeping order on the boat deck but there was still an emptiness in the bosun's eyes, almost a menace. He'd never yet spoken to any man about Chippie's death, keeping his grief private under an introspective, brooding calm. But it was an unstable, frightening sort of calm . . .

Yet many of *Lycomedes'* complement reacted equally superbly, adapting to the demands of the Cataclysm with enormous self-control as soon as that initial period of the first shock had passed.

Chief Engineer Barraclough had, and the second. Operator Kemp and Chief Officer McRac. Feeny and Harry Whatsisname, Apprentice Cassiday, Huang Pi-wu – still calmly preparing for survival even while the ship hung on the edge of a cliff . . . Eddie Ferguson, who, despite his fear-provoked logic, had still gone back to the galley to become finally trapped at the bottom of an impossible slippery slope . . . Fourth Engineer Bert Chisholme who'd proved that the greatest asset any man in hazard can possess is his determination to live, even though he had got a little fed up with the whole survival bit towards the end . . .

But the changing situation was changing again, now.

It was the time of The Leaving.

Until that twelfth minute they had still been able to cling to *Lycomedes,* and to the tenuous hope still offered to all but the brutally realistic. The ship had been their security in an unstable world, a familiar and comforting environment even despite the threat which hung over her.

Only now they were being forced to desert her. The Cataclysm left them no alternative.

Yet there are seamen who are afraid of the sea itself. Longtime seafarers have been known to draw back in horror under the very personal crisis of having to abandon ship.

Especially in favour of a flotsam, reeling balloon.

Junior Apprentice Cassiday was the first member of *Lycomedes*' crew actually to abandon her after the signal had been given.

He left her in fear, just as the captain had anticipated, because the spirit of the Great Adventure had finally drained away when the boy looked over the bulwarks and down to where the two already jettisoned liferafts swirled, almost on a level at one moment before dropping away – plunging some twenty feet and in under the overhang of the ship's side – the next.

While all around him the snow blasted horizontally, the surrounding wave crests reared higher and higher until eerily dissolving into the murk, and the strained, blue-cold faces of the second mate's team turned apprehensively outboard as they struggled with raft number three.

'Get in, Rupert,' Fuller ordered. 'Slip your shoes off first, then get in before the rest of them arrive.'

But the boy shook his head, staring fixedly at the jerking orange targets. 'I can't,' he blurted. 'I can't jump down there, sir.'

'Yes you can. Climb over and hang on to the rope. Wait till the raft comes up under you . . . an' let yourself go. It'll be easy!'

One of the seamen came over and held out his hand. 'Come on, son, an' get a grip. We knotted the line so's you won't slip by accident . . . Got your worms with you?'

Rupert blinked, so surprised he almost forgot about the danger. 'Worms?'

The seaman nodded solemnly. 'For fishin'. They got fishin' lines in each of those – except we'll probably get rescued before we've time to enjoy it, o' course.'

'You'll have to hurry,' the second mate said. Gently.

'Too right.' The seaman looked disgustedly up at the men now streaming down the ladders towards them. 'They're a selfish crowd've bastards. They'll *all* want to fish once they get aboard . . . '

Rupert climbed up on the rail and lowered himself until he was hanging over the sea. He felt the ship roll towards him and he swung away from the steel side with a squeal of fright, not daring to look down. Above him the two men watched calculatingly as the raft expressed upwards on a platform of swirling foam.

'Remember an' keep a hook f'r me,' the seaman called.

'No, *please* . . . ' the boy shrieked in uncontrollable terror as he heard the wave smash apart under him, felt the icy flail of spray booming up, around and over him . . .

Leggo NOW!' Fuller roared . . .

Rupert knew his clutching hands had opened even though he never meant them to. He knew that much because he sensed himself falling like a stone, eyes screwed tightly shut yet still retaining one appalling image of the whole ship poised above him . . . Funnel leaning outwards in a drunken spiral against the wild sky; the port bridge wing dropping vacantly like a tired scarecrow's limb from the white, hanging mass of the super-structure; empty lifeboats swinging jerkily under skeletal davits . . .

He landed in water and squealed again with the shock of it. Until he felt his legs crumple under him as they seemed to bounce back, throwing him awkwardly to one side. He opened his eyes hesitantly to find himself lying in a resilient black bath with an orange roof. Scrambling urgently towards the triangular entrance of the tent he stared up at the ship again, only it was much smaller now – much farther above him – while he seemed to be lost in a dark, hissing valley.

The boy started to shiver convulsively. The water in the raft was much colder than he could ever have believed. Then the whole bath began to express vertically upwards and the two heads still leaning over the rail got larger and larger with sickening speed . . .

'Thank Christ!' said the seaman as he grimly watched the liferaft with the boy in it swamping up towards them. 'Thank Christ the kid made it.'

'Get the next raft over,' Fuller snapped as men began to form into nervous groups beside the rail. 'God knows we'll need all the time we can get.'

The chief officer shouldered his way through the mob and shouted, 'Shoes off . . . Get your shoes off, and anything else sharp. Loosen ties and collars. First men in the rafts break out the rescue quoits – you'll find them attached to heaving lines – and stand by to throw them if anyone goes in . . . '

The third raft splashed over and Fuller tugged the painter sharply. Only this time it broke cleanly and the white canister began to float away to leeward, still uninflated.

'Christ!' the seaman standing beside him growled again.

'Try the last one,' the second mate snarled, dropping the useless cord. 'Quickly now.'

*Lycomedes* wallowed heavily into a trough and shuddered through every plate. The two released rafts – one with a small white face still peering through the embarkation opening – rose up and slammed into the rail itself, almost capsizing as the sea fell away again.

McRae thought, 'My God, it's hopeless,' then continued in a clear voice, ' . . . and there's probably water in the rafts themselves. Find the bailers an' get it out as soon as you can. Keep dry as you can, too . . . '

Somebody laughed. It seemed to help a bit. The mate felt a surge of gratitude towards that anonymous cynic and forced a mockery of a grin himself. 'Right. Start going over. Three men in each raft, then pass down any injured.'

A big greaser swung himself over, then winked at McRae. 'I reckon we oughter be signed off articles first, eh? And given a few bob in our pockets.'

'Just hurry up, Kennedy.'

The greaser held his nose dramatically. He was scared to hell but he was damned if anyone was going to know it. 'Don't forget the diver, mates.'

'JUMP!' McRae roared.

The head vanished.

'Next one . . . '

The rail a line of climbing, struggling figures now. Some going over straight away, others hesitating at the last moment as the terror of it all overwhelmed them . . . The deckhand Lindsay, the one with the shattered forearm, being eased outboard by his shipmates, moaning softly and in terrible pain . . .

'Bowline, Jock. Round an' under . . . '

'Easy, mate. Easy does it now.'

'Switch the TV on when you get there, Lindsay boy.'

McRae watched them. They were good men. He hoped very dearly that the ship would allow them just a little more time . . .


Huang Pi-wu had never slackened in making his preparations, not even when *Lycomedes* had begun to lie over.

Having found everything he needed he dressed quickly – warm sweater, heavy serge trousers, carpet slippers instead of shoes, woollen gloves – then he knelt down and lifted the hand painted tin box lovingly from the drawer under the bunk.

He opened it. The money lay neatly packed, all one thousand

three hundred and sixteen pounds, in bundles tied together with elastic bands. Huang reached for the empty plastic underwear bag and began to place the money in it. Having done so he folded the end over carefully and replaced the parcel in the tin.

Then he took the tin itself and placed that on Eddie Ferguson's vivisected lifejacket . . .

When the ship gave that second warning shiver Huang didn't even look up. Either he would go when he was ready, or *Lycomedes* would go when *she* was ready.

It was a very comforting philosophy. For a fatalist.

Kemp tested the reserve transmitter and found to his relief it was working. The whip aeriel on the bridge deck hadn't been affected.

Something touched his headphones and he whirled in shock. As far as he'd been aware the radio room should have been empty by now, other than himself.

Bentine looked apologetic as he slipped the lifejacket over the chief radio operator's head and then replaced the headphones. 'Sorry. It's just in case, though.'

Kemp snapped angrily, 'I told you to clear out, Johnny. I'll be there soon as I can, don't you worry . . . '

But he felt pleased, all the same. Bentine shrugged and put his arms round the chief's middle, feeling for the tapes.

'I thought it was tradition . . . the gallant operators hanging on to the bitter end?'

'Yeah? Well, *you* can, mate. I'm bloody off soon as . . . '

'Mister Kemp.'

They both swung to face the door. The captain stood there looking tired and drawn. His uniform jacket was soaked through and they could see he was shivering constantly. He reached for a pad and began scribbling with difficulty.

'Send this. As soon as you receive an acknowledgement you will leave. The liferafts are waiting port side after centrecastle.'

Kemp drew the pad towards him and glanced at it. 'Yes, sir.'

Shaw turned away until Bentine said hesitantly, 'Don't you have a lifejacket, sir?'

The captain smiled. It was a wistful smile. 'Everyone asks me that, Mister Bentine. I really ought to do something about it.'

He stopped at the door and looked back.

'Be as quick as you can . . . and thank you both.'

Then he was gone.

Kemp reached for the key and began to transmit. The second operator passed the jacket tapes around his chief and tied them at the front. Neither of them mentioned the captain.

But they both wondered if they would ever see him again.

Time . . .

It was running out fast now. Much too fast.

Chisholme and the second felt the ship falter as she dropped into that big sea. And they, probably better than anyone else aboard, knew what that could do to the overstressed number three's forward bulkhead.

The second, still agitated over Barraclough's abrupt disappearance, had just started to say, 'Maybe he's gone up to the bridge . . . ?'

But Bert only snarled, 'Oh, come *on*, f'r cryin' out loud. He knows what he's doing . . . '

He stopped talking abruptly, as if something was choking him. The second eyed him with growing concern until the fourth engineer lifted his head. Tears were running down Bert's cheeks, white furrows against the oil and grime.

For Bert Chisholme had already died far too many times. While now there was a grey rectangle very nearly within reach and, for the first time in twelve minutes – hope!

'Get me *out* of here. Please, Charlie . . . ? Because honest to God, I've bloody well had it.'

The second gazed back down the empty alleyway again. He couldn't forget about the chief. But he couldn't ignore his responsibilities either. He leaned across the stretcher between them and touched Chisholme's shoulder gently.

'Come on, Bert. Let's go.'

They started to run again, awkwardly angled against the sloping deck. The second didn't say any more to Bert – he didn't dare – but he could have sworn they seemed to be making harder going of it suddenly, as if they were trying to race uphill.

As if *Lycomedes* had begun to sink appreciably faster by the head.

But the amount of water entering her engine space couldn't have increased. Which only left one alternative.

That number three bulkhead had already begun to give way . . .

Eddie Ferguson slid back down the slide for the third time. When he reached the bottom he didn't try again, he just lay in the filth and began to sob.

Harry sat beside him with the bone sticking out of his leg and a deep frown on his face. He didn't really understand what was happening to them, the shock and confusion had all been a bit too much for Harry's mind to cope with. But he did gather Eddie wasn't happy and that worried him. Harry Whatsisname was a kind, warm-hearted man.

Eventually he nudged Feen. 'Why doesn't he go if 'e wants to, Feen?'

Feeny inhaled a cloud of smoke and coughed wheezily. If the sea didn't hurry the tobacco would get him first. 'Because it's too slippy, Harry. You can't climb up slippy tiles, an' there's nowhere to hold on to . . . where you going then?'

And even Feeny stared in surprise, because Harry was slowly beginning to stand up. A compound fracture in his leg and the sweat running in rivulets with the pain of it . . . yet

Harry was forcing himself, inch by agonized inch, to his feet. Propping himself against the topsy-turvy ship's side with enormous, almost lugubrious concentration.

Seadog watched him, too, brown eyes following every move, ears alert and suddenly cocked forward. He started to wag his tail hopefully in little jerky movements.

Huddled against the animal Stan patted it again, stroking the wet coat appreciatively. 'Good dog,' Stan murmured. 'Who's a good dog then?'

It was a very odd scene. A deranged man, a philosophical man, a hopeless man and a simple man – all mixed up with flour and grease and a dog and a leg of lamb only a spit from the bottom of the sea.

Harry continued to drag himself up. His eyes were full of pain yet there was something else there, too – a sort of pleased, triumphant look.

For the very first time Harry had thought of An Idea . . .

The captain left the radio room and hurried towards his cabin in the closing moments of the twelfth minute.

Huang Pi-wu wrapped Eddie's lifejacket carefully around the hand painted tin box, then, lifting the prepared ropes from the bunk, began to lash the whole thing firmly into a secure bundle.

Third Mate Wise tripped in his fluffy carpet slippers and fell cleanly between the two waiting liferafts at the end of that twelfth minute. He'd slipped his bulky lifejacket off so he'd be able to descend a trailing length of fire hose more securely, and sank like a stone before Apprentice Cassiday's horrified eyes.

Chief Engineer Barraclough began to . . . But nobody knew *where* Chief Engineer Barraclough had gone.

Bosun Skinner didn't do anything much during those last all-too-fleeting seconds. Other than stare bleakly at Second Officer Fuller as he rushed to the rail when his friend screamed. And then died, just like Chippie had done.

Another steel plate creaked, then exploded inwards under a torrent of water as a sea jolted squarely against *Lycomedes'* amputated forward end. It confirmed the second engineer's fear about number three's bulkhead.

Chief Radio Operator Kemp finished transmitting *Lycomedes'* last message to the world at precisely 1433 hours Greenwich Mean Time.

ALL SHIPS ALL SHIPS ALL SHIPS DE LYCOMEDES GBYD . . . AM ABANDONING IN LIFERAFTS . . . WILL FIRE DISTRESS FLARES EVERY FIVE MINUTES COMMENCING 1445 ZULU . . . PLEASE HURRY . . . SIGNED SHAW. MASTER . . .

'Acknowledge . . . ' Kemp grated, eyes fixed unblinkingly on the receiver. 'F'r Christ's sake ACKNOWLEDGE it . . . '


## CATACLYSM PLUS THIRTEEN MINUTES

'Mickey's gone!' Fuller whispered disbelievingly. 'Just climbed over the rail . . . slipped . . . He's *gone*, Dave.'

McRae winced at the agony in the second mate's tone. He could see Fuller slipping back into his earlier trauma and, shocked as he was himself by the third mate's violent death, searched desperately for a counter-point – anything to prevent Fuller from losing the will to fight.

And then he found it. The Cataclysm itself provided the solution with a sense of timing born of superb irony . . . when the fourth and last liferaft available on *Lycomedes'* midship section inflated precisely according to plan – only while still on board, wedged immovably across the confined space of the port alleyway.

The seaman who'd helped young Cassiday stared speechlessly

at his mate. The man waved his hand vaguely, still holding the activating lanyard, and stammered, 'It started to *roll*, f'r Chrissakes! I jus' grabbed f'r the canister to stop it . . . '

McRae ran over, thrusting the seaman aside. The raft was compressed in a tortured arc, bulging unyieldingly through the gaps between the outboard rails. He leaned out briefly, assessing the situation below where the two survival craft careered in nauseating swoops, juggernauting vertically one moment – hesitating while riding the swell so close under him he could make out the white knuckles of hands clutching the lifelines – then tilting hair-raisingly, glissading into the trough, snatching dangerously at the painters which still tethered them to the ship.

Eight . . . maybe ten men already in each. McRae swung, running a quick count of those remaining aboard *Lycomedes* . . . eleven, twelve . . . fifteen at least. And there were still groups to come, please God . . . The engineers from below. Four . . . five in the galley party including one burned man. The radio operators . . . Chippie. Where the hell *was* Chippie, anyway? And Apprentice Standish . . . the captain . . .

But McRae, like everyone else, had fallen a long way behind in the struggle to keep track of the Cataclysm's advance. A ship is a series of compartments on varying levels, each linked to the other by internal passages and external alleyways; there are stairways and ladders where men can pass within a flip of a coin yet each be unaware of the other's presence. It would be hopeless at any time to attempt to account for the whereabouts of each individual crew member. When a disaster strikes as suddenly as it had within *Lycomedes* – with events overtaking events, splinter situations careering uncontrollably towards sudden, isolated conclusions – the task becomes impossible.

McRae knew of only one certainty. Two liferafts could hold, in the extreme, forty survivors – there were fifty-two men on *Lycomedes'* muster list, less three known dead within the mate's limited sphere of information . . .

Yet there *was* one more certainty . . . Time. The bloody *time* was running out . . .

A terrible rage swelling inside him. An anger at the ship, and at the hands who stood so helplessly. At Fuller for wallowing in guilty martyrdom. At himself for feeling bound to wait for all the scattered remnants while the whole lousy ship tottered on a precipice . . . he started to push men brutally toward the well deck ladder roaring, 'Ten of you. Get aft an' launch the poop raft, dammit! You three . . . An' you, Rattray. An' you and you and you . . . MOVE yourselves!'

Lunging, seizing Fuller's arm and hauling him away from the rail. The second mate's eyes staring into his from a million agonized miles away, black hair plastered like dead tendrils across a marble brow.

'Go with them and take charge. That's what you're paid for, Mister. Get them together, launch the raft an' abandon. Fast!'

A sea passing under *Lycomedes*, suddenly rearing to leeward and curling back inboard over the well deck bulwarks, crashing thunderously among the seamen already running for the poop . . . One going down, dragging and rolling across the angled deck on a helter skelter of white water racing for the freeing ports . . . other hands grabbing for him . . . 'Stop *fightin*' Alfie! We got you, mate . . . '

Fuller saying slowly, almost vaguely, 'Ten men? But there's places here for . . . '

Shock. Slowing reactions, making even fear a conscious effort. McRae snarled, 'There's still more to come. I'm giving them one more minute, Fuller, an' by *God* I'm going to make sure there's space for them if they do . . . '

The second mate passed a hand shakily across his face, then nodded. He started to run, stumbling slightly, like a man in a dream. Or a nightmare. McRae became dimly aware of someone watching – not really doing anything, just standing watching as if time didn't even matter.

He swivelled, feeling the rage draining away and leaving only the sick foreboding. 'Go with Fuller,' he said bleakly. 'Do whatever you think needs to be done!'

Bosun Skinner nodded grimly.

But he'd had thirteen minutes to decide what that would be.

Kemp snapped tensely, 'That's it. They've both acknowledged.'

Snatching the headset off he dropped it on the table. Bentine started to run for the door, then stopped dead and blurted, 'Christ!'

The chief operator looked up, still sitting in his chair, just as the lights flickered again, then went out. The steady hum of the blowers died away and suddenly the whole ship seemed lifeless – eerie somehow, as for the very first time the static which had filled the radio room gave way to the fitful moan of the storm outside.

Kemp shouted, 'Generators shorted out. Switch to RP supply.'

The second sparks hit the battery switch-over and the set splurged back to life. Kemp screwed the key down to continuous transmission and finally made it out of the chair. *Lycomedes* would send a steady electronic guide to listening direction finders from now until the water finally exploded into the radio room itself.

Which wouldn't be long. Still isolated high in the ship's superstructure they could both sense her gathering herself for the final plunge.

The pencil on the abandoned operator's table rolled down the incline and fell to the floor. Above it the electric clock had finally stopped. Until it corroded to nothing it would show that *Lycomedes'* generator room had handed over to the sea at exactly twenty-six minutes to three on that winter's afternoon.

'Let's go, Johnny,' Kemp said.

They began to run.

'C'mon, mate!' Harry muttered. 'Like a ladder then. Hands first, step on me shoulders . . . an' you gotter chance ter grab hold've the door post.'

Eddie lifted his head slowly. They were nutters, all of them. All mad except him. An' none of them even scared of dying . . . except him. The dog between him and mad Stan Young began to whimper excitedly – an' *that* just about summed the day up in a nutshell. Dogs, death, an' bloody disaster . . .

Feeny on the other side of him said, 'Get up, lad! She'll go quick when she does.'

Eddie's head jerked right back until he was staring up at Harry. Only Harry was now lying back against the sloping galley deck, hands cupped in front of him and those neanderthal brows meeting in a gigantic effort of concentration. Yet the big seaman's eyes were the only sign of the pain he must have been enduring. The eyes, and the smashed white bone projecting from his leg.

'Like a ladder,' Harry urged again, almost appealingly. 'Right, Feen?'

'Right, Harry boy,' Feeny encouraged. He started to cough again and didn't get up to help. But the old man knew how much it meant to Harry – to have An Idea of his very own – and he didn't want to steal Harry's limelight when there was so little time left for them to be together.

And *that* was a new thought, too. For Feeny.

Eddie scrambled to his feet, hardly daring to believe he still had hope. The dog pulled away from Stan, scrabbling and skidding in the mess. The second cook looked hurt for a moment then shrugged and drew his knees up, hugging them tightly and crooning to himself. He'd forgotten about Seadog within seconds. But Stanley Young had even forgotten where he was, and what was about to happen to him.

For Stan's nightmare was finally over. His mind had broken down from the moment he'd realized it had all been for nothing, because Norrie Dempster had died anyway . . .

Eddie Ferguson blurted, 'Thank you . . . Oh, thank you for . . .'

He stopped abruptly, the sick fear flooding back as the galley lights went out while below him he could hear the throb of the generators dying away. Feeny snarled angrily, 'Get *out* if you're goin' to, steward.'

Eddie didn't know what was wrong with him. He started to shake yet he still couldn't bring himself to leave. 'I'll bring a rope. Get some help . . .'

'Hurry up! My leg hurts. Christ, it *hurts*, Feen . . .'

Harry was swaying now, starting to tilt sideways against the deck, face shiny with sweat.

Then Feeny scrambled to his feet suddenly, grabbing Seadog. Eddie shrank away in terror as the old man lifted the heavy animal bodily, swinging it like a sack of coal. The dog's whimper turned to an abrupt snarl of fright and Eddie caught the flash of bared fangs against the semi-darkness. Until Feeny literally hurled the creature up towards the galley door, paws skittering and clawing for a hold.

'You too,' Feeny roared. 'Get OUT!'

Seadog vanished into the corridor still growling and whining. Eddie squealed, '*Yes*, Feeny,' and put his foot frantically up into Harry's still-cupped hands. The big man moaned and buckled at the knees as the steward's other foot dug into his shoulder.

Eddie's clawing hand felt the door. It was slippy, too – everything was slippy to hands coated with grease – but he gripped it with vice-like desperation, unable to pull himself up any farther.

'*Push* meeeeeee!' he screamed, feeling the ship heeling farther to port as another sea came under her, increasing even more unbearably the strain on his arm.

But Harry finally went down like a felled tree, moaning in undisguised anguish now, sweeping the raging Feeny's legs from under him, too. They both sprawled helplessly at the bottom of the slide while, up at the top, Eddie Ferguson slowly swung like the pendulum on a clock.

Yelling dementedly.

'Cunard,' Stan suggested conversationally to his remarkably quiet friend. 'I reckon we oughter sign on a Cunarder next trip, Norrie boy . . . '

The captain heard the generators run down as he opened the safe in his cabin. Quickly he withdrew the ship's papers and stuffed them in his briefcase lying nearby. He hesitated momentarily, looking around for the last time at the place where he'd lived so many years of his life, then, reaching back into the safe, withdrew a neatly tied bundle of letters from his wife.

Methodically he closed the safe door and spun the combination wheel, tugging at the handle as an automatic check. It only struck him then, with poignant realization, that doing ordinary, simple things didn't matter any longer. That it just wasn't an ordinary day any more, and nobody would ever try *Lycomedes'* safe door ever again.

Rising to his feet he walked firmly from the cabin without even a backward glance, hurrying towards the internal stairway to the bridge. It had all begun from there thirteen minutes ago. When he'd just left David McRae after talking about . . . tomatoes, was it? And dried blood? And then arrived topside to meet Quartermaster Clements's familiarly reproachful stare because *Lycomedes* wasn't running on auto-pilot . . . as a perhaps unnecessary safety precaution. Until – suddenly – Fuller's chilling exclamation while he stared hypnotically ahead, through the wheelhouse windows . . .

'Oh, my *God* . . . !'

Only thirteen lonely minutes ago. Thirteen *minutes* . . .

Shaw went straight to the chartroom, lifting the ship's log from its rack and stuffing that, too, in his briefcase. The passage chart still lay spread out before him. *North Sea, Central Sheet No. 2182b*. A neat cross in pencil was marked on it to show Fuller's last range and bearing from the Vyl Light . . . A small cross. Like a crucifix . . .

The port of Esbjerg lay out there, over the invisible horizon. And the Danish ferries ran into Esbjerg from Newcastle and Harwich . . . The captain felt a little better in that moment. If one of them had met the sea-cliff instead of *Lycomedes* fifty men could have been five hundred. And women and children . . .

And it could so easily have happened. Even to ordinary people . . .

He moved quickly back into the wheelhouse. The radar stared blankly up at him for it was finally dead now, all power gone. *Lycomedes* had become blind in her last moments of life. Not that it had mattered even before because the Cataclysm had still struck just the same. But perhaps there was a lesson there for others who worked in modern ships: sighted men can run heedlessly into a quicksand; blind men feel their way . . .

A splash of bright orange caught his eye, lying discarded on the deck. He looked down and saw the lifejacket. Slowly he smiled a very small smile and, bending down, slipped it over his head. He turned and looked at the vacant wheel, and at the dead compass suspended above it. The deserted helmsman's grating still twinkled as the varnish caught the light.

The lifejacket wasn't really for the captain, it was only a gesture. To a strange and angry man he'd once known.

He began to walk towards the starboard wing, intending to ensure the boat deck was clear, moving with difficulty because of the list. But then he stopped again and frowned, because the ship felt suddenly different even more unresponsive to the sweep of the sea. Totally dead now, and slowly falling forward as well as to port . . .

Shaw whispered, 'Oh, my *God* . . . '

Just like Second Officer Fuller had done, thirteen minutes before. When it all started.

He stumbled towards the siren lanyard only nothing happened, for *Lycomedes* was also mute without power, as well as blind . . . But David McRae wasn't blind, or any of those men waiting in the liferafts . . .

The captain began to race downhill, towards the outer wing of the bridge.

Because he knew they'd finally run out of time . . .

Chisholme and the second virtually exploded from the accommodation with Halliday bouncing and swaying heedlessly between them. As they hit the open deck they could see a crocodile of men staggering and running along the after well deck towards the poop . . .

Bert sobbed, 'They're going. They've *left* us, Charlie . . . '

And then the second altered course, yelling 'Over there. Port side. The mate's waiting . . . '

Halliday began to splutter through his smashed mouth, bubbles of bloody foam trailing in windblown flecks across the stretcher. Outboard they saw a liferaft rise unbelievably above the rail, tilting crazily towards them. Bert just carried on sobbing, 'I told the chief, I told him he should've left me . . . '

McRae running towards them, two seamen following with bleached, taut faces. 'Rig lines on the Robertson. Top an' bottom . . . They'll need to guide him from the raft.'

'Three bulkhead's gone, Dave. I could feel it . . . You seen the chief, f'r Chrissake?'

'He should've been with *you*, dammit – anyone else down there? Ferguson or Feeny, the chief cook . . . Coming from the galley?'

'Knife! Gimme yer knife, over here.'

'Who *is* this, Charlie?'

'Halliday! Greaser on the eight to twelve . . . Steady, Bert. Steady as she goes, boy.'

The fourth engineer collapsed to his knees, shoulders heaving convulsively, vomiting his relief in the scuppers.

'Get over the wall an' stop hanging about, Chisholme. This bloody ship's sinking in case you hadn't noticed . . . '

'Lift. Gently now . . . carry 'im gently.'

'But where the hell *is* the chief. And Donaldson . . . you must've seen Oggie Donaldson, Dave?'

'Big greaser. Bloody humourist?'

'Little bloke. Scared to hell.'

'No.'

*'Christ!'*

Confusion . . . Shock . . . Grim determination . . . Time evaporating into nothing . . .

*Whoooooosh* . . .

The rocket exploding blood red against the grey screaming sky.

The captain's voice from the sloping bridge wing, commanding even the storm to be stilled momentarily as the pain it carried reached every man on deck.

'She's GOING, Mister McRae. Cast off the rafts . . . then save yourselves!'

# Chapter Eleven

We perished, each alone:
But I beneath a rougher sea,
And whelmed in deeper gulfs than he.
*William Cowper*

CATACLYSM PLUS . . . ?

. . . BUT PERHAPS IT WAS THEN THAT TIME FINALLY
DID LOSE ALL MEANING. BECAUSE THERE NEVER WAS
A WHOLE FOURTEENTH MINUTE.
NOT IN THE SPAN OF THE *Lycomedes* CATACLYSM . . .

As number three's bulkhead gave way, most of the cargo in
that hold was displaced violently into the sea. The solid mass of
water entering *Lycomedes* then swirled, mounted, exerted a
monstrous and virtually instantaneous pressure against cofferdam and forward engineroom bulkhead . . . and crushed those
structures back into the already partly flooded engine space
with the detonation of a five hundred pound bomb burst.

The trapped air – this time compressing with the speed of a
lightning flash – blew the whole engineroom skylight seventy
feet into the air along with the funnel deck, boat deck ventilators
and a section of the midships accommodation.

The huge funnel itself, abruptly stripped of support, slowly
crumbled backwards into the gaping cavity, toppling faster and
faster in a screech of buckling metal until it vanished under a
jetting black and white cloud of billowing carbon deposits and
spewing sea-spray.

*Lycomedes* didn't capsize. She simply tilted forward and began to gather speed, the sheer cliff face of her centrecastle and bridge smashing contemptuously against the seas bearing down on her, fragmenting them with a thunderous roar, scattering them high on either side of her in whirling tatters.

Her stern rose steadily above the surface, the golden bronze contours of her stilled propeller reflecting the cold winter light. Crisp white letters shouted defiantly towards the sky that she was . . . and always would be . . . LYCOMEDES, of LIVERPOOL.

A myriad of waterfalls twinkled and tumbled, a silvery-opaque curtain hanging between keel and sea.

A Gargantua in suspension.

While, even in death, she seemed to possess a terrible beauty . . .

Chief Officer McRae killed Greaser Halliday.

Oh, perhaps he didn't really. The steel door had already done that a long time ago – when Halliday decided to be a hero and act spontaneously, just like heroes do.

But McRae had heard the captain's last warning, felt the ship already lifting under him, and rushed to the side to see the stretcher line still connecting the rafts to *Lycomedes* like a jerking, wallowing umbilical cord.

He glimpsed the hunched figures of the second engineer and the two seamen frantically paying out the inboard end . . . a stark tableau of hands below hauling in confused, uncoordinated lunges . . . rafts expressing up and towards him one moment to stop short of the captive man in limbo . . . plummeting away crazily, rope burning bloody red grooves in the palms of those skyrocketing survivors who could still be dragged down. Unless . . .

McRae cut the line.

The rafts began to drift to leeward immediately, finally freed from the drag of the foundering ship. Halliday hit the water with a hardly noticeable splash and sank like a stone. Even if he had regained consciousness in that last, horror-filled second of his life he wouldn't have been able to move a finger as the sea closed over him.

The second engineer whirled even as the two seamen beside him began to scramble up on the rail.

'Murderin' bastard . . . !' Charlie screamed.

'Jump, Charlie . . . Get over an' JUUUUUUUMP!'

One of the seamen – the one who'd inflated a whole twenty-man liferaft high and dry on the deck of the ship – landed flat on the surface like a great big starfish. Slowly his lifejacket turned him face upwards and he began to drift away, following the scudding orange domes of the survival craft like an obediently homing sheepdog.

He was dead already. He'd jumped as a trough forty feet deep had opened up right underneath *Lycomedes*.

The second man half turned towards McRae and nodded calmly. 'See you shoreside, boss.' Then he stepped off the rail, hands gripping the front of his lifejacket and feet together in a perfect entry. He surfaced immediately and began to swim after the rafts, spluttering, 'Get them fishin' lines ready, kid . . . '

McRae stared towards the poop. The second engineer was still shouting at him but he didn't care any more, not now. He could see the men on the after end still struggling with the liferaft and he knew that if he'd let them stay they might have stood some chance of survival. Bosun Skinner . . . poor tormented Mike Fuller who'd allowed all this to happen in the first place . . .

The white canister of the raft tumbled seawards even as *Lycomedes*' stern rose higher and higher out of the water. He watched as two figures slid frantically down a trailing rope towards the inflating hope. Then one seemed to hang as he came to the end, clinging even now to the false security of the sinking ship. The other black figure began to kick viciously at the man below, trying to force him into the water . . .

*Lycomedes* gave a monstrous shudder and something exploded deep down inside her. McRae could see fragments spinning high into the air from somewhere up on the boat deck. The funnel tottered . . . started to keel over . . . a ventilator climbing further and further into the scud of blanketing snow in a crazy, slow motion ascent . . .

Going, now. Beginning to slide forward with a great, subterranean rumbling . . . the captain's lonely figure still out on the wing of the bridge apparently staring ahead . . . and down . . .

Someone screaming. A long way away.

Something else above him. A falling section of the ship. Coming right down on top of him and revolving all the while like a windblown autumn leaf . . .

More men leaping from the poop . . . *Everybody* leaping from the poop with the red flail of the ensign still streaming proudly against the scream of the wind.

No more shouting now from Charlie . . . McRae looked down and saw that the falling leaf had fallen. The second engineer's head still stared accusingly towards him, but curiously it was from behind glass now, and Charlie couldn't speak any more. The heavy steel skylight – still virtually intact – had crushed a large part of him completely flat. Then the unbroken window went very red and Charlie ceased to exist, even as a two-dimensional indictment.

The sea came roaring and leaping up the deck towards him.

Chief Officer McRae climbed up on the rail and stepped off.

His neck snapped as he hit the water. He drifted away in his lifejacket, totally paralysed.

It *was* a strange thing about Chippie, though. The way he'd seemed to disappear, right from the very start of the Cataclysm . . . ?

Eddie Ferguson finally managed to escape from the galley.

He didn't even wait to see if any of the madmen were trying to follow. He just started to run down the corridor hardly able to believe the nightmare was over and he would be outside again in three more steps. Free to survive under an unencumbered sky.

Behind him he could still hear Stan Young's crooning soliloquy ' . . . Bermuda with Cunard, eh? An' the Bahamas . . . You'll really like the Bahamas, Norrie boy . . . '

And Harry. In an agony of pride. ' . . . my Idea, it *were* a Good Idea, weren't it, Feen?'

The fear had left Eddie now. It went the moment he'd managed to get out of that hellish place. He even thought he could manage a smile so's they'd see he wasn't scared when he got out on deck.

He was just arranging it when the wall of water came round the corner and smashed him backwards, all the way back to where he'd come from.

And whirled him round and round and round along with Stanley and Feeny and triumphant Harry . . . Harry What-*was*is name again?

*And* all the plates and spoons, and the leg o' lamb and the cooked cook and . . .

Huang Pi-wu had timed preparations to a nicety.

As the bulkhead in number three imploded he'd just finished securing the hand-painted tin box inside Eddie Ferguson's unwanted lifejacket with the ropes he'd cut earlier.

He lifted his chin momentarily when *Lycomedes* shuddered and tilted forward. Picking up the bundle he passed the leather belt through the lashings and slipped his own jacket over his head. He then strapped his everlastingly buoyant one thousand, three hundred and sixteen pounds floating asset to that . . . and was ready.

He opened the cabin door just as the compressing air ripped through the ship. Stepping through he closed it carefully behind him after a final – but very inscrutable – glance at the bed in which he had spent so many happy hours with the everlastingly youthful Yeh Chun.

But, you see, Huang had really got life totally under control. Even though *Lycomedes* was going he still retained everything he ever needed. His freedom . . . his loved one . . . and his money.

He walked out on deck and saw the liferafts drifting quickly to leeward, sea-anchors tripped temporarily to enable them to blow clear of the sinking ship. It didn't bother Huang at all.

But that was another of Huang's philosophies . . . that even a fatalist – especially a fatalist who went to sea – should practise a little sensible insurance.

Consequently Yeh Chun's superb lover was an equally superb swimmer. Only for real this time, though. Huang didn't believe everything should be left to the power of the mind . . .

He waited until the sea rose to just below the rail.

And calmly walked off the ship.

The poop rose higher and higher as *Lycomedes* began her final run.

They got the liferaft over and all the men either jumped or slid down the few ropes they'd managed to rig outboard. You could hear one of them below you if you listened carefully. 'Leggo, Bernie . . . Leggo an' save yourself you stupid ba . . .'

Then a shriek. And a splash. And silence – apart from men choking and retching as they struggled in the icy water for the liferaft which was slowly blowing out of reach.

Second Officer Michael Fuller helped them go and then sat down on the deck under the board-flat ensign and waited to die. He wasn't frightened. He simply knew he had to. As a sort of apology.

And then a man walked up the deck towards him and Fuller looked up with a start. Bosun Skinner stood over him, eyeing him with a grim, unsettling expression.

Fuller said tonelessly, 'Go on, Willie. What're you waiting for?'

But Skinner didn't move. Only his fists revealed the tension building within him, grimly clenching into great knotted clubs.

'You, Mister. I'm waitin' f'r you to get up on your feet.'

And then the ship began to slide and the funnel fell over. They could feel the shuddering under them and the sea looked a very long way below them, but suddenly coming closer.

The second mate shook his head. 'I'm not coming. You get clear for God's sake!'

And it was then that the old man looked down and really saw into the young man's eyes for the very first time and suddenly, as he looked, all the rage and all the barely-suppressed resentment drained away to nothing. Oh, the grief remained for Chippie, but there was no malice. Not any more.

'Don't be silly, son,' the bosun said.

He helped Fuller to his feet, slipping awkwardly because the ship was angled so sharply now. A crackle above them made him glance up at the Red Ensign, and Bosun Skinner was very proud of that ensign. It had been seen by more people in more countries than any other flag in the world, and he'd served under it all his seagoing life.

'You don't give up, Mister Fuller. Not standin' under a flag like that, you don't.'

'I killed them all,' the second mate muttered.

'Don't be *bloody* silly,' Skinner said again. 'The sea killed them. It'll go on killing men like us for as long as we accept its challenge . . . an' we won't never stop doing that, will we?'

The young man smiled then, for the first time. While they stood there under Skinner's flag and waited for the sea to try to kill them.

And when it did try they both fought it very hard before it finally succeeded.

For Bosun Skinner had somehow given Second Officer Fuller a strength he thought he'd lost for ever . . .

Fourth Engineer Bert Chisholme had slid down one of the ropes trailing from the centrecastle deck feeling very, very bitter indeed. Imagine the mate telling *him* the bloody ship was sinking . . . Him – Bert Chisholme – who'd put more dedication into the art of surviving than the rest of *Lycomedes'* crowd put together.

And even then he'd nearly failed. Everything he'd tried to do had been neutralized by the shrinking time-scale of the Cataclysm . . . ladders straight out've nightmares that receded as you struggled towards them . . . unspeakable things that tripped you up when there shouldn't have been anything there at all . . . dead men who beckoned you . . . other dead men who reached out to clutch at you . . .

He was OK now, though. There was a sky above him and a beautiful orange liferaft below him. Nothing else could go wrong. Not now . . .

Until somebody fired a rocket . . . and Halliday plummeted past him trailing blood flecks and snaking, severed line . . . men began to jump . . . the raft got smaller and smaller, drifting to leeward as the ship's stern climbed into the sky . . .

Bert let go of the rope five seconds too late, screaming 'Ahhhhh *SOD* it' with a terrible bitterness. He never even tried to catch the rescue quoit they threw to him and finally drowned within a few feet of outstretched hands.

But it was only then that he realized he'd made a silly mistake. And gone to a lot of trouble for nothing because of it.

Because he should have realized that the knowing smile on Third Engineer Bowman's dead face had never been meant for Carbon Black at all . . .

No one ever did find out what had happened to Chief Barraclough.

Apart from Hermann the parrot, that was.

But nobody would ever have imagined that, once he'd satisfied himself that he'd done everything he could to help Halliday and Bert Chisholme, he would have gone back into the ship, running up the internal stairway even while he knew *Lycomedes* was tilting over the precipice . . .

For Hermann wasn't just another bird to Chief Barraclough. He was a flesh and blood personality that the chief could really hate. And the snag was that, if you can hate something that much, then you can't just pretend to yourself that it's simply a . . . well . . . simply an *ordinary* bird.

It meant that Hermann was real people to Chief Barraclough. And you can't leave real people trapped in steel cages aboard a foundering ship. Even if they do look a bit *like* birds . . .

So he'd just bundled through the open door of his cabin, already reaching for the cage and with Hermann delightedly spitting shreds of peanut and chewed feather in a vindictive screech of 'Screw you, Baldie!'

'Bloody PARROT!' Barraclough roared back desperately . . .

. . . and then the exploding air pressure had ripped through *Lycomedes*, slamming bulkheads flat down and tearing a great hole which reached from the bottom of her engineroom right up to her boat deck.

Hermann's cage toppled over and lodged firmly, projecting out over the edge of the abyss. He found that by screwing his head sideways he could fix one beady, still implacably hostile eye on a very familiar figure, still moving feebly while skewered twenty feet below him on a length of dislocated steel pipe.

'Whoooooooooo's a clever bird then?' Hermann crooned ecstatically, victory finally his until the very end of time itself.

But Chief Engineer William Barraclough surely didn't expect *sympathy*, did he . . . ?

Not from a bloody *parrot*?

Radio Operators Kemp and Bentine only got as far as the promenade deck when they felt the ship finally beginning to slide from under them.

Bentine skidded to a halt at the head of the ladder and yelled excitedly, 'I can see them. The rafts. They're still waitin' f'r . . . '

Then *Lycomedes* exploded right in her belly with a stunning roar and Kemp threw himself down because that uncanny sixth sense of his told him precisely what was going to happen in the split second that it did.

'*Geddown* Johnny an' mind . . . '

The rectangular windows in the empty passenger accommodation blew out in a cloud of scything, armoured glass fragments. Second Operator Bentine went clean over the rail like a twinkling red porcupine, screaming a long, arcing scream all the way down to the sea fifty feet below.

' . . . the windows,' Kemp finished dully.

He doubled over, still on his knees, and vomited into all the blood and the glass and the debris. Yet even then he found himself promising to drink a vodka for Johnny. Because he knew, somehow, that he would survive.

His sixth sense told him that, too.

Then he got to his feet. And jumped.

The captain watched the two rafts drift away until he knew they were clear of the ship. And then he turned to face forward, holding calmly to the sanded teak rail of the bridge for the last time as *Lycomedes* began her final rumbling slide towards the bottom of the sea.

The warship would find them. Or the Russian. And if it

didn't take too long then most of those men would survive the intense cold, and the wind and the rage of the sea. Shaw found himself praying that the young boy Cassiday would survive, but somehow he guessed that he would . . .

He felt the ship going then, and a great sadness came over him that she should have to go in such an untidy, confused sort of way, leaving so many loose ends and unattained objectives.

Oh, the objectives had all been the same. To reach the life-rafts, and survive. Only the captain understood that Cataclysms would never be tidy events, and that they fed on men's mistakes . . . and that there had been many mistakes made aboard *Lycomedes* during the last fourteen minutes . . . that there had been delays and prevarication, too-slow reactions and foolish acts committed under pressures too great . . .

He knew they would never make mistakes like that aboard an ideal ship, but he didn't feel quite so sad about that.

Because *Lycomedes* had simply been an ordinary ship. With very ordinary men sailing her.

And the captain knew that – if you read through the casualty lists – you'd find that the Cataclysm strikes at *that* kind of ship nearly every day of the year . . .

. . . then the bridge seemed to fall away from under him, and the white-whipped wave crests rose on a line with his eyes . . . reached above his eyes . . . rearing higher and higher . . .

He was dragged a long way down, twisting and tumbling as if in black, weightless space. All around him he could hear noises from the breaking ship . . . until he began to rise. Gathering speed. Shooting up while the black became greyer and greyer . . . and a sudden dazzling light striking him once again.

He felt the lifejacket holding him up. The lifejacket he'd only put on as a gesture . . .

Turning in the water he found he was quite a long way from

the ship now. And that she was almost under. Only her stern showed briefly, sliding steadily downwards into the white flower of foam which surrounded it.

There were still two men waiting for the water to rise. Standing together under the Red Ensign. It seemed to Shaw that they were holding on to each other. Waiting resolutely. Almost proudly . . .

And then a dog came swimming past the captain and he couldn't help staring at it in surprise. It seemed to be a very big dog, with floppy ears and soft brown eyes. Not really the kind of dog you'd expect to find swimming in the middle of the North Sea in the middle of winter.

The ship went, then. With hardly a ripple. While with her went the very last traces of Chief Engineer Barraclough and Chief Officer McRae, and the second and Bert and Stan and Feeny and Harry and Hermann the parrot . . .

The captain blinked away a curiously stinging tear of sea-water as he just managed to read LYCOMEDES . . . LIVERP . . .

Before she disappeared. For ever.

He turned and swam after the rafts with the out-of-place Seadog paddling behind him.

The captain knew he would die before he'd got very far.

But he hoped the dog wouldn't.

Because it was such an ordinary sort of dog. Just like the ship had been . . .